MY LIFE
ON MARS

MY LIFE ON MARS

*A novel of family entanglements—
and a second chance at love*

ALICIA
METCALF MILLER

A PLUME BOOK

PLUME
Published by Penguin Group
Penguin Group (USA) Inc., 375 Hudson Street, New York, New York 10014, U.S.A.
Penguin Group (Canada), 90 Eglinton Avenue East, Suite 700, Toronto, Ontario,
Canada M4P 2Y3 (a division of Pearson Penguin Canada Inc.)
Penguin Books Ltd., 80 Strand, London WC2R 0RL, England
Penguin Ireland, 25 St. Stephen's Green, Dublin 2, Ireland
(a division of Penguin Books Ltd.)
Penguin Group (Australia), 250 Camberwell Road, Camberwell, Victoria 3124, Australia
(a division of Pearson Australia Group Pty. Ltd.)
Penguin Books India Pvt. Ltd., 11 Community Centre, Panchsheel Park,
New Delhi—110 017, India
Penguin Books (NZ), cnr Airborne and Rosedale Roads, Albany, Auckland 1310,
New Zealand (a division of Pearson New Zealand Ltd.)
Penguin Books (South Africa) (Pty.) Ltd., 24 Sturdee Avenue, Rosebank,
Johannesburg 2196, South Africa

Penguin Books Ltd., Registered Offices: 80 Strand, London WC2R 0RL, England

First published by Plume, a member of Penguin Group (USA) Inc.

First Printing, April 2006
10 9 8 7 6 5 4 3 2 1

With gratitude to W. D. Snodgrass for permission to quote from his poem "April
Inventory." Copyright W. D. Snodgrass, 1959.

Ⓟ REGISTERED TRADEMARK—MARCA REGISTRADA

CIP data is available.
ISBN 0-452-28683-2

Printed in the United States of America
Set in Bembo
Designed by Eve L. Kirch

PUBLISHER'S NOTE
This is a work of fiction. Names, characters, places, and incidents are either the product of
the author's imagination or are used fictitiously, and any resemblance to actual persons, living or dead, business establishments, events, or locales is entirely coincidental.

For Bill, my North Star, with love

CHAPTER 1

"Sister?" It was my mother—who has called me Sister ever since my brother was born—phoning from Ohio. No respect for time zones, as usual. If it was 8:15 in Edgecliff, it must be 8:15 everywhere. But it was 6:15 in Santa Fe, and I'd been dead asleep.

"Hi," I said. "Are you all right?" Next to me in bed Sam hadn't even stirred.

"Did I wake you, Eliza? I hope not."

"No. It's okay. But what's wrong?"

"Bates Barker," my mother said, and then paused. "Bates died yesterday. I'm in shock."

"Mother, that's terrible." It *was* terrible, of course, but I was immensely, selfishly, relieved that nothing was wrong with her or my kids. "I'm so sorry." By then I was fully alert.

Bates Barker had been my mother's neighbor, a retired State Department functionary who had spent years on the Arabian Peninsula. When he retired, he moved back to Edgecliff to join his unmarried sister, Dorothea, who had died two years ago, just a week before my father did.

"Had he been ill?"

"Not at all. We went to the symphony together the other night. It was a stroke, apparently." She began telling me the details.

After Dorothea and my father died, my mother and Bates began keeping company. My father had always referred to Bates as an "odd bird," and I had never heard my mother contradict him. Yet after death struck them at almost the same time, she and Bates started taking walks together, going to museums and lectures and plays. At seventy-eight, my mother was still passionate about politics and history, and so was Bates.

I'd been gone for years by the time he returned to Edgecliff, so I scarcely knew Bates. But he had been kind to my mother. According to her, Bates had been writing a book, something about the way settlement policies in various Middle Eastern states had affected Bedouin tribes. He was a scholarly man, a lifelong bachelor, and rather stiff and formal the few times I'd seen him.

". . . Bates's cousin is making the arrangements," my mother was saying. "Someone he seldom spoke about. I don't know what he's planning."

"Would you like me to come?" It wasn't as if I was doing anything else at the moment.

"Oh, no, Eliza. I wouldn't want to disturb your work. You're busy, and I'll be fine."

"Not so busy, no." I'm a writer and illustrator of children's books. *Once upon a time* is the world I've inhabited for years. *Happily ever after*. But since our youngest child, Anna, left for college a few months earlier, I'd been feeling stuck, as if I'd run smack into a creative wall.

"Really," I added, "think about it. I could be there tomorrow. Have you called Mary?" Mary Talbot had been a good friend of both my parents since before I was born.

"Mary just left for Italy, remember?" my mother replied. "On her annual jaunt. She won't be home for weeks."

I was still on the phone when Sam sprang out of bed. He strode toward the windows, a tall, rangy man with broad shoulders and long, muscular legs. He jacked up the thermostat and opened the drapes, then left the room. A few minutes later he came back carrying a mug of coffee for me, something he'd taken to doing. Every night before we went to bed, he would grind the beans and set the timer—a gesture that, when it began, almost floored me it was so uncharacteristic.

"Your mother?" he mouthed.

I nodded and said, "Thanks," as he set the mug down on my bedside table and disappeared into the bathroom.

My mother replayed Bates's death again, "Right there in his vestibule, Eliza, discovered by Bea, who cleans for him. Tragic. Poor woman, she was quite beside herself."

We talked for a few more minutes, and eventually, nothing decided, we hung up. I sat in bed, sipping my coffee, staring out the window at the cottonwood trees tossing in the November wind. Off in the distance, I spotted fresh snow on the mountains. In recent years, my mother had lost not only her husband, but also a number of friends. Now Bates. I vowed to visit her more often, something I could easily do now that the kids were gone.

Showered and dressed, Sam came back into the bedroom and began packing. He was flying to Houston on business and would be gone for the week.

"What's wrong with your mother?" he asked. "Why so early?"

"You remember her neighbor, Bates Barker? He died yesterday."

"Peculiar little guy."

"But they enjoyed each other."

"Well, sure, but your mother could talk to a doorstop, don't forget. She'll find someone else."

"Maybe I'll go to Edgecliff," I said. "She sounds like she could use some company."

"Yeah, it might do you good to get out of this house."

I nodded. "It might."

"And after you're back, why don't you come with me when I go duck hunting? How about that?" He looked hopeful. For weeks, he'd been trying to jolly me out of missing the kids.

Late autumn mornings, as the sun was coming up and the mist was rising, were achingly beautiful in northern New Mexico. But I didn't enjoy slogging through marshes in the waders he'd given me a few Christmases ago, a gift that sent our kids into tailspins of giggles. I was squeamish—I hated watching him kill birds, and detested the bloody mess he made as he breasted the ducks he'd bagged. But this was his idea of a pleasant outing for the two of us. The weekend before, he'd invited me to ride up to Colorado on his Harley, even though he knew I was not fond of motorcycles. I wound up seeing him off as he rumbled out of the garage.

"Come on, Eliza," he'd said. "You can't mope about the kids forever. Let's enjoy our freedom."

"Maybe," I said. "We'll see." Then I paused. "Is that a new tie?" He was wearing a tie with sunflowers all over it, unlike any other one he owned.

He nodded. "I got it the other day. What do you think?"

"It's pretty," I said.

"Pretty?" He recoiled ever so slightly.

"Good-looking," I amended. "Smart."

"I'm glad you like it. It reminded me of you. You like sunflowers a lot." He hesitated. "Don't you?"

"I do." I nodded. "I love sunflowers."

"I thought so." He smiled and zipped up his suitcase.

"Have a good trip."

"Thanks," he said, kissing me on the top of my head. "I will."

Since Anna left for college, I'd been sleeping too late. I had been trying to accommodate myself to an empty house, or rather, a house to which no one came home but Sam, and I was having trouble getting the hang of it. In the past, I had worked religiously from eight in the morning until one or two o'clock, but lately all I'd been able to do was putter. I cleaned closets and cupboards, even ironed. I read anything I could get my hands on. I fixed elaborate dinners, which Sam adored, and gave several dinner parties, something I hadn't done for years. I was behaving like someone I didn't know.

When the children left, I had anticipated feeling relief. Instead, I experienced bouts of melancholy, sentimental episodes that sent me poking around their empty rooms, examining their leavings— drawers of mismatched socks, bandanas, and tie-dyed T-shirts. I would stare at the twins' collection of toy cars, or Anna's dolls, as if I expected a consoling message to materialize.

I didn't miss the chaos or the telephone's endless ringing. What I missed was some sweet image of my children, pre-adolescent and lit with a radiant innocence they hadn't possessed for years. Scenes from their infancy flashed through my mind, and I would have to catch my breath. I was haunted by their lovely talcum smells, their tiny hands and feet. Some days I could feel the heft of their small bodies on my hip so solidly that it frightened me. For twenty years, my children had been the measure of my days, no matter what else I was doing. Now the only thing measuring my days was the annoying tick of my late mother-in-law's banjo clock in the hall. My good spirits appeared to have deserted me; I felt mired in an unfamiliar gloom.

Other women I knew whose children had left home—a few friends and those at the AIDS clinic where I volunteered one afternoon a week—never spoke about their empty nests, but one day, I could no longer keep it in.

"I miss my kids," I ventured in a voice I hardly recognized.

"Come now," one of my friends said. "Aren't you glad to have them out of your hair?"

"Of course, Eliza," another said. "You always liked your kids more than I liked mine."

"I did?"

"Well, you all seemed to have a lot of fun together. I felt like a policeman, but you . . ."

"Your problem, Eliza," someone else said with a laugh, "is that you always say what the rest of us are thinking and won't say."

Then, like confessions of peculiar bereavements—when your dog dies, for instance, and you are utterly grief-stricken—stories began slipping out, the tellers often perplexed or embarrassed. One of the women confided that sometimes she missed her daughter so much she would sit on the floor of the girl's closet amidst her old jackets and prom dresses. Another woman said she would drive to the athletic fields of her son's high school, pretending she was on her way to one of his soccer games.

It was as if we hadn't known from the start that our children would grow up and leave home, just as we ourselves had. All of us were around the same age and had lived through a time when motherhood was not something you were supposed to admit was central to your life. Whatever we may have wanted to feel, or thought we should feel, the fact was your children leave home and you miss them. It didn't matter that you were aware they were only on loan, or that you could recall days when you would have been glad to get rid of them any legal way you could. It didn't matter that you were mostly content to hear the general outlines of their worlds without the details.

"A year," one of these women said. She is a bankruptcy lawyer and the first woman in her firm. A year to get her life back together after her daughter left. "Maybe two," a painter with work in museums around the country chimed in.

Two years didn't appeal to me. I wanted to sign up for the short course and get on with things. I wanted to work, I wanted to laugh.

"Frankly," someone said, "I'm surprised at you, Eliza. You have so much to keep you busy, I wouldn't think you'd have time to miss your kids!"

"That's right," another woman said. "Look at you. You're the picture of success."

"Brother," I said, "these days you could fool me."

CHAPTER 2

My career began as a fluke. After college I needed a job. Sam and I had just gotten married, and he was beginning law school in Boston. Jobs were hard to come by that year, but I finally found one illustrating children's greeting cards. I had minored in art for the fun of it and had never harbored any great aspirations, but I quickly discovered I had a commercial knack. As people who took their art seriously never would do, I treated the job as a lark, a stop along the way to something else.

After a year of designing greeting cards, I was contacted by someone at a publishing house who had spotted my drawings and liked them. She asked me to illustrate a line of inexpensive children's books, the kind you still find in supermarkets and discount stores. One thing led to another and, eventually, I quit my job and set up shop in our apartment. By that time, I was twenty-three, pregnant with twins and a little overwhelmed. Writing and drawing became my salvation.

Soon I grew bored by the stories I was sent, with limited vocabularies and sentiments as flimsy as their bindings would be, so I began making up my own. The third story I wrote was accepted by Rutgers & Hammond, a respected publisher. It was called *Betsy Blossom and Her Magic Seeds,* and it featured a spunky girl with bright red hair. Betsy had the habit of walking into the middle of disasters and setting things right by throwing down a magic seed, a slew of which she'd discovered one morning under her pillow.

Betsy Blossom was based on a character I had made up as a child. Before my brother was born, I—and later, even my mother—wove Betsy into stories. I adored Betsy, a girl who could fix any problem—put out house fires, fend off burglars, mend broken bones, miraculously find lost children and cats, that sort of thing. For years, Betsy had been my constant companion, one of several make-believe characters who kept me company. I spent loads of time in an imaginary world, which was safer and more predictable than the world I actually inhabited, with a mother who was frequently ill and a father who was often remote. I would cook up drastic situations that Betsy could fix—with my help, of course.

On one occasion, my mother heard me talking to Betsy in the downstairs bathroom, a situation she found suspicious. Betsy and I had been trying to figure out whether we could rescue two astronauts whose spaceship was stuck in orbit.

"I can't go throwing my magic seeds all over the universe," I said in what I pretended was Betsy's voice.

"You're just being stingy," I said for myself.

"Am not."

"Okay, keep your dumb old seeds," I said snootily. "They probably don't even work in outer space."

"Wanna bet? Just watch."

She threw down a seed and got those astronauts back to earth, quick as a wink. I flushed the toilet and washed my hands.

"Dear," my mother asked when I came out, "I heard you talking to someone in there. Did you take a friend into the bathroom with you?"

I was embarrassed. Until then, I'd kept all my imaginary friends secret. But finally—I never could lie to my mother—I told her that Betsy was someone I'd made up.

"Oh, delightful!" she exclaimed, to my surprise. "You have such a wonderful imagination." And that's how my mother and I began sharing Betsy. My mother was resourceful about disasters, but hers were more grown-up than mine, like the time when all the printing presses in town broke down and only Betsy could start them up again so that everyone could get the morning news. But making up Betsy stories was something we could do together, and we both got a kick out of while it lasted. Eventually, with my brother's birth when I was almost six and with other things on her mind, my mother's interest in Betsy dwindled. Not mine.

I had other imaginary friends besides Betsy, ones my mother knew nothing about: The weirdly named Moag, who sang like Barbra Streisand—or tried to. A family called the Treesomes, clothespin dolls with crayoned-on faces, with whom I'd replaced the perfectly respectable plastic figures that came with my dollhouse. The Treesomes were a little dim, so naturally it fell to me to advise them about everything from childcare to furniture arrangement.

There was also a stuffed monkey named Davey, who bossed everyone around, shouting orders and nasty remarks from his perch on my dresser. And Acme, whose name came from an orange crate I'd spotted at the store; she was a ballet dancer, and we danced, but mostly we jumped up and down on my bed. After my brother was born, a sinister character called Jimmy, an old boy-doll of mine whose right arm was missing, began to torment the Treesomes, routinely scaring them half to death.

But Betsy was my stalwart companion, my favorite, and later in life, when I began writing down stories about her, it was as if I'd reentered a wonderful world I'd almost forgotten.

To my complete astonishment, my first Betsy Blossom book won the Scholander Award for children's literature. The prize was ten thousand dollars, an enormous amount of money at the time for a young couple who by then were the parents of three-year-old twins, Jesse and Will, and their younger sister, one-year-old Anna. With the gold Scholander Award seal stamped on its cover, *Betsy Blossom* became a huge bestseller.

Licensing offers began pouring in—for Betsy Blossom dolls, bed sheets, gift-wrap, stationery, barrettes, lunchboxes, pencils, stickers. There was even a Saturday morning cartoon that I had nothing to do with. For some years, Betsy was everywhere. Even I grew a little tired of seeing her on T-shirts, lampshades, pajamas, backpacks, frilly socks. By then, she had taken on a life on her own, independent of me.

But I was launched. From a dabbler, biding my time, working during my children's naps and late at night, I'd become the woman behind the ubiquitous Betsy. Sam began to say that I'd been seduced by commerce—a strange way, I thought, of interpreting my success.

Possibly he was talking about himself. After law school, he did not go into legal aid work, as he'd always insisted he would, but took a job in his home state of New Mexico. We moved from Boston to Santa Fe when our kids were in pre-school, and Sam went to work for a boutique firm that assisted businesses in acquiring and selling oil and gas rights. He found he had a flair for maneuvering through the tax maze related to those properties and often referred to gaining maximum tax advantage for his clients as the art of winning without actually cheating.

When Betsy became such a hit, my mother was tickled by my success, which was hers, too, in a way, though she always pooh-poohed any hand she had in it. But my father was not impressed by Betsy and her magic seeds, which more than once, he referred to as "commercial guff." I have no idea what I could have done that would have pleased him. Maybe a Ph.D. dissertation on fricatives or the glottal stop; he was fascinated by linguistics. In any case, I wrote three more Betsy Blossom books and then stopped—not a decision my publisher approved of, but I wanted to move on to other things. Since then, I have written more children's books and won another prize, but nothing I have done has approached the Betsy phenomenon.

Illustrations are what I'm best at; I really love to draw, and have ever since I can remember. In recent years, my illustrations have become quirkier and more intricate; they reward the sharp-eyed with curious details and small surprises. But I have never grown used to my good luck, or taken for granted the accident of catching someone's eye in the first place. Luck is a curious thing to live with, a constant reminder of randomness and chance. Yet whenever I have actually voiced that thought, people object. They mention talent or a gift. I don't believe I'm particularly talented, merely a little clever—that and very fortunate.

After Anna left home, however, my luck abandoned me. Everything had gone so smoothly for years, and there I was, stymied, unable even to concentrate most days, doing anything I could to avoid my office.

There was something else, too, something I didn't like to think about: A few weeks before, I had driven up to Taos with a friend who needed to pick up a painting she'd bought. We left early and were gone until dinnertime. When I walked into the house, there was the distinct smell of gardenia perfume that wasn't mine. It was especially strong in the den.

Over dinner that night, I asked Sam if he'd been home during the day, and perhaps a little too quickly, he said, "Of course not. Why would you think that?"

I had never much noticed his comings and goings; his life was far busier than mine. But now something told me to pay attention. Over the next week, the phone went dead twice when I answered. Then the gardenia scent turned up on a sweater Sam had left on a chair, and, later, on a jacket he had worn to a meeting that lasted late into the night.

Although this was the first time I'd smelled trouble, it was not the first time I'd discovered he was fooling around. Two years before, it was a secretary at his firm, a beautiful Hispanic in her early twenties, Denise. I found out about it simply by walking into a restaurant at lunchtime with someone who was interviewing me for a magazine article, and finding my husband and Denise together, looking cozy. When Sam saw me, he turned a little pale. Denise mostly kept her eyes on her Caesar salad as I made pleasantries.

Call it a sixth sense, I don't know, but I felt sick, so shocked and disconcerted I could hardly get through the interview, let alone eat my lunch. Fortunately, I'd been interviewed so many times by then, that I could have talked about my work in my sleep. But that day, with my heart pounding away, I was a total mess. I kept blowing my nose and swiping at my eyes. "Allergies,"

I said to the journalist. "I have terrible ones this time of year. I apologize."

She nodded sympathetically. When the article appeared, she made a big deal of my allergies, as if they, not my work, were my claim to fame. Frankly, I was grateful I'd managed to remain upright through that ordeal.

That night, when Sam and I were alone, I said in a shaky voice, "So, what are you up to with Denise?" There were tears in my eyes, which he couldn't miss, though at first he appeared dumbfounded by my question.

"Meaning?" he said.

"Meaning," I answered, pulling myself together, "precisely what I asked."

He looked at me, but I kept still. Then haltingly, the story came out that, yes, he had been having an affair with Denise for two or three months, and, yes, it would stop, and "Oh-my-God-Eliza-I'm-so-sorry-so-sorry." He put his head in his hands, and strangely, it was all I could do not to comfort him.

I didn't realize it until later, but that day something broke inside of me that has never repaired itself. Slowly, over the months, and for all Sam's new attentiveness, it seemed as if my heart had turned into a block of ice. I couldn't forgive him, hard as I tried; I no longer trusted him. I loved him, but the fact was, I had never learned to like him much.

Sam's problem, other than his wandering eye—and how many times had that happened that I never found out about?—was that on some level he persisted in being a boy long after his childhood was over. He was funny, gregarious, a good father when it was convenient for him, but not very interested in anyone but himself.

We had met when we were students at Dartmouth, and I'd been wowed by his good looks and the exuberance he generated wherever he went. Around him, women fell all over themselves, as if bewitched. At the time, I was going through a brief party-girl incarnation of myself, and he presented a challenge I couldn't resist. Call it competitive zeal, I don't know. But I needed to win him, and I did: A week after we graduated, I became Eliza White Naughton.

Over the years, our relationship had devolved into trivial conversations and dutiful sex two or three times a week, during which I would sometimes imagine I was really with Denzel Washington, say, or Harrison Ford, or even the hunky FedEx man who regularly made deliveries at our house.

I attributed at least part of the distance between Sam and me to the fact that he had never come to terms with my early financial success. Betsy Blossom was our black hole. Sam resented that I'd made so much money when he was a struggling young lawyer—money my father had helped me invest and, that, not incidentally, had made our life a lot more comfortable than it might otherwise have been. But Betsy was only one of the things we didn't talk about as, increasingly, we went our different ways.

Sam was perpetually busy. Besides his work—and he probably qualified as a workaholic—he hunted, fished, did triathalons, played in an over-forty basketball league, and took long trips on his beloved red Harley; he was on the boards of the local hospital and the community foundation. Sam was far more social than I and couldn't wait for the next party. I thought I had made my peace with that years before, but as our life played out, I often stayed home with the children and my work while he went on his merry way. By the time of the Denise incident, I realized that what I valued most about Sam was this: He left me alone.

After our conversation about Denise, she vanished from the firm, and nothing was ever said about her again. When the strange perfume came along, I found myself overcome by conflicting emotions: curiosity about whose perfume it was, embarrassment, shame, and plain indifference. The truth was I hadn't been sure about our marriage for years. I worried about the kids, of course, and what kind of devastation it might cause them if we split up.

So there I was that chilly November morning, missing my children like crazy, having trouble with my work, and unable to figure out what to do about the scent of gardenia that seemed to be taking over my house. I was a regular train wreck.

CHAPTER 3

I got up and made the bed, feeling purposeful for a change, as if my mother's call had triggered a sense of determination in me. I walked Snickers, our old West Highland White Terrier, and fed him. By eight o'clock, the kitchen was clean, and I went into my office, the earliest I'd been there for weeks.

Once upon a time, went the story I'd fitfully been working on, *a girl named Lily decided to run away from home. She put her pajamas and toothbrush into a brown paper sack, picked up her favorite doll Sophie, and kissed her dog Moe good-bye.*

She finds her mother in the kitchen. *I'm running away from home,* Lily announces.

Why, Lily, her mother says, *what on earth is the matter?*

I need an adventure. You can't have an adventure at home.

Her mother thinks for a moment and says, *Can I come, too?*

No. Grownups can't run away from home. You stay here so I'll know where to find you, just in case. Besides, if you came with me, where would home be?

But I'll miss you, my Lily-bell.

The story goes on. Lily wanders around town and finally comes upon a group of homeless people. When she tells them what she's doing, they urge her to go back. *People without homes don't have any fun,* an old man scolds her. *No fun at all.* Eventually, Lily realizes she's made a mistake and heads back to her house. Her mother welcomes her home and gets off a line I couldn't decide upon, having rejected twelve or fifteen by then. It was a sappy story, but Helen Dash, my longtime editor, had been after me to do a picture book about something "relevant." I was not doing a very inspired job of it.

I had begun the story of Lily right before Anna left for college, yet whenever I worked on it, my attention drifted. Or worse, I would find myself overcome with doubts about the value of make-believe and even of stories themselves. Those stopped me cold. But on the morning I learned of Bates Barker's death, I was able to put such thoughts out of my mind. In the face of death, stories seemed indispensable, providing at least the illusion of coherence and a hedge against life's senselessness.

I went over my notes and moved to my drawing table. I lost myself in my work as I had not been able to do for weeks. After a while, I could feel, in almost a physical way, how my stalled story of Lily might turn a corner. What if she and her mother baked cookies for the homeless? Or took them lunch? That might make for interesting visuals. I tried some and became immersed in dozens of details. Lame ideas, probably, but at least I was engaged. When the phone rang around noon, I swam up out of my silent world reluctantly.

"Hello?" My voice sounded rusty.

"Sister. I'm glad you're there. I've been thinking about how you said you would come to Edgecliff if I needed you." She paused. "I've been thinking about a lot of things."

"Like what?"

"I've been thinking . . . well, I've been thinking I should probably sell this house."

I was stunned. Since my father's death, my mother had stubbornly resisted the slightest hint from either my brother or me that it might be time for her to move. Where was she thinking of going? Certainly not into a retirement home; she had enormous disdain for those places. The few times the subject had come up, she'd dismissed it immediately. "I didn't like living in a dormitory when I was in college, and I don't intend to live in one now."

"What I've been thinking," she said slowly, "is that I should move to Santa Fe. How would you feel about that?"

I was doubly stunned. Santa Fe? As many times as she and my father had visited, my mother seemed to show little interest in Santa Fe. Oh, she thought it was quaint; she loved the clean air and mountains. But live here? With Sam and me, and our shaky relationship?

"Really?"

"Don't worry, Sister, I would never move in with you. But there must be a little house not too far from yours where I'd be comfortable."

"I'm sure there is," I replied with what I hoped didn't sound like relief. "I'll call Ellen right away if you'd like." Ellen was a good friend and a real estate agent.

"I'd like you to do that, yes. You know what I want—a snug little place. Two bedrooms, a view of the mountains."

"But you'd need to see it before you bought it, right?"

"Not necessarily. I trust your judgment. You've always had good sense about matters like that. You and your father. Much better than mine."

Things were speeding along a little too fast for me, but my mother could be very decisive.

"And, Sister? I hate to say it, but I'd need your help on this end, too. Over forty years in one place makes for quite an accumulation, I'm afraid."

I'd been looking for a distraction, something to take my mind off my own rattled life. Maybe this was it. "Of course I'll help."

We talked for a few more minutes. It was decided that I would call Ellen, and my mother would find a real estate agent in Edgecliff.

"Wait, Mother," I said. "Does Bin know about this?" Bin is my brother, an actor who lives in New York.

"Oh, Bin," she said and laughed. "You know Bin's been trying to get me out of this house since Davidson died. But no, I haven't talked to Bin yet—I'm talking to you."

After we said good-bye, I just sat there. My mother's news was too much to digest all at once. Eventually, I phoned Ellen, and the next afternoon, she and I began looking at houses. Three days later, after going through fifteen or sixteen, we found one I was sure my mother would like, near the center of town and more or less the right price. Not that I knew anything about her finances; discussions of money had always been off-limits. But I did have an idea what her big house in Edgecliff, on a bluff overlooking Lake Erie, might be worth. And I knew I could help her if she needed me.

CHAPTER 4

When we'd finished writing up an offer for the perfect little house we'd found, Ellen said, "Come have a drink with me." We walked from her office to the bar next door, which, at shortly before five, was almost empty, and we both ordered margaritas.

I had known Ellen ever since I'd moved to Santa Fe, and we had spent a lot of time together when our kids were small. She's a tall woman with green eyes and my idea of dream hair: dark and straight as a stick, bobbed as if someone cut it using a plumb line. (My own hair is blond, curly, and unruly.) Her two boys, Win and Carey, were the same ages as the twins and Anna. Ellen and I used to share a babysitter so that we could play tennis and run; we bicycled for miles. Later, we suffered through endless playgroups and PTA meetings. Once our kids were older and Ellen got a job, we'd seen less of each other, but I've always liked her screwball sense of humor and her kind heart. She was very outspoken, shrewd too, and we'd had a lot of fun blowing off steam together.

"Here's to this house," I said, raising my glass. "I hope we get it, and I sure hope my mother likes it."

"Oh, she will, she will; it's an adorable place."

"To adorable places, then." We drank.

Then hesitantly, narrowing her eyes, she said, "Are you okay? You seem a little, uh, subdued. For you."

"I'm fine."

"Why don't I believe you?"

I took a deep breath. "Because I'm lying is why."

"Okay. So tell."

"Well," I said, not really wanting to talk but feeling I owed her some explanation after she'd scoured the city with me for the past three days. I sighed heavily and held up a finger. "Number one: I miss my kids." I held up another finger. "Two: My work is not going well." And a third. "Three: I think Sam is fooling around again."

"No!" she said. "I thought he was done with that."

"Apparently not." My eyes filled with tears.

"Oh, Eliza, Eliza. I am so sorry."

I nodded slowly, then finally pulled myself together. "Four: This thing with my mother kind of throws me."

"Wait," Ellen said. "Go back to number three."

I was holding up four fingers when the waiter came by our table. "You want four more margaritas?" he said and winked. The bar was starting to get crowded.

"I do," I told him, "but I'd settle for one. One for her, too." I nodded at Ellen.

"There's a number five," I added when he'd left. "I have to go to Ohio to help my mother move." I actually laughed. "What a pathetic inventory. I bet you wish you hadn't asked."

"You know, Eliza, you're always so cool and calm, it's hard to tell when you're upset."

I nodded. "That's a problem, I guess."

"Well, sometimes not. Do you remember the time when we were trying to play tennis without a sitter and had all our kids with us? And when we weren't paying attention, the boys climbed on somebody's motorcycle that was parked on the grass?"

"And knocked it over and broke off a mirror," I remembered.

"And when the guy said we had to pay for it, you gave him one hell of a lecture about leaving his bike where little kids could get to it. You actually told him it was a safety hazard! The guy was scared to death."

"Did we pay? I can't remember."

"We did not," she said. "The guy took his bike and slunk away." She shook her head. "Those were the days. You got me through a lot of hard stuff. I know you figured this out long ago, but I never really appreciated my kids when they were small. I do now. I'm nuts about them."

We talked about our kids for a while. Mine were scattered all over the country, but her boys were both at the University of Colorado, majoring, she swore, in skiing.

"How are you?" I asked.

"Me? I'm great. I love my job, I don't mind that the boys are gone, though I did at first. Shep is good old Shep. I'm not going to Ohio, and my mother wouldn't dream of leaving Malibu. But listen, don't be so evasive, what is this about Sam?"

"I don't really know, but something's going on." I told her about the gardenia perfume.

"You don't think you're maybe jumping to conclusions?"

"Jeez, Ellen, who would have been wearing gardenia perfume? The dog?"

She just looked at me.

"Besides," I went on, "my hunches aren't usually too far off." We were halfway through our second margarita; I was feeling a little more cheerful and no longer much cared what I said.

"Frankly," Ellen said, "I don't know how you've put up with him all these years, not that it's any of my business. Is he ever home? I mean, this is the man who couldn't even make it to the twins' high school graduation!"

"Yeah, he was doing that endurance thing in New Zealand." I shook my head.

"You know? I've always thought he acted like someone from a different generation, when fathers were, you know hands-off," she said. "All that don't-bother-your-father-he's-busy crap that I grew up with."

It struck me that she had just nailed Sam. I sighed.

"What are you trying to prove, anyway? Are you aware that in some circles you're known as the Widow Naughton? I kid you not."

I raised my eyebrows, appalled. "Oh God, Ellen, that really hurts." And it did; I was stung.

"You've always been extraordinarily tolerant of him. And, please don't tell me it takes two to tango, or any bullshit like that."

"This was never a tango for him," I said. "I've always known that. No pas de deux at our house. This was Gene Kelly doing a solo. Fred Astaire without . . ."

"Mark Morris dancing in a sarong, alone?" Ellen interrupted. "God, how I love Mark Morris."

"Yeah, well." Dance-wise, my marriage sounded dismal. Who was I kidding? My marriage *was* dismal.

"So, who do you think belongs to the gardenia perfume?"

"Beats me," I said. "Though, since he was practically a child molester the last time, she's probably young."

We sat and stared at each other for a long moment, both of us—I could tell—recalling when we ourselves were young.

"How about another?" Ellen pointed to her empty glass. "I'll call Shep. He'll come join us. He's always been crazy about you, you know."

"Better not. It could turn out to be like the night you and I sat on my kitchen floor, swilling that cheap Gallo wine. You remember that?"

"Where was everyone that night? The kids, I mean? Oh my God, I got so hammered." She paused. "I had some desperate moments when the boys were small. If it hadn't been for you . . . You were such a good example. Of a mother, I mean. That whole period of my life nearly did me in."

"But look how nicely you've recovered," I said, gathering my coat and purse and leaving money on the table.

As we were walking out, Ellen stopped and looked at me. "Listen, if there's anything I can do, just let me know. I mean it. You'll be all right, I know you will. I have a ton of faith in you." She gave me a big hug.

"Sure," I said. "Dancing in the dark, alone. I'm a whiz at that."

"*I'll* always dance with you, Eliza," she said a little tipsily, and we both laughed.

I called all the kids the next day to tell them I was going to Ohio. I had to leave messages for the boys, but I actually spoke to Anna.

"Nana's moving to Santa Fe?" she said. "Wow!"

"I'll feel better with her here."

"But, Mom, when you leave, what about Snickers?" Anna had always been very attached to Snickers. When she was little, she used to dress him up in old baby clothes and talk to him for hours. What a sight: poor woebegone Snickers in a sailor suit.

"Snickers," I said. "Oh my God, I forgot all about him!" He was at my feet, snoring, with a fuzzy white toy known as Dumb Bunny clutched in his front paws.

"I guess your father will have to take care of him."

"Mom. Are you crazy? He's hardly ever home."

"I'll put him in a kennel then."

"No," she wailed. "Those dogs won't understand him."

"Anna," I said. "What else can I do?"

"I know! Ask Ellen to keep him. He's always liked Ellen. And she likes him, too. Remember the time she helped me tie him in the baby buggy? We laughed so hard."

"And your brother Will thought you were both being cruel."

"Oh, he's always been too serious," she said. "So, what about Ellen?"

"That's a great idea. Thanks."

Which is how I wound up taking Snickers, his bed, his food, and half a dozen dog toys, including Dumb Bunny and a reindeer named Legs, to Ellen's the day before I left.

"No baby clothes?" Ellen said.

"You want the ASPCA on your doorstep?"

She rolled her eyes. "Have a good trip," she said, picking Snickers up and making him wave his paw as I drove away.

In the meantime, Sam came back from Houston and handed me a velvet-covered box; inside of it was a pair of very fancy gold and pearl earrings. Guilt is a powerful motivator. Judging from the jeweler's name, these had probably cost a fortune. I put them on and felt freakish, like a child dressed in grown-up things, but he kept saying how beautiful I looked.

"Thank you," I said. "What an amazing surprise."

Yet there was that goddamn perfume again, everywhere. I smelled it on his underwear as I threw it into the washing machine, and on his sport coats and ties. When I took his suit and shirts to the laundry, the car reeked of it. The whole thing made me livid.

Then, the next day, a strange apathy descended on me—apathy mixed with contempt. I didn't know what I wanted to do, but I wasn't about to confront him, not yet. Given the mood I was in, I would only sound like a scold. Let him have another midlife crisis, or whatever it was. I would go to Edgecliff and help my mother, and he and his perfumed bimbo could screw their brains out for all I cared.

CHAPTER 5

Two days later, I was sitting in a hospital room in Edgecliff, holding my mother's hand. I couldn't tell if she was asleep or just resting her eyes. She looked remarkably the way she had decades before, when I would barge into her room after school. "Are you asleep?" I would say. Her shoulders would give a little start, but her eyes would remain closed. "Of course I'm not asleep," she always said, "I'm just resting my eyes. My head . . ."

Careful not to inquire about her head and just as careful not to bounce the bed, I would lie on my stomach next to her and tell her about my day at school. As I did, I would study her face, her eyes still shut, and marvel at her white skin, her dark, arching eyebrows, her perfect small nose. At six or seven, I was almost as big as she was, large-featured, blond. We didn't look as if we were related at all.

My mother was a beautiful woman; she still is. Yet for some reason—a lack of vanity, perhaps nothing more complicated than that—she has always refused to acknowledge it. When people complimented her on her looks, and people still did, she would reply with genuine incredulity, "But I'm so old!" At seventy-eight, she appeared twenty years younger, even in the harsh light coming in through the hospital window, a tiny woman whose hair was still naturally dark.

But on those afternoons years ago when I lay on her bed, I was consumed with worry over her. Next to me, she seemed dangerously lifeless, and so I talked nonstop, as if I might vanquish the headaches that rendered her helpless. Sometimes, as I told her about my day, I would close my own eyes, but I always had to open them quickly, because, eyes closed, I would feel giddy, sprung loose from the world. I believe my mother was interested in my life, but with her eyes shut, she was strangely remote. I know now that she was sick and holding herself in; but then, with a child's logic, I suspected she was shutting me out.

After telling my mother about school, I would slide off her bed and start to wander downstairs. Usually, that was the moment she would open her eyes and say, "I guess it's time to think about dinner." Holding her head, she would get out of bed slowly, and I would hope that my talk had revived her, as one of Betsy Blossom's magic seeds might have done—or as I myself could have done if I had been smart enough or good enough or powerful enough. But nothing I was able to do fixed my mother.

Bin, almost six years younger than I am, refused to become involved in my concern for our mother back then. Much later, he said to me, "What the hell was I supposed to do? It was clear from the get-go that you had a goddamn monopoly on worry. Besides, I was a little kid." He was right, of course.

As an actor, Bin makes a good living doing what he does— movies, plays, commercials, soaps, as well as the occasional MTV video, to the delight of my kids and their friends. I adored my baby brother when he was born and continued to as we grew up, even though he could be a handful: high-strung, moody, and

often short-tempered. Mostly, I succeeded in ignoring his prick-
liness, but sometimes, he really got to me.

As a child, Bin had stubbornly refused to acknowledge the fact
that our mother was different from other mothers, or that she
needed quiet. He would bang around, yell, even drag his dusty-
smelling friends into her bedroom; he treated her as if she were
perfectly healthy. For her part, my mother led me to believe that
a boy couldn't understand and that we should excuse his behavior. Not that my mother and I talked much about things like
that then. We spoke very little about her condition, as if men-
tioning it would make her headaches more real than they already
were.

My mother was my first love, and almost from the start, it was
a desperate affair. She was not like other mothers. Not even when
she was headache-free and up and about, as she would be for a
week or so at a time. Out of bed, my mother spoke her mind. She
had strong opinions; she was well read and did not attempt to
hide it. I admired that part of her, but what I did not admire, what
caused me nearly to keel over with embarrassment even before I
became a self-conscious adolescent, was that when she felt well,
she talked to everyone: clerks, waitresses, cab drivers, doormen,
people standing on corners waiting for traffic lights to change.
Even today, she is the kind of person who consults the mailman
about investment opportunities or the gardener about foreign pol-
icy. This constitutes more than filling a void; she genuinely likes
people and is curious about them. But as a child, I would beg her
to stop talking to strangers. Sometimes I would say nastily, "Be
quiet!"

"Now, now," she'd say at moments like that. "I'm from a small
town, and I know how much people enjoy being spoken to." And

they did. Even I could see how much others appreciated her friend-liness. She had, in effect, willing accomplices wherever we went, eager to engage in conversation with her at the drop of a hat. But I didn't want to share her; I was jealous of the attention she gave away so freely.

Maybe all children feel that way, I don't know. With my own sons and daughter, I have made it a point to err in the other di-rection, focusing perhaps too much attention on them. That had the effect, I believe, of sending them bolting out the door at eighteen, in a rush to see the world. A few days before Anna left home for college, she grew jittery about the prospect before her. I said, "Okay, Anna. Stay home, and we'll play beauty shop. I'll do your nails and braid your hair. We can learn to sew."

She looked at me as if I had lost my mind, then burst out laughing. I laughed, too, and that was the end of it as far as she was concerned. Still, I could almost imagine playing beauty shop or baking cookies with Anna for years. I did so little of that with my own mother. Instead I witnessed her pain, part of me always holding my breath, afraid that she would disappear. "You over-identified," a therapist-friend told me. "We're not talking logic here." Well, yes. If I hadn't had a monopoly on worry, as Bin suggested, I'd certainly had a thriving franchise in it.

Now, as she lay in a hospital bed, I had no day at school to tell her about. Not much of a day at all: I had taken her poor dog, Duke, for a walk, then brushed him, which it appeared no one had done for months; I had gone to the liquor store for cartons to pack books in and had even filled up a few; I'd walked Duke again, made a trip to the supermarket for some groceries, bought my mother flowers. I had spoken briefly on the phone to Sam. I also finally talked to Bin. "Trouble," I had said to his answering machine the day before, in the jokey way we often communicate with each other, "Here in River City. Call me as soon as you can." He didn't return my call until that morning. It turned out he had been in Paris, doing an American Express commercial, and had just returned to New York. When I filled him in about our mother's broken hip, he asked if he should fly in.

"No, stay put," I told him. "Come later in the week, maybe. I'll keep you posted."

"I hope you managed to find her adequate care," he said, in a tone of voice which suggested that, left to my own devices, I would choose a doctor whose license had been revoked.

"I think so. Yes. Geoff Ewing, your old tennis pal. It's not complicated, at least according to him."

"So," he said, "how is Geoff?"

"He seems fine," I replied. "I was surprised to find him in Edgecliff."

"Depressing place, yes. What do you suppose people do there? Seriously."

"Live lives, apparently," I said, knowing that living a life is what my footloose brother hadn't quite gotten around to yet. "I'll call you later." I gave him the hospital number, and hung up.

So there we were once again, my mother in bed with me looking on. She was far sturdier than she had once been, and I was now an adult, so why was *my* left hip throbbing in sympathetic pain? I disengaged my hand from hers and went to the window. Edgecliff's gray November sky was roiled and angry, churning so fast it looked like time-lapse photography on the Weather

Channel. The trees were leafless and blackened with rain. Three floors below, in the middle of the street, steam rose in clouds from a manhole cover. I remembered this cold, leaden weather; it was one of the reasons I was glad to live in New Mexico, where the sun shone blindingly almost every day.

I turned from the window and toyed briefly with the idea of lying down on the other bed in my mother's room. I was tired. I had not slept much since I arrived in Edgecliff. I had flown in on Saturday night. On Sunday, my mother and I were sitting at the breakfast table, both of us in bathrobes, mine a bedraggled terry-cloth thing that had been hanging in my old closet since high school. A pale light hovered over the slatey expanse of Lake Erie that extends beyond my mother's backyard for miles, to Canada. Off in the distance, I could see two ore boats, miniatures on the horizon. A torpor seemed to have fallen over me. I complained that my eyes ached.

"Mine do, too," my mother said. "My eyes have ached ever since your father died. It's probably all those unshed tears." She made a puzzled sound. My mother had not cried when my father died, at least not in my presence. She'd always claimed she had trouble with tears.

"Let's get dressed and start in on the downstairs closets," I suggested. Her house had gone under contract after only a week on the market, and she needed to be out before the end of the year.

She made a pained face and sighed. Just then, Duke, my father's old black Lab, came into the kitchen, his rheumy eyes glistening, his claws tapping on the floor. My mother concentrated on her cereal.

Duke began to bark. Over the years, his bark had become a strange moan, trailing off into hoarseness or sadness, as if the poor thing lost heart, or breath, midway through. It was an awful sound, impossible to ignore.

"Oh, calm down," my mother ordered him and delivered another spoonful of bran flakes to her mouth. Eating has always been an effort for her. She regarded food as fuel and was largely indifferent to it.

The dog barked again, louder this time. Since my father's death, Duke had been all turned around. He paced the upstairs hall in the middle of the night and often refused to come when called. The evening before, when I'd arrived, I went to hang up my coat and found him sleeping on his back, paws in the air, on the closet floor.

"Do you think Duke is losing his marbles?" I'd asked my mother as I stooped down to rub his stomach and fondle his velvety ears.

"Why should he be exempt?" she said dryly. She called his name two or three times, and with my help, he got to his feet and left the closet. Most of the time, she reported, Duke lay next to my father's leather chair, looking confused. My mother was not much of a dog lover, and I think she largely ignored Duke, which saddened me. He was fourteen, old for a Lab. The hair around his eyes and mouth was gray, his hind legs stiff. He often bumped into things because he was going blind.

Duke tapped around the kitchen. Evidently, my quick excursion up the street with him earlier hadn't done the trick. I rose from the table. My mother set down her spoon. "Stay, Sister," she said, getting up. "I'll take him."

I strode ahead of her into the front hall, intending to take Duke out myself. "No," she said firmly. Duke moaned and twitched while my mother put on a scarf, a knitted tam, a down coat, gloves, and a pair of fur-lined boots. At last she was ready. I clipped Duke to his leash, and the two of them went out the door. Only when I saw them together did I realize how mismatched they were. Duke was a big dog, with an enormous head; he probably weighed twenty pounds more than my mother. I watched them go down the porch steps and across the lawn to the driveway—a small woman in a brilliant red coat, being pulled through the sullen light by a huge black dog. I thought of all the mornings this scene had been enacted since my father's death, and inexplicably, tears filled my eyes.

Unlike my mother, I don't have a problem with tears, though until recently, I'd never been much of a crier. Bin can produce tears on demand and has done so more than once in the movies. "Part of the job," he'd said when I asked him about it. "It's easy." I have no idea if Bin cried when our father died. He was at a film festival in Singapore and only just made it to the memorial service a week later.

I returned to the kitchen and slowly, as if I were half asleep, began to unload the dishwasher. My mother's house was clean but never neat; it had too much stuff in it. I felt over my head as I anticipated sorting through the residue of my family's life. I needed to dive in and get to work.

With my mother out of the house, I inventoried the contents of her refrigerator: tiny custard dishes containing only a dollop of this or that, a Baggie holding one carrot stick, two strawberries, odds and ends I was sure neither of us would eat. When my father died two years earlier, neighbors and friends sent dish after dish—casseroles of rice and noodles, roasted chickens, baked beans laced with bacon and brown sugar, a ham—as if we would be feeding large groups. Even with Bin and Sam and the children there, we couldn't make a dent in all that food.

"What can people possibly be thinking?" my mother had said. "That we're holding a wake?" "Wake" was one of my parent's code words for things people like us didn't do because we knew better.

I suggested we might be better off holding one. "We could tear our hair, we could wail. Isn't that what the Irish do at wakes?"

"You read too much," my mother had replied. "You and your brother are hopeless romantics. Your view of the Irish is right out of Synge." She bustled around, wrapping things—a turkey breast, a loaf of garlic bread—in foil. She eyed a chocolate cake in a bakery box, enough for twenty people.

"Tell me," she said, "what am I supposed to do with all this food?" She seemed momentarily frantic, but then, before I knew what was happening, she was on the phone to a homeless shelter. "I'll have my daughter drop it off," she said. That was how I wound up taking the funeral meats, as I could not stop thinking of them, to the address she handed me, then hurrying away.

But now, as my mother walked Duke, I grabbed three or four small packages from the refrigerator and threw them, wrappings and all, down the garbage disposal. While it churned, I felt a pang of guilt, not for being wasteful, but because (and I could hear my father's voice), I was jeopardizing the workings of the In-Sink-Erator with plastic wrap and Baggies. I encouraged the disposal along, reflecting on the contrast between my mother's need to tuck things away and my own tendency to throw things out, habits that must skip every other generation: My children saved everything.

I was roused by the doorbell and wondered why my mother hadn't intercepted whoever it was in the driveway. I wiped my hands and went to the door to find my mother, her tam askew, in the arms of a darkly handsome man with striking blue eyes. Beyond the porch, Duke sat on the lawn.

"She fell," he said. "The dog tripped her, I think." He smiled as if he wanted to put me at ease. His unusual eyes captivated me. His teeth were brilliantly white, and he wore a brown leather jacket. But I was unable to place his faint accent.

"I think something's broken," my mother said and winced. "The pain is excruciating."

I ushered them into the living room and pointed to the couch. "No," my mother said. Not even in emergencies was anyone permitted to lie down on her living-room sofa.

I beckoned the man to follow me into the library, where under stacks of magazines, books, and catalogues there was a couch a person could safely lie on. I removed the clutter, and he set my mother down gently.

"Nine-one-one," he directed me. I must have appeared addled.

"This is Robbie," my mother managed to say. "Rob, this is my daughter Eliza."

"Hi," he said and smiled.

My knees felt rubbery, and I had to sit down. Irrationally, I longed for Betsy Blossom to rescue us with one of her magic seeds. I unearthed the phone from under stacks of papers on my father's desk and dialed 911. When I looked up, Robbie had vanished, but as I was talking to the dispatcher, he reappeared, carrying two glasses of water. He handed one to me and knelt by the couch to offer the other to my mother, lifting her head so that she could take a sip.

"They'll be here in a minute," I said when I hung up. "Everything will be fine," I added, going over to my mother, who was very pale. Robbie stood up and I knelt down. "Mama," I said. "Dear thing. What happened?" I noticed that her left leg looked shorter than her right and that her left foot splayed out at an odd angle.

"Where's that dog?" she said.

I leaped up and ran out onto the front porch, calling Duke's name just as he rounded the corner of the house, his leash wrapped around one of his hind legs so that he limped pathetically. I untangled him and got him into the house, where I found Robbie patting my mother's hand. "Don't worry," he was saying.

The doorbell rang, and before I could answer it, two EMS medics walked right in. I pointed to the library. My mother said, "Be careful of the woodwork," when they lifted her onto the stretcher. As they maneuvered her out of the house, I told them what I thought had happened. One of the medics asked if I wanted to ride along in the ambulance.

"Dressed like that?" my mother piped up through her pain. "You get dressed properly, Sister, then come along. No one wants to see two of us in our nightclothes. I'm in good hands." I kissed her cheek. By then her teeth were chattering and she was white as a sheet. "Don't forget my purse and house key, and oh yes, make sure the stove is off."

"We'll take good care of her," the driver assured me. Robbie and I stepped back as the ambulance pulled away. Duke began howling mournfully behind the storm door, and Robbie bounded up the steps and into the house. Only then did it click: This person was not a stranger. He was someone my mother knew.

One of the neighbors, Frannie Eckles, suddenly materialized at my elbow, wanting to know what was going on. She wore a coat over her nightgown, apparently the neighborhood uniform that morning.

"Well," she said when I'd told her what happened, "at least your husband's here." She nodded toward the house. Frannie was older than my mother, and for all I knew, her eyesight was bad. There wasn't time to explain, so I told her I'd talk to her later.

I ran back into the house, my bathrobe flapping. Robbie and Duke were in the front hall. "I don't know how to thank you," I said. I was freezing. Duke collapsed on the slate floor with a heavy groan.

"Don't worry," Robbie said. "Your mother is—how do you say it?—a hard cookie." His smile disarmed me. I had trouble looking away from his eyes.

"Tough," I said. "Tough cookie. And you're right. How do you know her?"

"I've worked for Mr. Barker, her neighbor, for years, doing research. And now I am cleaning up some things. He died, you know."

I nodded.

"But your mother and I are friends," he added.

"I'd better get to the hospital."

"Would you like me to go with you?" he asked. I still couldn't put my finger on his accent, but I was pretty sure "Robbie" wasn't the name he started out with.

"No, but thanks." I was freezing. "Leave me your number, though, and I'll let you know how she is." I ran to the kitchen and got a pad and pencil so he could jot it down.

"Where are you from?" I asked as I opened the front door for him. His eyelashes were amazingly long. I couldn't tell how old he was. Younger than I was, though.

"Moon," he said.

"Moon?"

"Moon Lane, you know, up by the reservoir?" He grinned.

I vaguely remembered there was a street called Moon, one of those narrow streets in south Edgecliff, away from the lake. There were streets in Edgecliff named for everything in the night sky; my mother's house was on Mars Avenue.

"No, really," I said.

"Really," he said smiling. "I'm the guy from Moon."

"But before that," I pressed, no idea why. My feet were icy.

"Oh, before that," he shook his head. "All over the place."

I suddenly realized I didn't have time to chat. "I'm sorry, but I'd better run. Thanks again for your help."

He went out the door, then turned around and waved with such an exuberant motion he seemed to be waving to someone besides me, someone out in the middle of Lake Erie, or far off in Canada.

I closed the door and on numb feet, went to check the stove. I knew it was off, but I had to make sure for my mother.

CHAPTER 6

At the entrance to the emergency room, a receptionist directed me down a long hall, and before I could ask where to find my mother, I heard her voice coming from one of the examining rooms. She was lying on a gurney, talking to a doctor. "Probably should have put him down when my husband died. A dog in mourning, well . . ." I could tell it was an effort for her to talk.

"Mother," I said.

"Ah, there you are." She introduced me to the doctor. He was blond, with a runner's build, and seemed immoderately young.

"How is she?"

"I think she broke her left hip," he answered, and my heart fell. "There seems to be an intertrochanteric fracture." He pointed to several x-rays hanging on the wall. I asked him to write down that word for me, which he did on a Post-it. "We're waiting for the orthopedist," he added. "Here he is now."

I turned around to find Bin's old friend, Geoff Ewing. "Geoff!" I exclaimed.

"Good gravy," my mother said, brightening up. "Geoffrey Ewing!" And then to the ER doctor, "If this old friend of ours knows as much about bones as he did about tennis, I'm in good hands."

Geoff bent down and gave my mother a peck on the cheek, then studied the x-rays. I had not seen Geoff for at least ten years, and he seemed taller than I remembered him; better looking, too, as if he'd grown into his face and made friends with his once gangly body. While Geoff and the ER doctor examined the x-rays, I sat down next to my mother.

"I'm sorry," she said to me. "That was a cheap trick to pull. And all to get out of cleaning closets."

"Are you all right?"

"Well, obviously, I'm not all right," she said. "My hip hurts like the devil. But I feel better than I did when I left home. Of course they gave me a shot for the pain. That g.d. dog knocked the pins out from under me."

"You look better," I said.

"You're the one who looks better. I bet you're glad you spruced up before you came here." She nodded in Geoff's direction.

A moment later, he ambled over and pulled up a chair on the other side of my mother. In a calm, comforting voice, he told her she had a fractured hip and asked if she had any osteoporosis.

"Not according to those bone-density people," she replied.

"Well, that's a testimony to diet and exercise. And your charm, of course," he said.

"The same old malarkey," she replied, pleased by his flattery. "Just genes and luck. Not that I'd call this luck."

I was quieted by this large man, and curious, too. Why was he back in Edgecliff? And what had he done with his life since I'd seen him last? My brother and Geoff had been inseparable before

Bin went away to prep school, and after that, during the summers all through middle school and high school. I didn't know if they still kept in touch.

Geoff explained to my mother that he would fix her hip with a compression screw and a plate and that she would have to remain in the hospital for three or four days. He also added, in a throwaway tone, that special care might be required. A nursing home, I immediately thought, and my heart sank. "Physical therapy, I mean," he said.

"Now, Geoffrey," my mother said, "you and I are old friends. Don't tell me I have to stay in the hospital. I hate hospitals. Besides, that will bollix up Sister's plans something dreadful. She came to help me move. To New Mexico. Davidson died two years ago, and I've sold the house on Mars."

"I know. I'm sorry. But just think of this as a small delay," he said reassuringly. "I'm confident Lizzie will work things out."

"Of course," I said. Lizzie. Geoff had picked that up from my brother, who'd often called me Lizzie years ago.

"Excuse me," I said to him, "but what are you doing in Edgecliff? I thought you were in Boston."

"I'll tell you about it later," he said. He turned to my mother and asked whether the pain was bad.

"Not quite so bad since they drugged me."

He smiled. "Well, it's probably going to hurt more after I finish with you. I apologize in advance."

"Let's get it over with, then," my mother said.

He asked her when she last ate, and when he heard she'd had some breakfast, he said he'd wait until the afternoon to operate. "In the meantime, we'll get you settled and prepped."

"Can Sister come with me?"

"Naw," he said, "Lizzie can come back later. She'd just be in the way right now."

I took my mother's hand and kissed her. She smelled like freesia, peppery and fresh. I would recognize her scent anywhere.

"The dog," my mother said to me. "Don't forget to walk that beast around noon." I nodded, and we all moved out into the hall, where my mother was wheeled away.

"Thank you," I said to Geoff, "for being so kind and reassuring. I'm assuming you were telling the truth?" Looking up at him, I was momentarily disconcerted because he seemed to possess two faces, the one I had known years ago and another belonging to a man in his late thirties whose dark hair had flecks of gray in it. I was lifted out of the hospital corridor by a memory of my mother lying in bed, and Geoff and my brother at age nine or ten perched on the steep gabled roof off her bedroom, balanced precariously on snow shovels. There had been a blizzard, and my mother was certain the roof over the dining room was in danger of collapsing under the weight of the snow. My father was away, and I hated heights. Responsible Geoff had insisted on getting rid of it, and he'd dragged Bin out to help him.

"Absolutely," he said. "She's a wonderful woman, your mother. And you haven't changed at all."

I made a face. "I'd like to think I'm a little smarter now."

He patted my shoulder and told me where to meet him after he'd finished operating. "We'll take her in around two. You should be there about four or so."

"And you're sure she'll be okay?"

He stared down at me soberly. "Hasn't she always been? Hasn't she always rallied?"

"Eventually, yes." I smiled. "You were always so good to her." And then, without thinking, I stood on my tiptoes and kissed him on the cheek. He grabbed my hand for a second. As he walked away down the hall, he turned and said, "I want to hear all about Bin later. I haven't talked to him in a couple of years. About you, too."

Only when he had disappeared around a corner did I realize I was shaking. Nevertheless, I managed to find my mother's insurance information in her wallet and give it to someone in Admitting. Then I fretted for the next six hours.

Around 4:30 that afternoon, Geoff located me in the waiting room where we'd agreed to meet. I had forgotten a book, and I was going through a third issue of *People* magazine as if I were about to be tested on the material.

"Your mother's fine," he said. "In a good deal of pain and groggy, but her hip should heal nicely. It was a clean break. The internist who checked her over said she's fit as a fiddle. She's in the recovery room now. You can run in for a minute, but why don't you come back this evening? Or better yet, wait till tomorrow. Get out of this place," he added. "You must be tired."

I stood up and my purse fell to the floor, its contents scattering. He stooped to help me pick things up. My wallet had flopped open, and out dropped the photos of my children. He saw them and nodded appreciatively. "She's a beauty," he said about Anna. "And these guys here," he pointed to a picture of the twins horsing around by the pool last summer, "they look like your clones. It's amazing."

"They're a lot bigger than I am. They have more muscles, too." I slipped the photos back where they belonged. "But tell me about your life," I added, "your wife, your kids."

"A boy six and a girl eight. They have all of your books, naturally. My mother made sure of that. My little girl is crazy about Betsy Blossom." He grinned.

"But how do you happen to be in Edgecliff?"

"Last year my father decided to sell his practice so he and Mom could move to Florida and play golf every day. I was ready for a change, so we came back here a couple of months ago. We're living in the old house on Jupiter."

"Does it feel strange?"

"Strange? Sometimes. There's a sense of déjà vu about a lot of things—the same country club, the same Browns' seats, the same Thursday-night orchestra tickets. Even the same old metal backboard at the end of the drive. I haven't gotten around to getting a new one yet."

Suddenly, I could hear the precise clang that backboard made when a basketball hit it. For hours at a stretch, Geoff and my brother would shoot baskets, and sometimes when I went to pick Bin up, they would invite me to play Horse with them. Whoever missed a shot got a letter and the person who spelled "horse" first lost. Even though they were young, they were both tall for their age, and except for the rare times they let me win, I always lost.

"How's Bin? It seems like every time I turn on the TV, I see him. He's looking good."

I filled him in on Bin's activites. "That SOB," he said. "Who would have dreamed it? A star."

"Oh, you know Bin. He's always been a star, at least in his own mind."

"Still giving him a hard time?"

"Not really," I replied. "Some things never change."

"Everything changes, Lizzie," he said. "But how are you? Still happy out West? You sure look like life agrees with you."

"At least the sun shines there. Vitamin D—wise, I'm set."

We both laughed. "I'll talk to you soon," he said. "Call me if you have any questions. Your mother will be out of bed tomorrow. We'll have her home in no time. Scout's honor."

That calmed me down. "Really?"

"Really."

I went to see my mother in the recovery room, but she was so drugged she couldn't talk, so I stayed only a few minutes. Then I drove back to the house and took Duke for a walk that, not accidentally, led me down Jupiter, past the Ewings' house. Except for a new silver Volvo in the driveway, it looked the same as it always had, a rambling white clapboard house, shaped like a barn and set sideways on the lot. I spotted a wreath on the front door, one of those jaunty twig things with painted wooden hearts all around it.

In the waning light, I walked back to Mars Avenue, feeling like a visitor from outer space on my own childhood streets, or like Mandrake the Magician from the comics, who had a cloak that rendered him invisible. I imagined people glancing out of their windows. If I'd had a cloak like Mandrake's, they would only see Duke moseying along, sniffing at every tree, a big, old dog in no hurry to go any place, his leash suspended in the air by an invisible hand.

Edgecliff is a suburb to the west of Cleveland, and its homes range from the large ones along the lake to small up-and-down duplexes on the south end. In between are streets full of well-maintained houses. Except for the tall apartment buildings on the lake, almost everything was built before World War II.

When the city was laid out in the 1880s, the east-west streets running parallel to the lake were given numbers, First Street to Eighth Street; the north-south streets, dozens of them, were named after famous people: Lincoln, Emerson, Euclid. But shortly after the turn of the last century, a man named Josiah Walker became the mayor. An avid astronomer who had actually named his daughter Universe, Walker introduced a proposal to rename Edgecliff's streets after heavenly bodies—planets, stars constellations. He was persuasive enough to get his way. In a celestial state of mind the chamber of commerce dubbed the town "A Heavenly Place."

Heavenly or not, Edgecliff never felt quite like home to me, though it's not an unattractive town as Midwestern suburbs go. There is plenty of green in the summer—beautiful oaks and maples, lush gardens, manicured lawns; cooling breezes come off the lake. Still, Edgecliff always felt like a spot on the map where I'd merely happened to land, one that could easily be confused with other spots.

My parents claimed to have moved to Edgecliff because they loved the lake. But who knows why people choose the places they live? As a boy, my father had lived all over the West, where his father, an engineer, built railroads. Born in Montana, my father attended eight different schools in four states before he was nine. A feeling of belonging—that deep sense of place that frees us, and enables us simply to *be*—was something my father never experienced growing up.

He was fond of Edgecliff, though his fondness always seemed arbitrary to me. I can see now that was because it had nothing to do with sentiment. Rather it was the result of a conscious decision to stop and settle. Work drew my father to Cleveland, not love or a dream, or the claim you make on a place when its beauty haunts you. It could have been any of a dozen places.

My mother, on the other hand, came from a small town in southern Ohio. Before the Civil War, her great-grandparents built the house she grew up in. They had been fierce abolitionists, and the house had been a station on the Underground Railroad. An only child, my mother lived in that house with two grandmothers, a great aunt, and her parents. The name of the street where the house stood bore her own last name.

That experience gave her a sense of home that no other place could rival, and so she tried to superimpose the town in which she was raised onto Edgecliff. It was a terrible fit, but she refused to acknowledge that. When I was small, she offered her town in lieu of where we actually lived. And I, so eager to be some place, learned that town like the back of my hand.

Thus, I have in my head two places, Edgecliff and, infinitely more vivid in my mother's telling and retelling, her town, a tenth of the size of Edgecliff. No wonder the suburb where I was raised didn't live up to my expectations; it would never be the place my mother made it clear we belonged—her own small town, worlds away.

So there I was: a child with a father who had little notion of home, and a mother with one so firmly rooted in her memory that no other place would do. I understood none of this when I was small. I blamed Edgecliff, failing to understand that the true source of my nagging homesickness was largely my mother's; unable to see that my sense of Edgecliff's randomness stemmed from my father's decision to choose a job, and then, as an afterthought, a place to live.

Throughout my childhood, Edgecliff remained stubbornly at odds with a certain richness I felt must exist; not any richness I myself had experienced, but rather my mother's version, enhanced by nostalgia, of abundant life in a little town. Naturally, I couldn't live in my mother's town; besides, I knew the times she talked about had long since vanished. Then one day, when I was fifteen, the town itself nearly vanished, wiped off the map by a devastating tornado. At the time, I could not understand why my mother wasn't grief stricken. Later I did: The place she loved wasn't so much a real town; it was made up of fragments of dreams and memories, peopled by those who were gone for good.

When my mother's town disappeared, Edgecliff became far less bothersome to me. I began to see it as something I would have to wait out, and I did. Eventually, I got married and started a life in the kind of sunny, rich place I'd always dreamed of. But that November day, walking Duke, I puzzled over my lack of connection to Edgecliff. That seemed odd, because in high school, I had done almost every activity it was possible to do; I'd been so involved that my mother began calling me a whirling dervish.

Yet now my past seemed murky and vague, as resonant as an amnesiac's. Or, as if it might belong to someone else.

Jesse phoned from Northwestern around dinnertime. It was good to hear his voice.

"Hey," I said. "Where have you been?"

"Around," he said. "Going crazy studying. How's Nana?"

"Doing well, I think. You should call her tomorrow."

"I will," he said and then paused. "Uh, Mom? Listen. Don't get hysterical or anything, but I'd like to take flying lessons. I know they're kind of expensive . . ."

"Flying lessons?" I said. "Not on my dime." I was horrified.

"Aw, Mom, come on."

After a while I said I'd think about it, and, in a better mood, he brought me up to date on his classes. Jesse was pre-med; he'd always been fascinated by science and math, unlike his twin brother, Will.

"By the way," he said. "My roommate Dan? He got a concussion mountain biking, but he's okay. I mean, he must be since he called to tell me his doctor sucked."

"I'm sorry to hear that, but I suppose he wasn't wearing a helmet," I said, suspecting that Jesse often went without one, too.

"You know Dan. He's kind of irresponsible."

"Well, I hope you're not. You wouldn't want to wind up in a hospital bed with a crummy doctor, would you?"

"Not me, Mom. But think about the flying lessons, please. I really need to do this."

"Oh my," I said. "Oh my."

CHAPTER 7

Visiting hours at the hospital didn't begin until two o'clock, so I had plenty of time on my hands. Alone in the house, I moved from room to room, packing things fitfully, going through old boxes of tax returns and bank statements from as far back as the 1960s. I started two piles in the living room, one of things to keep, the other to throw away.

I ran across a carton of my father's little pocket-sized date books—almost forty of them—in which, along with lunches, meetings, and trips, he had meticulously recorded daily temperatures, odometer readings, his weight. Strange markings—X's and P's, M's and ★★'s—dotted the pages, a private code I would never decipher.

On the second night my mother was in the hospital, I started in on his desk, which my mother appeared not to have touched since his death. For more than an hour, I found only packets of canceled checks, minutes and financial statements from various boards, ancient receipts. I read everything, as though I were searching for a sign from the dead, but nothing shed any light on my father, and nothing—why should it?—had anything to do with me.

Then, at the bottom of a drawer, under a pile of annual reports and clippings, I discovered a think manila envelope with "Expenses" printed on it in my father's neat hand. I put it aside for the throwaway pile, then changed my mind and opened it.

Inside were dozens of letters, mostly business correspondence addressed to my father, some still in envelopes. Near the top, though, was a letter from me, dated July 8, 1971, written on the stationery of the summer camp in Vermont where I'd gone for years.

"Dear Daddy," I had written,

I'm sorry that mother is sick again, or believes she's sick. I know how hard this is for you. The fact that she has been mostly an invalid has affected us all, even Bin, though he does a good job of pretending not to notice. I wish I could lighten the burden for you somehow . . .

The letter went on in that vein for a page and a half, full of pity for my father, never a kind word about my mother, only the suggestion that she could have been feigning illness for years. Reading it almost thirty years later, I was appalled by its tone, so full of disloyalty and betrayal. The letter ended with a sentence that made my face flush: "I just wanted you to understand I'm sorry you have to put up with all this."

All this. How could I have been so callow?

I suddenly recalled writing that letter. For the zillionth time I had been reaching out to my father, hoping for a response, and I'd obviously been ready to sacrifice my mother to get one. But this letter represented a quantum leap in my girlish campaign to establish a measure of intimacy with him. Had I meant what I said in the letter? Not as much as I'd intended, at whatever cost, to get his attention.

I also recalled receiving no direct answer to it. Several days later, a short note from him arrived—it could have crossed my letter in the mail—asking me if I had heard the joke about the man whose golf partner drops dead on the twelfth hole. "So what did you do?" his friends ask him when he gets in. "Putt one, drag Charley," he replies. "Nine iron, drag Charley," and so on. My father frequently sent me jokes, so it could have been merely a coincidence that this particular one came on the heels of my sorry letter.

But how could my father have kept this, I wondered. Of all the letters I ever wrote to him, the last one I would have wanted my mother to read. Why hadn't he thrown it away? Especially under the circumstances, because that same summer, not two weeks after I took up my fickle pen, my mother had a convulsion. She was taken to the hospital and put through many tests, and for once the tests revealed what had been wrong with her all along: a brain tumor. In a matter of days, she was operated on. The tumor was large and had been there for years, the doctors said. Blessedly, it was benign.

My father didn't call me at camp until several days after the surgery. When he did, I spoke with my mother, who sounded groggy, her voice thick. "Just wait till you see my new hairdo, Sister. Just wait," she said.

I reeled at the speed at which my mother's predicament had been resolved, and felt giddy with gratitude that she was all right. Several weeks later, when I returned home, my father picked me up at the airport. "She doesn't look well," he informed me. "Be prepared for that. But she'll be better soon, she will."

I found my mother lying in bed. Her head had been shaved and there was a new growth of stubble. A raw scar severed her forehead, and there was a noticeable dent near her hairline. He had been right; she was a frightening sight.

"Don't worry, Sister," she said, patting my hand. "It won't get any worse than this. In six months, I'll look like Rapunzel, the doctors swear it."

"Oh, Mama." I was close to tears.

"I hear little noises in my head," she said. "God's knitting needles, the surgeon told me."

I stared at her and then braved the questions. "Why didn't someone discover this before?"

"Shhh," my father admonished me.

"Technology caught up with me," she said. "And Sister? I may not look it now, but I'm lucky. Just think: I get a whole new life, or so I'm told. In a few weeks, I'll be up and around." She closed her eyes and smiled. "A whole new life," she repeated.

My brother Bin walked into the room. "Hey, baldy," he said to my mother.

"God, Bin," I said. My father turned and left the bedroom.

"Bin's fine," my mother said. "Bin understands things."

"Name one," I said bitterly.

"Reality," she replied.

"Reality?"

"He understands it's merely a temporary condition." She smiled.

Bin looked at me and laughed loudly. "What she thought, Mom," he said, "is that you meant reality is a temporary condition." Then the two of them laughed.

"Ouch," my mother said. "Don't make me laugh. It hurts my head."

I gave Bin a dirty look.

"Bag the tragic glances, will you?" he said to me. "This is a celebration, or haven't you noticed?"

"Fix me a cup of tea, will you please, Bin?" my mother said, and at once he was up out of the chair, nearly knocking over a lamp.

When he had gone, my mother took my hand. "I love you," she said. "And you know, I'll tell you the oddest thing. When they were about to put me under, I began reciting an old poem to myself. 'Go not, like the quarry-slave at night, / Scourged to his dungeon, but sustained and soothed / By an unfaltering trust, approach they grave . . . ' "

"Mother," I interrupted. "Don't." The word "grave" had cut through me like a knife. "Please."

"Oh, Sister, please yourself. Don't be so sensitive. I thought you'd be interested. The mind is such a strange place."

"Yes, but—"

"But nothing. Anyway, when it was all over and I was awake, the first thing I remember is saying to your father, 'How's Sister?' " She squeezed my hand. "You take everything too much to heart," she added. "You need to learn to take things in stride."

I stared at her, shocked that my brave little front had been exposed for a sham.

"Listen," she said, "I may look like the wreck of the *Hesperus* now, but quick as a wink, I'll be out of this bed. Life isn't so bad if you don't weaken."

She was right. Within a month, she was bustling around. Her hair came in even darker than it had been before and grew out in a pixie cut that perfectly suited her tiny features. She looked younger than I could ever remember, and bubbled with energy. She seemed an entirely new person. It was clear she was not looking back; she was aimed straight ahead.

My parents must have made many adjustments to their marriage when my mother miraculously became a healthy person. Certainly her recovery altered both their lives—they began traveling, they entertained friends, they went to parties and played bridge. My mother's world, once limited to the house on Mars, expanded dramatically. She volunteered at the library where she'd worked before I was born, read to the elderly, and became active in their church. She was like someone who had lit out into a new country.

After I finished reading my shameful old letter, I felt unutterably sad. I got down on the floor with Duke and buried my face in his coat. As communications went, I thought, what could have conveyed more clearly the limits of understanding in my family than my pitiful letter and my father's joking response? And whose limits had they been?

Not my mother's.

I put on my coat and fled the house with Duke. We walked for half an hour before I could bring myself to go back. I tossed the manila envelope into a garbage bag, but not before removing my thoughtless letter, which I ripped into shreds and buried under the trash in the kitchen.

The phone rang. It was Bin.

"Where have you been?" he said. "Out on the town? I've been trying to get you. The old girl needs to get herself an answering machine."

"I was walking Duke."

"How's the patient?"

"Didn't you talk to her earlier? She told me you called."

"You sound edgier than usual," he said. "Are you okay?"

"Just tired," I said.

"Yeah, well. Rest up. I'm coming to town."

"Mother will love that." She would, too. The two of them still sparked off each other.

"Getting bored, is she? Needs a little oomph in her life? Well, I'm her guy."

"You are her guy," I said. "No question there."

"Christ, don't be so theatrical. Have I ever told you that almost everything I know about drama I learned from you and Dad? Not, comedy, God knows, but the heavy stuff. The two of you elevated ordinary household affairs to goddamn Greek tragedy."

"Calm down, Bin."

"But I'm serious," he said. "And even grateful."

"Of course you are, but for once I would just like not to be your whipping person."

"Whipping boy is the expression," he said.

I figured he'd been thrown for a loop by our mother's accident.

"Or it was before genderless prose," he added. "Ah me, genderless prose."

"So when are you coming?"

"Saturday," he said. Mother would be home by then. "I've got this tryout, then this two-day gig on *Days of our Lives,* then I'm free. Will you pick me up at the airport?"

"You know I will. Just tell me what time, and I'll be there."

"With a big brass band?"

"Right," I said. "And a rose between my teeth, since it's been a while."

"Oh, I'd recognize you anywhere. I've got your number, remember?"

"Of course you do, but cut me some slack and don't call it," I said.

There was a pause. "It's not like you to mix metaphors. The old man must be spinning in his grave."

"Let's stop this, okay?"

"What? And have all the fun go out of our relationship?"

"I'm not the enemy, Bin," I said, hoping to shake him out of his mood.

"No," he said with a sigh, "but you do pretty well. Not as well as the real one, but you have the same knack." Even death hadn't diminished Bin's anger toward our father.

"I'll see you Saturday."

"We'll have a great time together," he said. "Relive three-fourths of the primal scene. All that."

"Sure." I put the phone down, feeling unsettled. He was almost thirty-eight. I was forty-three. Why couldn't he let go of his anger? And why couldn't I stop being offended by it? Maybe, by the weekend, he'd be over his anxious little snit.

I locked the doors and turned off the lights. I helped Duke up the stairs, pushing him from behind. On the landing, I let him rest while I looked out the window toward the lake, where lights twinkled from distant ships. In a few months, it would freeze over.

That night I had trouble going to sleep. My thoughts were so jumbled and disturbing that finally I dragged my quilt into my parents' bed to see if I could fall asleep there. After ten minutes, I gave that up as a more desperate idea than I wanted to be credited with. I moved into my brother's old room, which no longer bore any trace of him since it had been transformed into a comfortable guest room. Strangely, I kept imagining I smelled gardenias.

Eventually I stumbled back to my own room, where I tossed fitfully in my old bed, beneath a bulletin board on which my faded purple-and-gold high school banner was tacked, along with wilted ribbons for athletic events and academic honors. There was a photograph of me in my cheerleader's outfit alongside yellowed newspaper clippings. The room remained the way I'd left it when I went off to college.

"It looks like a shrine," Bin had said to me several years earlier on a visit to Santa Fe. I laughed in agreement, but lying in my old room that night, I could understand the impulse to preserve a childhood that was gone for good. Then I caught myself: My mother was not particularly sentimental. The room was just one more thing she hadn't gotten around to—like my father's desk, or the closet where his clothes still hung, as if he might rise from the dead one morning and put them on.

CHAPTER 8

S am called almost daily. "Why don't you fly to Chicago and visit Jesse," he suggested.

"Jesse's busy," I said. "Actually, I'm busy too. There's a lot to do here." I didn't add that I was not ready for a discussion with Jesse about the Wright Brothers yet.

"Oh, come on," he said, as if I were just whiling away my time in Edgecliff.

"Have you seen Snickers?"

"Am I supposed to visit Snickers?"

"I don't know, but it might be nice since Ellen and Shep aren't used to having a dog around. Maybe you could take him for a walk."

"Listen, I'm sure Snick's okay. I've got a lot of work piled up."

I bet you do, I thought. Affairs take time.

"I can't leave Edgecliff," I said. "Who would my mother have if I weren't here?"

"I suppose Bin could stay a while," he replied and laughed. Bin might be coming, but he wouldn't hang around for long. He guarded his time jealously; we all knew that.

Sam assured me my mother was fine. "Anyhow," he said, "Mary Talbot should be home soon. And face it, as nice as it may be for your mother to see you all the time, this is keeping you from things."

"What things?"

"Well . . ." he began, and then stopped.

What I didn't say to Sam that day was that I didn't *want* to leave Edgecliff, and it wasn't only because I couldn't abandon my mother. I needed to be by myself for a while, and Edgecliff seemed as good a place as any to hole up. Besides, going through my parents' house had begun to possess me; it was a diversion I could give myself over to completely. In the grip of sorting and cleaning, other things were blotted out, or at least seemed less dire and gloomy.

Two days after my mother's fall, she was clipping along with a walker, doing something the physical therapist called touch-down weight-bearing, which my mother had taken on as a serious challenge; she might as well have been in training. She would come home in two more days, and though it would be with a cane, as she kept reminding me, she couldn't wait. Her spirits were high, and I felt good about her when I left to take Duke for a walk.

As I was headed for the elevators, Robbie stepped out of one, on his way to visit my mother, carrying a bouquet of red tulips, his blue eyes like headlamps. I had called and left him a message to thank him for his rescue work the day of the accident, but I hadn't yet spoken to him in person.

By then, my mother had filled me in about him: He was thirty-five, a postdoctoral student in metallurgy at Case Western Reserve, and he had worked part-time for Bates Barker for the last three years. A Palestinian originally from Israel, he'd emigrated to this country as a boy, via Germany to Pittsburgh, where he had relatives. His name was Rabi, not Robbie.

"Hi," I said, pleased to see him. "What pretty flowers! Mother told me about you," I said brightly. Then ridiculously I added, "You must speak Arabic."

"Sure," he said, looking amused.

"I've never heard Arabic," I said, "except on TV. No, wait. Didn't someone in *Lawrence of Arabia* speak it?" I was dithering, and a little breathless. "Anyway, how do you say, uh, 'Get well' in Arabic?"

"Salamit albik," he replied.

"Oh my gosh," I said. "Say it again." He repeated the phrase.

"And that really means 'get well'?

"Actually, word for word, it means 'the safety of your heart.' "

"What a sweet thought. How many other languages do you speak?"

"Just a couple. German, French, English—or I try." He smiled. "How about you?"

"Oh, I'm an idiot. Most Americans are. I can read French, and I speak a little Spanish—where I live, everyone speaks a little Spanish. *Un poquito español.*" Why was I going on like such a moron? "But basically, you know, English is about it." We had to separate to make room for an orderly who was pushing two wheelchairs into the elevator.

"So what have you been doing?" he asked as we moved back toward each other.

"Mostly going through my parents' things. You wouldn't believe all the stuff in that house. It may be another forty years before I can get it cleared out! What a job."

"I can help you, Eliza," he said enthusiastically.

"Oh, no, that's not what I meant at all. You've got your hands full already. But thanks."

I wasn't eager for company, but his offer made me realize I actually could use some help hauling things down the stairs. So I asked if he knew anyone who could give me a hand. "A friend or neighbor. Someone strong."

"But I'm strong," he said, and laughed. "And I'm serious. I'll do it." He tapped his finger on his chest emphatically.

"No, really," I said.

"Come on, now." He looked puzzled. "You can't do all that alone." He seemed a little chagrined by my refusal, and I thought, Oh, what the hell.

"All right," I said. "But only if you let me pay you."

"Please. Your parents have been so kind to me. You can't pay me. No."

"Of course I can."

"You are very stubborn, aren't you?" His gaze was so direct, my instinct was to turn away, but I didn't. I noticed a pale sickle-shaped scar intersecting his eyebrow; aside from that, his features were perfect, and his cheeks were rosy against his olive skin. All the same, he didn't seem vain. On the contrary, he appeared unassuming, his engaging buoyancy veering toward humor, or, even more disconcerting, wonder. Reluctantly, I agreed to his offer to come over that evening around half past six.

I was on the phone when he arrived, talking to Will, who was writing a paper for a course in the history of the English novel. He wanted to know what I thought of his take on Conrad's *Heart of Darkness*.

"I'd need to look at the book again," I said. "It's a somber novel, isn't it?"

"Yeah, it's kind of creepy." He sighed. "Listen, I'm stressed. The stuff I'm taking this year is overwhelming. I'm probably the dumbest person in all my classes. Physics alone will kill me."

"I doubt that," I said. "You're very bright, and you know that."

"Oh, sure," he said, sounding so glum I wanted to fly through the phone and hug him.

"Your brother's determined to take flying lessons," I said, hoping to distract him. "What do you think of that?"

"Oh, Jesse," he said, disparagingly. "He told me about that the last time he called. The wild blue yonder, sure. He has that macho, daredevil thing, just like Dad. Are you going to let him?"

"I don't know. The whole idea gives me the willies. But people do fly."

"He probably just wants to get high without taking drugs."

"Will, it's not like you to talk that way about your brother."

"Yeah, well, I'm sorry, but I already said the same thing to him."

"Hon," I said, "you're just pooped. Why don't you go for a run?"

"Because it's pouring here. All it does around this place is rain, like I told you. Then it snows. Rain or snow, that's the entire weather spectrum in New Hampshire. It's depressing."

"I'm familiar with the weather in New Hampshire, remember? But I wish you weren't so grumpy."

"Hey!" he said suddenly, sounding like a different person; Will could change moods just like that. "There's this dog in this bookstore here, named Dickens. The dog, not the store. He looks exactly like Snickers. It's weird. I dreamed about Snickers the other night, about the time when he was a puppy and fell into the pool. You had to rescue him, remember?"

"Oh my gosh, I'd forgotten. Poor little thing."

"You know? I wish it were summer, and I were in that pool right now," he said.

My mother's doorbell rang. "Hold that thought in your mind, Will."

"Yeah?"

"The pool. Sunshine. Heat. Got it?"

"Got it," Will said. And then, "Mom, I love you. This paper'll be okay."

"Of course it will. It'll be brilliant."

Rabi stayed for four hours, and together, we accomplished a lot more than I'd anticipated. I was so grateful for his help I forgot I hadn't wanted him to come. When I again mentioned paying him, he said, "Please, do something about this irrational desire of yours." I said we'd talk about money later, and he shook his head as if I were in need of serious help. You could tell he liked women.

He was surprisingly easy to be with, efficient and quick. He glanced at things and seemed to know immediately what to keep and what to throw away. Sorting through years of my family's detritus with him seemed to take the nostalgic sting out of the process. I was flabbergasted that so much had been saved.

We talked very little, but at one point, I said to him, "So how do you say 'pack rat' in Arabic?"

"You mean someone who saves things?"

I nodded. "Like my father, I suspect."

He looked puzzled. "Rat pack," he said thoughtfully.

I started laughing. He stared at me questioningly. "No, no, *pack rat*," I said when I'd recovered. " 'Rat pack' was what Frank Sinatra and his pals were called. You know, Dean Martin, Sammy Davis, Jr. . . ."

By then he was laughing, too. "Did I really say 'rat pack'? I must be losing my grip." He shook his head. "Okay," he added, straightening up, "I'm getting serious now: How about . . . hmmm . . . *hawi*?"

"Don't look at me," I said, and started giggling again.

"Or," he said, brightening, "maybe *mjamme*'?"

The word had a strange, gutteral ending. "And what does that mean, exactly?" I managed to ask.

"Someone—a man—who collects things," he replied. "Not good enough, though."

"Not as good as 'rat pack,' that's for sure. But thanks, anyway. Arabic sounds like an amazing language."

"And I seem to be losing it," he said dryly, and we both began laughing again. It felt wonderful to laugh; I hadn't laughed for weeks.

After a few minutes, I calmed down enough to say, "I'm wowed by your ability with languages. Seriously."

He looked at me sideways. "You're easy to impress. Too bad I don't speak more of them. Too bad I don't speak . . . fluently."

"Please," I said, on the verge of losing it again.

Eventually, we pulled ourselves together and got back to work.

That first night, we went through carton after carton in the attic—years' worth of canceled checks wrapped in neat packets, business papers, tax returns. I was amazed by how much my father had kept. I was also dismayed that my mother hadn't gotten around to going through any of it in the two years since his death. What had she been doing?

Among these papers, we found carbon copies of letters, none of them personal. In fact, there was nothing that spoke much of my father's inner life, except his inclination to accumulate things; just dry, brittle business correspondence: A letter dated March 1970, correcting a statement from the long-defunct Halle Brothers' Department Store; a recommendation for someone I'd never heard of who wanted to join Edgecliff Country Club; a carbon copy of a note written in 1963 to *Time* magazine threatening to cancel his subscription if he was billed again for the same time period. "At this rate," my father had written, "I'll be a qualified subscriber to *Time* into the 2000s, long after I'm dead—like those people the Democrats resurrect in Chicago every election day." Clipped to this was a handwritten apology from the subscription manager, a quaint reminder that before computers, there were actual people, real handwriting.

When I mentioned this to Rabi, he seemed baffled. "Who do you think runs computers?"

"Other computers, of course."

"Ridiculous person," he said and laughed.

I found several locks of curly, white-blond baby hair in an envelope. On the outside, my father had written, "Eliza's first haircut, June 8, 1959. Not much to her liking."

I dragged a large box from the attic corner. In it, to my surprise, were all the report cards my brother and I had ever received, filed away neatly along with certificates for perfect attendance, class photos, pins, prizes. There was a fat folder of *Edgecliff High Chronicles,* which I had edited my senior year, and it looked as if every single one of them was there. I leafed through several of them before consigning them to the trash. I was shocked by all the things my father had squirreled away.

I uncovered a large envelope full of newspaper clippings about Bin's prep school basketball career; dozens of programs from his performances at the Edgecliff Children's Theater, others from high school and college. I found two black-and-white photos of me as homecoming queen in 1972. I had a crown on my head, a large bouquet of red carnations in my arms, and I was wearing a short, lacy dress. My hair was piled high, and my smile seemed slightly blurry, like a child's smile, still new to the world.

"You look like a movie star," Rabi said. "But you're much prettier now."

"Come now," I said and shook my head as I shoved the homecoming photos in the trash. Rabi immediately retrieved them and set them on the pile of things to be saved.

I reached to put them back in the trash. "No, don't," he said a little sternly. "You're being disrespectful of the past. You really are." He touched my hand, and I suddenly felt completely unglued. I got to my feet and walked toward the attic stairs.

"Be right back," I called over my shoulder.

I went down to my mother's bathroom and pressed my forehead against the cool tile wall. My life seemed jumbled, pieces of it loose and floating everywhere, my past careering weirdly around inside of me: My father, dead; my father, almost the same age I was now, writing out checks and filing our schoolwork and prizes. My forty-three-year-old self, my adolescent self; my mother sick—the drawn blinds, the admonitions to be still, both of my parents in the clutches of her illness. And there I'd been a child, unable to penetrate either his worry or her pain.

I drank a glass of water, staring out of the window, past my own reflection, at the large oak outside. I heard the mournful whistle of a train in the distance, and the sound steadied me. Who knew the truth about their childhood, after all? My own wasn't in all those boxes; it was gone, and all that remained were memories I needed to keep at bay. Memories I *had* kept at bay, or thought I had, until Rabi startled me.

A perfect stranger took the remnants of my past more seriously than I did—I, who acted as if all the years marked by bills and receipts, programs and photographs, meant nothing. If I wasn't careful, I could tumble into the past and never come back. How had that happened? It seemed that I had momentarily lost control of the interior narrative I'd constructed to domesticate the sadness I'd experienced years ago.

I had thought I might discover some truth among my parents' belongings, but all I'd found were my father's magpie tendencies and my mother's haphazard housekeeping. Rabi and I were not handling treasures or uncovering family secrets; we were only rummaging through stuff that should have been thrown away long ago.

I climbed back up to the attic and sat down on the floor in front of a carton of old paperback mysteries that both of my parents had been briefly addicted to. Rabi was rifling through a stack of annual reports from the steel company where my father had worked before he opened his own law offices.

I felt better; it didn't matter what Rabi thought. Who was he, anyway? No one I'd probably ever know or needed to take seriously; not quite real, either. Like Moag or Acme, or the other friends I'd had when I was small.

I could almost imagine I'd made him up, too.

★   ★   ★

In retrospect, I might as well have been standing on the railroad tracks that bisected Edgecliff, facing down one of those hundred-car freight trains that streaked through the town twice a day. I felt it coming. I felt the faint vibrations on the track. I felt it coming and stood there anyway. Like a person who couldn't wait to be flattened.

CHAPTER 9

The next morning, I was awakened by a phone call from Geoff Ewing. "Lizzie. Bad news, I'm afraid."

"Oh my God." I was sure my mother had died.

"Your mom's temperature spiked to over one hundred and two degrees early this morning, and when the nurse checked her wound, she found some drainage."

"Wait, Geoff. Is she okay?"

"She'll be fine, I expect. It's a complication that happens, but I'm sorry it happened to your mother." He went on to say that she seemed to have a superficial wound infection, and that he was taking her back to surgery to drain it. As he kept talking, my racing heart began to slow down.

"I'll be there right away," I said.

"Take your time," Geoff said. "But you need to know this will substantially delay her going home."

Frankly, I was so glad my mother wasn't dead or dying that I didn't listen to much else he said. I got dressed, took Duke for a quick walk and fed him, and then, without even a cup of coffee, I went to the hospital, where I waited nervously for my mother in her empty room, trying hard not to imagine all the things that could go wrong.

As I was pacing around, a nurse's aide brought in a large vase of yellow roses. She left and returned almost immediately, carrying a white box. The roses—two dozen of them—were from Bin, and the box, which contained three gardenias in little water tubes, was from Sam. If I'd been up for comic relief, the gardenias might have done it, but as it was, they seemed like a sick joke. Knowing Sam as well as I did, however, I suspected gardenias were one of the few hothouse flowers he could think of. Besides, he obviously had gardenias on the brain. After debating whether or not to pitch them (I actually liked gardenias and so did my mother), I let them remain—a fragrant reminder of something I didn't want to think about but knew I should.

My mother was wheeled back into the room an hour or so later. She was woozy, but squeezed my hand and gave a little smile. "Go, Sister," she managed to say. "Get out of this depressing place." Then she nodded off. I sat for a while, holding her hand, waiting for Geoff to appear. When he did, he motioned me out into the hall.

"Everything went well," he said. "It looks like a mild staph infection, but we'll know for sure tomorrow when we get the culture back from the lab. I had to pack the wound open. She'll be on heavy antibiotics for a while."

"Open?" It sounded grisly to me.

"Yeah," he said. "There'll be whirlpool treatments to clean it, and then, in ten or twelve days, I'll go back and close it, assuming it's healing."

He kept reassuring me. "These things happen, but, as I told you earlier, she won't be going anyplace for a couple of weeks."

"And after that?"

"You're talking about the move?"

I nodded.

"Well, she probably could get on a plane a couple of weeks after that, depending. By Christmas, for sure."

I sighed and said, "Damn."

"Look," he said, "I'm sorry your plans are fouled up. I know you're anxious to get back home."

"I wasn't thinking of that," I said. "I was thinking how I hate for her to go through this."

"Me too, but these things usually aren't too painful. She's in great shape otherwise." He patted my arm and told me to take care of myself. "I'll be in touch. By the way, you should come over for dinner one of these nights."

Later, after I had pinned one gardenia to my sleeping mother's pillow and the other two on her drapes, I went home to walk the dog. I returned to the hospital afterward and spent most of the day there, watching her sleep, haunted by the scent of gardenias, which by then permeated the room.

When my mother finally came to, she asked me about the flowers and told me to remove the one on her pillow. "What were you trying to do, Sister? Suffocate me? I like gardenias, but that was too much."

I could tell her about too much, I thought. Could I ever.

The next few days went by in a blur. My mother complained about the whirlpools and dressing changes, but good-naturedly.

She placed great importance on being what she called "a good scout," and claimed to feel fine except for the antibiotics, which bothered her stomach. I wanted to stay with her, but she persisted in sending me away, so I was in and out all day long.

Rabi came to the house in the evenings, and after several nights, we had succeeded in clearing out most of the attic. Eventually we moved downstairs to my bedroom closet, which was full of old clothes in garment bags, most of which I hadn't looked at since high school. I was amazed to find them, along with small jackets and shirts my brother had worn in grade school. On a shelf was a collection of children's artwork, crude finger paintings and watercolors, all neatly dated on the back in my father's handwriting. As I wrestled the stiff paper into a trash bag, I caught a whiff of ancient classroom chalk.

"Maybe your brother wants these?" Rabi said, showing me a pad of charcoal drawings Bin had done of himself in high school. Narcissus, I thought, but he had captured himself perfectly. Bin had always been good at art, better than I was, though he hadn't pursued it.

I took the pad and put it aside. "He probably won't," I said. "He's not very sentimental, but I'll show them to him."

"Two cold-hearted children," Rabi joked. "Your poor mother."

"She may be more cold-hearted than we are," I said. "After all, she wasn't the one who saved all this. Maybe my mother kept the clothes, but more likely, she never got around to giving them away."

"So, your father really was the sentimental one."

"Frankly, I never realized he paid attention to things like this," I said, gesturing at the trash bag full of artwork. "I didn't know he cared enough to save anything. He seemed so aloof from the world."

"Your father *aloof*?" Rabi said incredulously. "No." I kept forgetting Rabi had known him.

"Except for jokes, my father was mostly cold and distant with us."

Rabi stared at me. I could tell we had two different people in mind. At last he said, " 'Avoid suspicion and do not speak ill of another in his absence.' "

It was obvious he was quoting something. "What's that from?"

"The Koran," he replied.

"Say it in Arabic, would you?"

" 'La tajassasoo wa la yaghtab ba'dukum ba'daan.' "

"Why am I so fascinated with the sound of that language?"

He laughed. "Beats me."

"I take it you're Muslim?"

"No," he said. "I was raised a Christian, but gave that up after my father was killed." With his foot, he flattened the artwork to make more room in the bag. He said his father had been killed when he was ten.

"I'm so sorry. Tell me about it."

"Another time. Let's get this cleaned up."

"You're sure?"

He nodded. "This is a mess," he said as we began clearing out a dresser drawer full of battered games and their pieces. Monopoly, Scrabble, Trivial Pursuit, Go. Dominoes were scattered all over, marbles and poker chips. Checkers, chess pieces, dice and Monopoly money all jumbled together. Rubber bands, playing cards, pencils, too. The amount of stuff exasperated me.

"Why in God's name did they keep all this?" I didn't expect an answer, so I was startled when Rabi spoke up.

"Because it's a home," he said quietly.

"And this is what homes come to? *Garbage?*" I was taken aback by the anger in my voice.

He was silent for a moment, and then he said, "Homes are places where you can throw things in drawers, and it's okay." He paused. "What a luxury," he added. Things, in the first place, somewhere safe to put them. Safety itself." He seemed to be talking to himself. "You claim a piece of the world, and it doesn't disappear, it's yours. You can be whoever you are, keep things or throw them out. Live your life." He sighed as if speaking was a great effort. "You Americans take so much for granted."

"We should talk about that," I said, but he didn't answer. By then he seemed as obsessed as I was with getting rid of things. He ripped another trash bag off the roll, and we began scooping the games and their annoying little parts into it—for the moment, beyond any discussion of homes or fathers, ridiculously consumed by the task at hand.

Yet I was brought up short by the harsh facts of his life. We might both be hostages to the past, but what Rabi had been through—losing his father, leaving his home, shuttling across the globe—made my own past merely a slight inconvenience. I was ashamed to have put us in the same boat. I had wanted only a carefree smoothness between us, nothing complicated or tricky, nothing substantial. I'd been unprepared for his troubled childhood and the tragedies he'd endured.

What had I been thinking, I wondered. Because even in fairy tales, hazards cropped up—unexpected, baffling, sometimes throwing lives completely off course. Why had I thought Rabi would be immune?

CHAPTER 10

During the time my mother was in the hospital, I did several inexplicable things, as if an unfamiliar version of me had surfaced. I watched myself as if I were a bystander, wondering what in the world I might do next.

One morning, for instance, I found myself in an Edgecliff real estate agent's car, secured by a seatbelt that simulated strangulation. The agent's name was Betty Morris, and her camel-colored coat was soiled around the hem, her leather boots water-stained. Slips of paper stuck out of her purse, Post-its littered the dashboard; the backseat was piled with maps and phone books and several metal FOR SALE signs. I found something comforting in all that disarray, or maybe it was that Betty herself was so unremarkable that I believed I was, too. She seemed so scattered, I had trouble imagining she could make a living selling real estate.

For Betty's benefit, I had invented a life for myself: I said I lived in San Francisco, that my husband was being transferred to Cleveland, and that we might be interested in living in Edgecliff. I made my children five years younger than they really were and gave myself a job working in an art gallery. I could have gone on and on, I realized; fabricating a life came so easily to me that it didn't feel as if I were lying but simply presenting alternatives.

The reason a total stranger was driving me around the town where I was born was because, the afternoon before, when my mother fell asleep after a whirlpool treatment, I grew restless. I picked up the Edgecliff phone book, and it fell open to real estate firms. Before I knew it, I found myself dialing the number of one of them and heard myself telling the agent to whom I'd been connected that I was looking for a home. I gave her a price range, and we set a time to meet the next morning. My mother's eyelids fluttered, and I hung up, certain I would cancel the appointment.

But I kept it, which was why I was being shown the main business street of Edgecliff, listening to Betty tell me things I would want to know if I was thinking of moving there: population, police and fire department response times, municipal and state taxes. She included a pitch for the Edgecliff school system and another for Edgecliff's proximity to the airport and downtown Cleveland. She said she herself loved living in Edgecliff.

Betty turned north and headed in the direction of my mother's neighborhood along the lake. "It's a choice residential area," she confided. "A real bargain compared to San Francisco."

A large tree-trimming truck blocked the street she'd turned down, and along with several other cars, we had to stop. We were on Mercury, and I realized the house we were temporarily parked in front of was Kevin Pace's old house. I didn't recognize it at first since it was no longer gray, but rather several shades of muted Williamsburg blue. Kevin had been a friend of mine in high school; we were on the student council together and shared a ride to church every week. Sometimes we would walk home from school together. I liked him; he was much smarter than most of the boys I knew.

"Edgecliff has beautiful trees," Betty volunteered.

Two men clambered like monkeys high above us. It made me queasy to look at them. "How long have you lived in Edgecliff?"

"Six years," she said. "Since my husband decided to move here. Of course, I'm not married to him anymore." She gave a brittle laugh.

Kevin Pace attended Princeton on a scholarship, then went to Berkeley to get his Ph.D. in Asian studies. I had not seen him since college, but for a while, there was gossip that he had become an undercover agent for the CIA. When I'd asked my mother some time ago if she'd heard he rumors about Kevin, she'd said, "Sister, you know the way people talk." My mother attributes much of what's wrong with the world today to unfettered gossip, so it came as no surprise to me that she wouldn't even speculate about Kevin. Still, it was odd; he and his whole family seemed to have vanished from the face of the earth, as some people from your past do. As the past itself does.

"I'm sorry about your husband," I said to Betty, since that seemed to be the response her tone had invited. Chainsaws whined above us.

"Ha!" she said, as if I had just said something hilarious. Then she proceeded to unburden herself of a story about the bad husband who had brought her to Edgecliff and the good one she was married to now. I only half-listened. I was sorry I'd come. More cars stopped behind us, and, from the looks of the men in the trees, there wasn't a chance we'd be moving soon.

"Can't we get there another way?" I said, knowing we could if we simply turned around and went down Pleiades.

"Oh, this will just take a sec." She seemed glad to have company; I had to wonder about her happy new marriage.

I was growing more uncomfortable by the minute because I couldn't think of anything to say to Betty. "There's a house down on Mars," she said, pointing north, "that I think you might have liked. But it was snapped up last week. A big old thing with good bones, right on the lake. Needs a little updating, but . . ."

I suspected she might be talking about my parents' house, so I asked her if there were a lot of houses on that street for sale.

"On Mars? Never. This was the first one to go on the market since I've been in the business." It *was* my parents' house. Odd that she would bring it up.

Eventually, the tree-trimming truck moved, and we were motioned around. Betty turned right onto Mars and proceeded to pull into my mother's driveway. "Here it is," she said. "Isn't it a handsome old thing?"

I studied the house I'd grown up in with a stranger's eyes. "It is," I said. "It looks comfortable."

"Well," she said, backing out of the drive, "unless that deal falls through, it's gone now. I just wanted to show it to you; I thought you'd like it."

"Thanks."

She drove back down Mars and turned up Orion, where she parked in front of one of the houses she wanted me to see. As we cut across the patchy brown lawn toward the front porch, the wind off the lake whipped our coats around and literally pushed us up the steps. Betty fumbled with the lock box, finally retrieving a key, and let us in.

It was chilly inside and very still, as if no one had lived in it for some time. There were signs of habitation everywhere, of course—in the abundance of chintz-covered furniture, in the dark green living room walls right out of an old Ralph Lauren ad, in the framed photographs of no one I recognized clustered on a mahogany table. But for all its cheerful *House & Garden* touches, the house seemed bereft.

Betty practically had to shove me into the dining room because by then, I felt really ill at ease, like the interloper I was. I cast around furiously for some way to extricate myself from this crazy situation, which, according to Betty, included two more houses. I trudged behind her, forcing myself to remark on various features, but finally I'd had enough. I told Betty I did not want to see the third floor, or the suite over the garage, or the finished basement. I told Betty it was a lovely house, but not my cup of tea.

She looked startled, then quickly, a little annoyed. "Saves us both time," she said. "Your honesty, I mean."

We climbed back into her car and went to the other two houses. They were both enormous. The one I went into was dark and dirty and smelled of stale cigarette smoke. Nothing had been done to it for years. The kitchen appliances were avocado green and so were the steel cabinets. I shook my head no. We simply drove by the third house because I told Betty I was running out of time.

"How about tomorrow?" she asked without much enthusiasm. I told her I had appointments in Shaker Heights and Chagrin Falls the next day. I said my husband was leaning toward someplace on the east side. She didn't seem surprised. We drove back to her office where I'd left my mother's car and stood for a moment in the parking lot, the wind sending leaves from a large oak swirling around our feet. I thanked her and said good-bye.

"I didn't think you'd like Edgecliff," she said to my back.

Clearly, her nose was a little out of joint. "You don't look the type," she added.

"What's the type?" I asked. In spite of myself, my hopes rose. Maybe Betty had information I'd been looking for.

She stared off in the distance and screwed up her face. At last, she said, "I think you may be too . . . Oh, I don't know." She was struggling. "Edgecliff," she finally blurted, "Edgecliff's really an old-hat kind of place."

I got into the car and waved.

"Lots of luck in finding a home," she called with more animation than she'd shown all morning. "Lots of luck!"

After I left Betty, I drove to a nearby shopping mall to buy my mother something to keep her warm on her way to and from therapy because she'd complained that the hospital halls were chilly. I located the sporting goods section in a large department store and found two extra-small, fleece-lined hooded sweatshirts. When I went to pay for them, I found myself staring into the eyes of a woman I had gone to high school with but whose name I could not recall. Her hair was gray and she'd gained a lot of weight, but I recognized her right away.

"Why," she said, "aren't you Eliza White? I remember you!"

Without thinking, I turned around, as if she had been speaking to someone behind me.

"I mean you," she said. "You're Eliza White. Of course you are."

I stared at her blankly.

"Edgecliff High?" she tried. "Class of '73?"

"Not me," I said. "You must have me confused with someone else."

"Really? You're sure?"

"Positive," I said.

"Well, I'll be. I could have sworn you were someone I went to high school with."

I handed her money, and she shoved the sweatshirts into a bag. "Sorry about that," she said as I put my wallet away. "But, boy, you must have a double walking around! You're a dead ringer for this girl I knew. I hear she's a famous writer now. I always knew she'd be famous for something."

I said good-bye and walked away, not a clue as to why I hadn't admitted who I am. What had come over me? I had no idea who the person could be who had engaged in the charade of house-hunting with Betty Morris or who had just denied I was me.

On my way out of the store, I walked through the cosmetics department, where a heavily made-up woman was passing out samples of perfume. Strangely—though what else could be strange on a day like the one I was having?—it was a heady gardenia scent that, unless my nose failed me, was identical to the smell I'd discovered in my house and on Sam's clothes. I took the sample to the perfume counter, where I bought a bottle of it and had it gift-wrapped and sent to Sam. On the card, I wrote, "Thinking of you. E."

When I went home, I called Ellen, ostensibly to ask about the dog, but what I really wanted was a sanity check. The dog was fine, she said; by next week, he'd be eating at the table with them, he was such a good conversationalist. "And he doesn't drink much of the wine, either," she added.

"Ellen? Why didn't you ever get a dog?"

"It was Win, remember? He was allergic to everything when he was little. Now that he's left home, maybe we will. But couldn't we just kidnap Snickers?"

"I'm sure that would be fine with Sam," I said. "Has he called, by the way?"

"Called? Called for what?"

"To see how the dog is getting along?"

"You've got to be kidding."

"Oh," I said. "I thought he might."

"Dream on, friend."

Earlier in the week I had told her about my mother breaking her hip; now I told her about the infection and how I would be away much longer than I'd planned. After she said how sorry she was to hear about my mother, she told me not to worry about the dog. He could stay forever, as far as she and Shep were concerned.

"You don't know how grateful I am," I said.

"What's wrong with you, Eliza? You know I'd do anything for you."

"You would," I said pathetically. "I know you would."

"Jeez, friend, you sound like you're in the dumps, not that you don't have reason to be, with your mom and all."

"I guess I am."

"Well, snap out of it. She's healthy. She'll be fine. I know she will." She paused. "Is it Sam?"

"I can't even bear to think about Sam."

"Well, then, what is it?"

"It's Edgecliff," I said. "I'm feeling a little unhinged here at the moment."

"Listen, pal, get over it. This isn't a life sentence. Nosiree. I'd recommend a very dry martini, double olives. It always works for me."

By the time I hung up, I was smiling.

CHAPTER 11

Bin never called to tell me what time he was getting in; he simply showed up. Around noon on the day he said he'd arrive, as I was leaving the house to take Duke for a walk, a cab pulled into the driveway and out stepped my brother. Spotting me on the porch, he dropped his bag and bowed deeply. He wanted me to clap and call "bravo," which, of course, I did.

Chances are you would recognize my brother, although you might not know his name. You have probably seen him dozens of times. If he's never achieved top billing, he has worked steadily for fifteen years, and I'm sure he still holds out hope that the role he gets next week or next month might catapult him to stardom. And it might.

I crossed the lawn, tugged by Duke. Bin looked handsome and tan. He's slim and tall, six foot four, and he projects the vivid aura acquired by people who are used to getting a lot of attention. Every time I see him, I want to stand back and admire him. My daughter bears an uncanny resemblance to him; she, too, is long-limbed and slender with straight, dark hair—utterly delicious to look at. Seeing Bin, I suddenly experienced a pang of longing for

Anna that made me wish I could switch the two of them—as Betsy Blossom would have done in a flash.

Duke recognized Bin and began panting and moaning, too weak in the hips to jump up. "Dukie," Bin said, stooping down to embrace the dog. He rubbed his flanks roughly. "Dukie," Bin repeated. Duke nuzzled his neck and licked his face.

Bin and a woman he used to live with, a dancer named Wendy, had bought Duke as a puppy. When they split up, Bin took the dog. But Bin was out of town a lot, and Duke was unhappy left in the care of dog-walkers. So Bin finally brought him to Edgecliff and deposited him with my parents. My mother agreed to take Duke only because he was Bin's. My father intended to ignore Duke, regarding him as one more mistake my brother had made.

You can guess what happened next: Duke immediately took to my father, shadowing him night and day, lying at his feet the moment he sat down, sleeping next to his side of the bed. Perhaps the dog confused my father with the other tall man in his life. In any case, my father softened and became genuinely fond of him. Duke was one of the few things, maybe the only thing, my father and brother ever agreed upon.

"Jesus," Bin said, standing up. "Duke's breath smells awful." Duke whimpered. "What are you feeding him?"

"He's getting old," I said. "His teeth probably need cleaning."

"Someone should see about his hips, too," Bin said. "They're shot."

"Maybe you could take him to the vet while you're here," I ventured.

"I'm just in and out," he replied. "I probably won't have time, but you . . ." Duke wound himself around Bin's legs.

"He's glad you're here," I said. "It's the happiest I've seen him since Father died."

"Yeah, well, I was pretty happy then myself," Bin said.

That seemed a new low, even for Bin.

"Just kidding," he added and smiled broadly.

Pretend you're deaf, I said to myself. For Bin, I'd often been a substitute for our father, the main object of his anger, but that was a role I'd never gotten used to. I liked to think I tried hard and that Bin was simply a difficult person, but in reality, I frequently reacted childishly to his goading.

Bin *was* difficult, though, and always had been. Ever since I could remember, he had made no secret of the fact that he disliked our father, although it wasn't until later that he could articulate the reasons: The man never paid enough attention to him, never had enough time for him, was seldom around. Bin's emotions felt a little raw and scary to me. Even as a child, he had treated our father with chilly politeness, and our father, in turn, had mainly disregarded his son, distancing them even further. I believe that my father, as the adult, should have vaulted the wall that separated them. But he wouldn't, or, more realistically, couldn't. Perhaps he didn't know how, although why he hadn't spent more time with Bin had always been a mystery to me.

As Bin grew older, be became increasingly condescending toward our father, whom he always called by his first name, Davidson. I don't know why my father never socked him, except that was so clearly what Bin was begging for—to see the man's composure crack. But my father refused to fight back; instead, he would leave the room, sometimes the house itself, when Bin acted up. What Bin had needed was the kind of fatherly interest a boy could understand, not the cold shoulder our own father routinely turned, which amounted to one long, endless rebuke.

Our father might have been trying to set an example by rising above his volatile son's anger. Or perhaps he was waiting for Bin to grow out of it, though his silence toward his son ensured that, in some respects, Bin would be stuck in adolescence forever.

At prep school, where he was sent primarily because of the tension between him and my father, Bin refined his slash-and-burn sarcasm and withering putdowns. He could be clever—no one disputed that—but verbal daggers aimed straight at the heart aren't terribly amusing when the heart belongs to you.

I never knew what to expect from him. One minute he could be charming and witty, the next he was at my throat. His behavior was dramatic and flighty, pitched too high for me. Oddly enough, with our mother, Bin has always been pleasant and loving.

My own initial reaction to my brother's assaults was to remain silent; something inside me often shut down. I knew this reminded him of our father, but, unlike our father, I couldn't remain silent for long. I snapped back feebly, no verbal match for Bin. Hours later—often, days—I would think of the perfect response.

I hooked Duke's leash over an outdoor spigot and went with Bin into the house. He threw his jacket on a table and turned and gave me the once-over. I was wearing jeans, sneakers, and an old brown canvas jacket of our father's with the sleeves rolled up.

"You look tired," Bin said, certainly the least endearing remark you can make to anyone over the age of eighteen. "Are you feeling okay?"

I just stood and stared at him.

"And what happened to your hair?"

My hair is very curly, the kind that used to be considered a regular tragedy but in recent years has become stylish. It was longer than it had been the last time I saw him, and I'd pulled it up in a knot. "Tired" I could take, even "sick." But the crack about my hair got me, for some silly reason.

"And what's with Davidson's jacket?" he added, as if he couldn't quit. "Some kind of memorial tribute? Wearing the vestments of the dead?"

"Why didn't you call?" I said. "I would have been happy to pick you up."

He didn't bother to answer.

"I hadn't realized how shabby things had gotten around here," he said, examining an antique needlepoint chair in the hall that had been threadbare all his life. By this point, I was nearly rigid, the muscles in my legs as taut as if I were doing isometrics.

He surveyed the living room that was by then stacked with cartons. Rabi and I had rolled up the large Oriental rug to get it out of the way and moved most of the furniture to one end of the room. We'd taken down paintings and leaned them against the walls.

"I thought you were here to straighten things out," Bin said. "This place looks like a cyclone hit it."

I took a deep breath. "You smell good," I said. "What is it?" I couldn't put my finger on the scent but it was familiar.

"Oh, that Eliza," he said, addressing an invisible audience. "Isn't she something? Speak to her about reality, and quick as a wink, she'll change the subject."

I was speechless.

"It's nothing but Old Spice, actually," he added, his tone

softer. "Of course, you remember Old Spice." Our father had worn Old Spice all his life; not even our mother could get him to use a fancier brand of aftershave.

"You're wearing Old Spice?"

"Just to throw you offtrack." He winked theatrically. "What do you want me to wear? Some overpriced product hyped by naked guys fumbling with each other?"

"Listen," I said, "I'm going to take Duke for a walk. You get settled. I'll be back in a while and then we can go to the hospital."

"But I want to come with you," he said, as if he were speaking to a demented person.

"Please," I said, "give me a break." That was typical of my brilliant responses to Bin.

He laughed as if I'd said something uproariously funny. My inarticulateness amused him. I turned and walked out of the house, where I unhooked Duke and started down the drive. And then, like the child my brother seemed to have rendered me, I found myself thinking about Betsy again. She would have thrown down one of her magic seeds and made him vanish. Or better yet, given me the wits to ignore him.

"Hey!" Bin called from the front porch. "I was serious. Wait for me!" He caught up, zipping his leather jacket and shoving his hands in his pockets. A cold wind blew off the lake, which was the same gray as the sky. We walked for several blocks in silence, Duke poking around bushes, peeing on trees.

"This is really a depressing place," Bin finally said. "Like what Sartre must have had in mind when he wrote *No Exit*." He took Duke's leash out of my hand. "I can still almost taste the way I felt here when I was fourteen or fifteen," he went on. "People so incapacitated by boredom all they could do was operate by rote: golf on weekends, Sunday nights at the country club, bridge every Tuesday." He was describing our parents' lives.

Bin and I had never talked much about Edgecliff. I assumed he had forgotten all about it.

"It was a place where we lived," I said. "Now we don't."

"I never felt at home here," he added.

"Me neither, actually."

"Seriously?" He stopped and looked at me. "I always thought you liked it here. Christ, when you were in high school, you practically *owned* this town."

"No," I said. "For me there's always been a drabness about the whole place, something melancholy. Why is that, I wonder?"

"I'm not sure," he said, "But it reeks of attenuated desire. You know? Of dreams that trail off into nothing or come smack up against a brick wall."

"Some people like it."

"Oh, Eliza, some people just got off the bus here."

We crossed the street and went into Edgecliff Park with its enormous municipal swimming pool and its eight WPA tennis courts, where we both used to play, and where Bin and Geoff Ewing regularly won the city championship. The park was deserted.

"Dad once told me," I began, daring to bring up the unmentionable, "that happiness wasn't a function of geography. I think he wanted to believe that, but it always sounded wrong to me."

"He was wrongheaded about a lot of things," Bin said, far less abrasively than I would have expected.

I knew I was risking it, but I didn't care. "Maybe not as many as you thought."

"Yeah," he said, "I know. But he was a stubborn, stubborn guy. You don't fight with little kids; you don't neglect your own son."

"But he *didn't* fight with you," I said. "Wasn't that the whole problem? Though he *did* seem to try to ignore you."

"The poor bastard was such a passive-aggressive. I think he really believed silence was power, when all of us know, or most of us do, that silence is empty space."

I had never heard my brother talk about our father so calmly, and it occurred to me that his death might have taken some of the sting out of Bin's feelings.

"He was a mystery," I said.

"The Shadow Dad," Bin replied ominously, in the voice of an old radio announcer. "He was probably a bigger mystery to himself than to anyone else." He hunched up his shoulders against the wind. "Christ. The energy he couldn't be bothered to spend on you and me! Always his nose in a goddamn book, if he happened to even be around, which was rare. He could have been on the *planet* Mars, he was so far gone. Not that you were much better, off in your own little world when we were little or, later, running around overachieving. Man, I felt like an only child most of the time! But him—poor guy."

"It sounds like you've made some kind of peace with him," I ventured.

"Peace? Hey, he's dead, after all." We scuffled through a large pile of fallen leaves. "I've been seeing a therapist," he added. "I don't know if I've made any peace with him, but he wasn't a load I wanted to lug around forever. It was beginning to bore even me."

"Did you ever feel guilty about hating him?"

"I didn't hate him," Bin said. "I was just trying to get his attention. I was this wise-ass kid and he wouldn't give me the time of day."

I was struck by the sadness of the situation. But sadness for what? For our father being the person he was? "I expect he did the best he could," I said.

"Doubtful, Pollyanna," Bin said as he walked off with Duke. I sat down on a bench and watched them move past the swings and the old picnic pavilion, wondering if Bin had changed and decided to grow up at last. Or had I simply caught him at an odd moment? He could be so mercurial. The last of the brittle leaves showered down from the trees.

Bin and Duke stood for a while looking out at the lake, then turned and headed back toward me. When they came alongside the bench, I got up and joined them.

"The whole thing with Davidson," Bin said, "it's not something I'm particularly comfortable talking about. I mean, turn on the TV any day—I don't want to sound like those poor assholes on talk shows, whining about their childhood decades later. Really, you know, as stories go, mine isn't so bad."

"No."

"And you?" he said, turning and punching me lightly on the arm. "How are you?"

"I'm fine," I said.

"Eliza." He stopped walking. "You're always fine."

Here it comes, I thought.

"I mean, you're the one person I know who is always fine, even when you're a wreck. Isn't it about time you got a new line?"

"Cut it out," I said.

"What are you doing here, anyway?"

"What do you mean, 'What am I doing here?' Isn't it obvious?"

"Come on," Bin said. "Movers could do all this. You could hire packers. Why don't you just ship it all out west and worry about it there?"

"Too much stuff," I replied. "Anyway, there's Mother." I glanced at my watch. "We should probably be getting up there. Visiting hours are starting."

"You're hiding out here, aren't you?" Bin asked, narrowing his eyes.

I almost said, "How did you know?" For a second, I was ready to blurt out how displaced I felt in Edgecliff, how rocky things were with Sam, how much I'd missed my children when I was in Santa Fe, how badly my work had been going, how oddly I'd been acting lately. But of course, I didn't. Instead, I said, "Don't be silly."

"Christ, Merry Sunshine," he said. "You really are hopeless." He and Duke plowed through an enormous pile of leaves, so deep the dog had to hold his head up as if he were swimming. I skirted them, my eyes tearing, the wind was so strong. I felt weighed down with the knowledge that my confusion was so transparent that Bin had noticed it.

We walked out of the park and along the street. Here and there, colorful banners flew from houses—one with a Thanksgiving turkey on it, another with autumn leaves. I had seen these curious banners all over Edgecliff, and I waited for Bin to make a remark about them, but he didn't.

"It's okay," he said as we approached our driveway. His voice was soft and reassuring. "Sometimes we all need a break from our lives. You're lucky—you get to run away from home with an airtight excuse." He reached for my hand and held it.

"Your hair actually looks pretty cool," he said, as we climbed the front steps. "For problem hair," he added, and slapped me on the back.

CHAPTER 12

The day before Bin arrived in Edgecliff, when I'd gone to the hospital to visit my mother, I took along my old copy of *Heidi,* a book I thought might amuse her because we had read it many times together when I was small. My mother did not watch TV except for the nightly news, and I'd wracked my brains for something that would cheer her up.

When I showed her the book, she said, "Why, Sister," and looked at me as if I'd gone off my rocker. "That silly old book."

"But we loved it," I said. "Don't you remember?"

"*You* loved it," she replied. "Good Lord, you made me read it to you over and over again. I became quite sick of it, to tell you the truth. There were days when I could hardly see, and you would drag that book into my bed and ask me to read it. I had page after page memorized and would skip great chunks of it until you caught on."

"Really?"

"Your father and I used to joke about sending you off to the Swiss Alps."

"But it wasn't Switzerland that appealed to me," I said. "It was the grandfather. He was so kind."

"Come now," she said without much interest. Dismayed, I stuck the book in my purse. "Has Bin called?" she asked. "Isn't he supposed to be here tomorrow?"

"That's what he said. He'll show up. He's been busy." Seeing Bin would give her a big lift.

"Well, when he does, I hope you two will be friendly. He's your brother, after all."

"Of course I'll be friendly," I said.

"You take him the wrong way, I've always thought," she said. "You're old enough now that you shouldn't let him get your goat."

My mother had been waging this campaign for some time but, frankly, her stake in my relationship with Bin had never seemed that high; our little spats seemed to faintly amuse her, though maybe I only imagined that. I had to keep reminding myself that my mother was an only child.

"You worshipped him when he was born," she said. "You would race home from school and wheel him up and down the street in his baby carriage. You carried him—"

"Mother, I love Bin. But you know as well as I do, he can be tough to deal with sometimes."

"Not for me," she said, giving me a meaningful look over the top of her reading glasses. "You just take him too seriously, Sister. Relax, relax." She took off her glasses and wiped them with a tissue. "I should take my own advice. This hospital . . . I can't wait to get out of here."

"Soon enough, Mama," I said. "When your infection clears up and the physical therapists are through with you."

"Oh, them," she said. "They give me such a pain. They talk to me like I'm a five-year-old. 'Mrs. White,' she mimicked, 'can you point to your left foot?' They must think I'm senile." She pulled the blanket up. "Your father could have dealt with them," she added. "Oh dear, your father. I miss him, Sister." She sighed heavily and closed her eyes. After a few minutes, she began snoring softly.

My father died suddenly while he was swimming. He swam a mile almost every day, but on that particular day, his heart stopped and he drowned. The emergency squad managed to get his heart beating again, but it stopped for good in the ambulance on the way to the hospital.

He was eighty, yet there was still a radiant promise still about him. As he grew older, the bones in his face had begun to assert themselves, but the high color in his cheeks remained, and his white hair was thick. I loved my father with the kind of intensity reserved for things just beyond your reach. Unlike Bin, I didn't find his silences annoying, but challenging. I felt he was somehow disabled, and that instead of holding back, he simply found talk too difficult. All my life I tried to bring him around.

But it was his intelligence I loved best—fine and probing, the connections coming clear as a bell for as long as I knew him. His memory was formidable; even he laughed about it. He could quote whole speeches from Shakespeare; he read Latin for amusement and taught himself Greek. He practiced law for more than fifty years, but his true loves were elsewhere, in literature, linguistics, and math. My mother always said he should have been an academic, and I suspect she was right.

When I was five or six, my father tried to explain quadratic equations to me, spacing these attempts between the chapters of *Treasure Island* and *Lorna Doone* that he read aloud. Of course, math made no sense to me then; it still doesn't. But as a child, I would stare unfathomingly at the sharp lines on the pages of the book he propped up in his lap, desperate to comprehend them.

Could he really have expected me to understand, or was he merely amusing himself? I never had the heart to ask him. Still, in all the years I knew him, my failure at those early math lessons seemed a barrier between us, though I'm sure my father would have found that ridiculous on my part. For all I know, he might have been looking for a way to connect with me that didn't involve words.

I was an only child for almost six years, and perhaps I paid too much attention to what was absent, in this case, my father's voice. I knew what I wanted my father to say: that he loved me better than his books, better than his work. Better than my mother. All my life, I chased after him with my heart on my sleeve.

He was a robust man, yet even as a child, I was gripped with fear that he might disappear. I saw him as vulnerable and unprotected, despite the fact that for years I watched him function successfully in the world.

I'm not unmindful that I might have my father all wrong. Children—and I know this from my own—are given to grave misinterpretations: Their memories turn the odd moment into long-standing tradition; the isolated swat into frequent spankings; the cry of a frightened adult into anger; the preoccupied parent into someone who doesn't care about them. Children are not reliable witnesses.

After Sam and I moved to Santa Fe, my parents made annual visits, at first staying in our guesthouse, later renting a condominium for a month each summer. For years, I acted the dutiful hostess, squiring them around town to galleries and museums, introducing them to the best restaurants and to people I thought they might enjoy. I was motivated by kindness, but also by a lack of faith that the two of them could possibly get along on their own.

Then one day I looked around, and they had friends in Santa Fe I didn't know; they talked about concerts I hadn't been to, operas, plays. One summer they took a seminar on Henry James's *The Ambassadors* at St. John's College, which my father, if not my mother, thoroughly enjoyed. The next summer they signed up for one on Thomas Mann's *The Magic Mountain*. I began to realize how overbearing I'd been—all to avoid my own discomfort at the thought of my parents loose in the world. They were tolerant of my meddling; they heard me out patiently, then went their own way.

The phone by my mother's bedside rang. I jumped, but she didn't move. It was an old acquaintance of hers, Nell Ward, the mother of my high school friend Callie. I told Mrs. Ward that my mother was sleeping, and I asked about Callie.

"She's still in New Delhi, at the embassy there. She loves the foreign service. Still footloose and fancy free, too. Al and I worry ourselves sick over her, of course, but don't tell her." Callie had been married briefly, but divorced years ago.

"I wish you could drop by and say hello," Mrs. Ward said. "Al and I don't drive anymore, but we're still in the house on Orion. I know you're busy, but we haven't seen you since . . ." She appeared to lose her train of thought. Mrs. Ward had always seemed overwhelmed; now she sounded a little dotty. "Oh, I remember! Not since your father's memorial service. That was the last time we saw you." She paused for a breath. "What a nice service," she added. "Your father. Such an unusual man. No one like him, Al and I always said. A real brain, way over my head most of the time. But he could be so funny, Eliza. Those jokes of his! He always left me in stitches. He's gone, oh dear."

I told her I'd try to drop around for a visit, and promised to have my mother call her.

"Poor thing," she said. "And all alone, too."

"But I'm here," I said.

"Yes, you are; that's right. I'd almost forgotten. Edgecliff's big celebrity. You and that brother of yours."

I would never say that my father was funny; I would say he was shy, which was why he felt comfortable telling jokes, of which he knew hundreds. What was far more impressive to me than his jokes, however, was the poetry he knew. My mother, too. From the vast store of poetry that had been drummed into their heads when they were children, they would pluck appropriate passages; almost every occasion elicited from them a spontaneous quotation, often in unison. My father dismissed this as merely a parlor trick, something anyone could do if taught early enough.

He managed to teach my own children poems, and Will was an especially good student. Inspired by my father, Will learned poems by Kipling, Frost, Sandburg, and Longfellow, but his crowning achievement, one that flabbergasted us all, was his committing to memory many verses of Hart Crane's "The Bridge." It's a difficult poem, and it doesn't rhyme or often even make much sense. Yet, at my father's urging, Will learned it in the seventh grade, for the only memorization assignment any of my children ever had.

"How many dawns," it begins, and I can still hear Will shouting these lines in order to fix them in his memory, "chill from his rippling rest / The seagull's wing shall dip and pivot him / Shedding white rings of tumult, building high / Over the chained bay waters Liberty . . ." When Will started in on these recitations, Jesse would often turn up his hip-hop music, until I thought the din would deafen us all. But Will prevailed and got an A+ on that assignment.

My children visited Edgecliff at least once a year as they grew older. Jesse and Will were wild about baseball, and my father always made sure their visit coincided with an Indians' doubleheader. All three of the kids loved the Rock and Roll Fall of Fame, to which my father dutifully took each of them after it opened, never once complaining, as far as I know. As a small child, Anna was fascinated by the mummies at the art museum, then later by the art. Both my parents seemed at ease with my children in all sorts of ways they hadn't been with Bin and me. They enjoyed being grandparents, and my children were extremely fond of them, as if they were dealing with completely different people than the ones I grew up with. And possibly they were.

The year before my father died, he and my mother drove Will all over Ohio to look at colleges. Their trip included my parents' alma mater, Oberlin, to which they remained warmly attached throughout their adult years. College was home to them in a way it never was to me, and no vision I have of my own college is as vivid as the one I sustain of my parents' reunions when I was a child: the large grassy square in the middle of the small town hung with glowing Japanese lanterns, their colors deepening like jewels as the evening grew darker, a breeze swinging them gently in the humid June air.

The last time I saw my father alive was in Santa Fe the summer before he died. We were at my house, and he and I were alone together on the deck, having a drink before dinner. The sunset was spectacular that night—a double rainbow in the east, brilliant white thunderheads, and silvery rain falling over the foothills of the Sangre de Cristo Mountains. Beyond them was a sky so blue it looked as if you could dive right into it.

The windows in the house across the street suddenly flamed gold from the setting sun, and my father and I were nearly blinded by their light. We stood captivated by the show.

My father remarked that he had tried to watch *The Portrait of a Lady,* a movie based on the Henry James novel, on TV that afternoon, and he hadn't liked it; he called it a miserably dreary attempt.

"You know," I finally said, "it's too bad that Jesse will probably never read James, or most of the other writers you and I love. It bothers me that he doesn't like to read." Though they look alike, Jesse and his brother Will, who's a big reader, are not identical twins, and their interests have always been different.

My father and I watched the rainbow fade and the mountains turn from pink to scarlet as the sun sunk in the western sky. "Everyone's different," he said.

"It disappoints me, is all."

My father didn't shift his gaze from the mountains. After a pause, he said, "Eliza, don't you realize by now that the nature of relationships between parents and children *is* one of disappointment?"

I was stunned. For a moment, I was unable to say a word. "I guess that means," I finally bristled, sounding like a child myself, "that you're disappointed in me."

He cleared his throat. "I meant only that, generally speaking, one's children, like one's parents, are seldom the people one might have chosen."

At that point, my mother and Sam joined us, both of them ooh-ing and ah-ing over the sunset, and I was not about to pursue a discussion of disappointment. I was stung, and my father's words cast a pall over the evening. Had I known I would never see him again, I would have persevered. But I let it drop, the last personal message I ever received from him.

Later, I realized I might have overinterpreted a casual remark on his part. He could have been disappointed in his own parents, who had trundled him all over the country; certainly he gave every indication of being disappointed in Bin. But it seemed ungenerous, at the very least, for him to be disappointed in me. Didn't he realize I had knocked myself out trying to please him?

Later, too, I thought about my own children. If my father had been right, were they simply still too young to be disappointments? Hard as I tried, I could not foresee them disappointing me in any significant way. My expectations for my children are only that they live lives that engage them as kind, decent people. If one of them doesn't like to read—my God, how trivial.

"Sister," my mother said thickly, without opening her eyes. She patted my hand. "You didn't come here to watch me sleep." Inexplicably, I felt on the verge of tears.

If I'd trusted myself to talk, I might have said that I was an expert in watching her sleep, in holding vigils while she drifted off. Instead I squeezed her hand and said, "I'll be right back."

I took the elevator down to the hospital gift shop where I bought three identical postcards of Edgecliff, an aerial view of the bluff along the lake, in which the roof of my parents' house was visible. I circled the house, and then wrote a few lines on each card. "I love you and hold you close in my heart," I ended all of them, and signed my name.

Suddenly, my children seemed achingly close to me. I saw the back of Jesse's neck, no longer downy and soft as it once was, but muscular, and almost out of my reach, he's so tall. I saw Will's long legs, now covered with golden fuzz, and Anna's dark hair, straight and heavy like my mother's. As quickly as these visions of my children came over me, they vanished, and I was alone in the lobby of the hospital where I'd been born.

Outside, a fierce wind whipped through the treetops and sent people scurrying in through the heavy glass doors. As I dropped the cards into the mailbox, it struck me that if I wasn't falling apart, I was doing a pretty good imitation of it.

My cell phone rang while I was in the elevator.

"Mom?" Anna said. "Mom?"

"Hi there," I said and immediately felt better. "What's up?" There seemed to be another conversation going on through the static. What was wrong with these phones, anyway? How could they send a man to the moon and still not make a cell phone that worked properly? I got off the elevator, hoping the reception would improve.

"Breaking up," I heard her say, then gibberish. I thought she was talking about the phone.

"No, you're okay. I can hear you now, hon, but barely."

"I said, I'm breaking up with Sean."

Sean was the good-looking boy whom Anna had gone all through school with in Santa Fe, and they had dated pretty steadily for the past year. Now he was at Stanford with her, on a tennis scholarship.

"Gee," I said. "I'm sorry." Through the strange electronic noises and static, I heard her begin to cry. My heart fell.

"Oh, Mom," she wailed. "He's been seeing some other girl, some slut who lives in my dorm. I saw them together. He told me it was nothing, but . . ." I lost her again amidst the garble.

"Mom? Mom? Are you there?"

I moved down the hall to a window. "I'm here," I practically shouted.

"So I broke up with him. He's nothing but a player!"

"And?"

"And I'm miserable."

"Well, I'm sorry, but it sounds like you did the right thing. This isn't the first time he's treated you shabbily. Remember the after-prom, when he went off with that Zoe?" Actually, I had never liked Sean much. He was cocky and took Anna for granted. Her brothers weren't fond of him either.

"You're right, but . . ."

The phone began making weird noises again. "Come on, sweetheart," I tried to say through the crackling. "Where's your pride? You don't want to be with anyone who'd sneak around with someone else. It's tacky. It's dishonest."

I could have been talking about Sam and me, I realized, and thought, Listen to yourself, Eliza. Listen.

"I know, I know, but it hurts."

"It hurts badly, I'm sure. But consider . . ."

"What?"

"I said . . . oh hell with it." I wanted to throw the goddamn phone out the window.

"I wish I were there with you," she said.

"Be my guest, but you don't want to be someone who runs away when things get tough, do you?" This, asked by her mother, who had effectively run away from her own predicament.

"No, but he's a shithead."

"Attagirl," I said.

"What?"

"That's the right attitude." I yelled so loud that several people in the hall turned around.

"The right *what*?"

"I'll call you back later from a real phone. In the meantime, if you can still hear me, hold on tight. You're a strong person. You don't need someone who'd treat you like this."

"But he dumped me," she wailed.

"He was disloyal, and you dumped him. Keep things straight." She said something incomprehensible, then we were cut off.

I went back down to the cafeteria and got some coffee before returning to my mother's room. Poor Anna, I thought, and wished I could help her. But what kind of tawdry person was I, anyway? Giving her advice I couldn't take myself. Was I a coward? A person without principles? Whatever I was, I seemed incapable of focusing on Sam at the moment.

After chatting with my mother for a while, I went home and called Anna on a land line. By this time, she sounded mad, not weepy.

"He called me," she said, "after I talked to you. To say he was sorry again."

"So what did you do?"

"I told him he could drop dead, for all I cared. I told him I never wanted to see him again!"

"Well, good for you," I said.

"And I don't," she added emphatically.

After I hung up, I was nagged by the fact that I was going nowhere, while Anna had taken charge and stood up for herself. It occurred to me that I was as bad as my goddamn cell phone: Something just wasn't getting through. The connection was lousy or, worse, nonexistent—as if the line had gone dead.

CHAPTER 13

Bin spent five days in Edgecliff, but we didn't spend much time alone together until the night before he left. He stayed at the hospital during the afternoons and, as I expected, my mother perked up enormously. She loved showing Bin off, introducing him to nurses and doctors and fellow patients. One of her physical therapists recognized him from a soap opera. An orderly reported he'd seen him in the teen-movie *Hanging Tough*, in which Bin had been one of the few adults in the cast. A number of people asked for his autograph.

My mother suggested that Bin read to her, even though she'd rejected all my attempts to do so. He chose Raymond Chandler's *The Big Sleep*, and he read it in a wonderfully sinister tone. My mother loved it. Chandler was a favorite of hers, but the story hardly seemed to matter; she probably knew it by heart anyway.

When Bin wasn't at the hospital, he wandered around the house, poking through drawers, reading old playbills and press clippings, all of which he tossed in the garbage. "I don't know why she saved all this stuff," he said to me. "She knows I have a clipping service."

"I don't think Mother saved anything," I said. "Father did most of the saving around here."

"Oh, come on," Bin said.

For dinner the first night he was in town, he insisted on fixing himself a sardine sandwich slathered in mustard, which I didn't point out had been our father's favorite. He ate the sandwich in front of the TV, sitting on the edge of my father's old leather chair. He kept the TV on mute and channel-surfed endlessly, as if he were looking for something. I stayed mostly in the living room, rooting through a box filled with hundreds of letters I'd sent my parents while I was in college, relics of another era. Now, with e-mail and cell phones, the only real pieces of mail I get from my children are bills. At some point Bin made a phone call in a low, private voice. I wondered if there was a woman in his life, but didn't ask.

Mainly, I tried to keep my distance because I didn't want to risk upsetting the equilibrium we'd stumbled upon during our walk with Duke, even if I was convinced it couldn't last for the duration of Bin's visit. I moved around the house quietly, like a ghost; Bin remained polite, even friendly, if somewhat preoccupied.

I had forgotten to tell Rabi not to come, and when he appeared at the door Sunday night, Bin seemed pleased to see him. It turned out they had met before when Bin was in Edgecliff and had run into each other earlier that day in my mother's hospital room.

Bin got three beers, and we all trooped down to the basement. Rabi and I had come across a stash of boxes in the jelly closet earlier in the week, and we wanted to see what was in them. Years before, the shelves of that closet had been filled with jars of canned stewed tomatoes, creamed corn, sardines, anchovies, and various jams and jellies. Damson plum was my parents' favorite, and my mother made it every year, no matter how sick she was. She left the pits in the tiny plums—the only proper way to do it, she informed me—rendering it effectively childproof. Undaunted, my father spread damson plum jam on his toast every morning, then carefully picked out the pits with a spoon and the tip of a knife.

We each carried a box from the closet into the finished part of the basement, a paneled rec room that smelled musty. I opened mine to find it was full of black-and-white marbleized notebooks my mother had used in college. We wound up spending almost an hour pouring over my mother's art history notes. The pages were dense with handwriting except where she'd pasted blurry reproductions of whatever the subject happened to be—the Parthenon, Chartres, the Palazzo Vecchio; paintings by Giotto, Turner, Monet. We decided there hadn't been a textbook.

The notes were so clear and coherent that Bin insisted on reading pages of them aloud. There was such a touching earnestness about them it was like visiting my mother as a child. She was only seventeen her freshman year, when she took art history.

"God," Bin said at one point, "I never took notes in college, let alone in complete sentences. This is amazing."

"I took notes," I said and was immediately sorry.

"Eliza has always done everything right," Bin said to Rabi. "By the book, that's our Eliza."

I wasn't offended by Bin's remark; it was true, more or less. Except for a lapse or two, I had actually observed most of the rules. My life had been relatively humdrum, if you didn't count my success as a writer.

"Then again," Bin said to Rabi, "you probably took notes, too."

Rabi laughed. "I couldn't take notes," he said. "When I came to the U.S., I didn't understand English very well, and it was hard to translate what people were saying into Arabic or even German or French, which I'd studied in school. I don't know how I made it through that first year. I was some kind of language orphan. That's why I ended up in chemistry and math. You don't have to translate formulas and equations."

"But your English is fine now," Bin said. "Your accent is pretty cool. Mysterious. A little of this, a little of that." As he spoke, Bin perfectly imitated Rabi's lilt.

"But I write like an idiot," Rabi volunteered. "My ear must be better than my eye. Maybe I have dyslexia." He pronounced the first syllable of that word "deeze."

"*Dis,*" Bin corrected him. "*Dis*lexia."

Rabi tried once more and got it right. He and Bin seemed to be having a good time together. I'm not sure why that surprised me. I guess I had expected that Bin would be wary of Rabi, or view him as a competitor for my mother's affections. I watched them carrying on like old friends—bright, engaging, handsome men, both dressed in black.

That evening, I felt cheerful, like myself again, instead of someone who'd been acting a little erratic. My excursion with the real estate woman was nothing more than a lark, I decided. Refusing to acknowledge who I was at the sporting goods counter, a momentary whimsy. My inability to think about Sam, temporary; something I'd eventually get around to. All of it caused by a glitch in the lunar cycle, planetary misalignment. Who knew?

"Anyone want another beer?" Bin asked.

Rabi nodded, but I declined, and Bin went upstairs to the kitchen.

"I haven't a clue what to do with all this," I said to Rabi, gesturing at my mother's notebooks.

"Save them," he said. "For a change, save something." He taped up the box and with a magic marker wrote on it, COLLEGE NOTES. "I like your brother," he added. "It feels like I've known him for a long time. When I first came to this country, I watched a lot of TV, trying to learn English. One of my favorite programs was *Windy City Blues*."

Windy City Blues had been a police sitcom set in Chicago, on which Bin appeared now and then.

"Oh, and *Sandler & Manning,* too," Rabi said. "Bin was on that a lot. He was amazing as that tough lawyer."

"Something in the genes, maybe," I said and laughed.

Bin came down with fresh beers in his hand, his head grazing the ceiling above the bottom step. He opened another carton, this one of full of more photographs—of Bin and me when we were small, of my parents in college and when they were first married.

"We must sort these," Rabi said, probably fearing that Bin and I would shove the jumble aside. We spent most of the rest of the evening ordering the photos according to the dates on the back, neatly recorded by my father, making it easy. I had to promise Rabi I would buy albums for them the next day.

Around ten o'clock, Bin went upstairs again and brought down the small TV from the kitchen along with two more beers. He turned on the Cavaliers-Lakers game from Los Angeles. Bin was a big basketball fan, and it turned out Rabi was, too. Half an hour later, when I announced I was going to bed, they were both so engrossed in the game that neither of them did more than nod in my direction. We hadn't got a lot done, but it had been a good evening, better than I would have predicted. Rabi had put my brother at ease, but then Rabi had a knack for being so at home in himself, he seemed to put everyone at ease. I went to bed and for the first time since I'd been in Edgecliff, slept soundly.

It wasn't until Tuesday night, when Bin and I were having dinner alone, that he told me what he had found in the third box, the one he'd opened after Rabi left.

I'd arranged the table with two place settings of my mother's china and silver, and had hunted up a tablecloth and candlesticks; I'd bought flowers and two bottles of good wine. Then I'd cooked a meal I thought Bin would like—a rare tenderloin with basil sauce, roasted new potatoes, baby string beans, and a salad.

"Nice," Bin said as we sat down.

We didn't talk much; Bin seemed unusually preoccupied. Midway through dinner, he removed an envelope from his shirt pocket and shoved it across the table. "The old man was a sham, Eliza," he said quietly. "Look at this."

What I saw gave me a raw feeling in the pit of my stomach. There, on a heavy cream-colored envelope, was my father's name and office address in Mary Talbot's fat, back-slanted writing. "Personal" was written in one corner and underlined. Everything about the postmark was blurred, except the year, 1992, four years before my father died.

"Go ahead," Bin said, "open it."

I wanted to bolt from the table, but instead I unfolded the note. "Dearest D," it said. "I cannot go a day without telling you how much I love you. Year after year after year. Of all the songs

I'll never sing, I am grateful beyond words that our love isn't one of them." There was no signature.

I looked at Bin. "So," he said, and it was clear that he felt vindicated. "There were dozens of those, all sappy like this, all unsigned and sent to his office. I don't know who wrote them, but how could the fucking bastard have saved them?"

Bin must not have recognized Mary's handwriting, but that wasn't so strange; they hadn't been friendly since Bin was small. Mary had disapproved of Bin's attitude toward our father, and she'd let Bin know it. The two of them wound up without much relationship at all.

Mary and I, on the other hand, had always been close, and we had corresponded for years, since I first went to camp in Vermont. I had been enthralled by her handwriting, which made my own forward-leaning Palmer penmanship seem woefully lacking in flair.

Rereading her note to my father, I realized that everything suddenly fit: their long evenings together when my mother was sick; their lighthearted banter, so uncharacteristic of my father; Mary's unwavering solicitousness toward my mother, her kindness toward me. I recalled a night when Mary and my father were both out of town, and how my mother, in spite of her headache, made a joke about trysts, a word that sent me to the dictionary, looking under t-r-i before I found it. I must have been twelve or thirteen.

I sat at the table with Bin's eyes on me and felt as if something I'd known all my life but never been able to articulate had now been said aloud. Amidst all the confusing feelings careening through my mind, I experienced a strange sense of relief: My father had been human, after all. He'd had a life; he'd had an affair. But, like Bin, I was shocked.

"You know who wrote this, don't you," Bin said, his eyes narrowed.

"It doesn't matter," I hedged.

"Tell me," Bin said.

I took a sip of wine and stared into the candlelight. Who I was trying to protect? Mary? Bin? And then I knew it was my father, who was far beyond my protection. "Mary," I finally said.

Bin slapped the table so hard that the wineglasses leaped and the candles flickered. "Oh, shit," he said. "Of course! The guy was leading a double life with his wife's best friend! No wonder he didn't have time for us."

"Mary has never been Mother's best friend," I said, as if precision mattered at the moment. "Mary was their friend, but it was always clear to me that she was closer to Father than she was to Mother."

"For Christ's sake, Eliza, get a hold of yourself! So she wasn't Mother's best friend. Does that mean this was okay on a technicality?"

"When did you get to be such a moralist?" I said.

"Eliza," Bin said with exaggerated patience, "listen. The man was duplicitous. He billed himself as a person of immense integrity and virtue, but he wasn't. Nobody was good enough for Davidson because he himself wasn't good! Don't you get it?" Bin poured more wine into our glasses.

"He was the fucking moralist here," Bin went on, "and he found himself seriously lacking. I'm sure he punished himself, but don't you see?" Bin was nearly shouting now. "He punished me, too. And not for anything I did, but because of this own guilty conscience!"

Bin's voice reverberated in the nearly empty room so that for a moment we both stopped and listened as if it were a judg-

ment call echoing through the house. Bin opened the second bottle of wine, then reached over for the note and put it back into its
envelope. He rose and stuck a corner of it in the candle flame and
walked into the kitchen, the paper burning in his hand.

Looking at my brother, my heart caved in. He seemed frail and
unprotected without his armor of glibness. For a moment, I saw
the skinny, angry child he had been. When I heard the water running, I got up and went to where he stood by the sink and put my
arms around him. He tried halfheartedly to pull away, but I held
on, and we stood that way for a minute or two. When I dropped
my arms and looked up at him, I saw there were tears in his eyes,
but he was smiling.

"Shit," he said, "I could have saved a lot of money on therapy
if I'd known about this sooner. I guess it wasn't all my fault."

"Of course not," I said. "It never was all your fault. Even
without Mary or anyone else, it wouldn't have been your fault.
He was . . ." I stopped because I didn't want to say it.

"He was what?"

"Not a great father," I finally got out. I half expected the roof
to cave in.

"Poor bastard," Bin said. "Maybe he did the best he could,
with Mom so sick and all."

"Bin," I said, "I know this sounds feeble, but his best wasn't
good enough." I couldn't believe I'd said that even though I knew
it was true. It was as if Bin and I had changed places.

He looked at me curiously. "That doesn't sound like you," he
said, "but thanks anyway."

Bin was right. I hadn't sounded a bit like the person who had
endlessly defended and protected my father. But I didn't care. If
I'd been honest, I would have admitted his failure years before.

We walked slowly back to the dining room, where I sat down and Bin began pacing around the table, wineglass in hand. "You know? I think I went into acting because I was looking for a family. The theater was like a home for me, one where I didn't have to be sullen or angry."

"You were smart," I said.

"It's like your books," he said. "Like you've been trying to get your childhood right after all these years." I was taken aback; I'd never thought of my books that way. He stopped and looked up at the chandelier. "But, hey, you know? Theater, fairy tales— they're still not the real thing."

"It's what we have," I said. "Maybe it's what we've made because something was missing. You figure a way around things, if you're lucky. I remember Mary once told me that she'd never married because she couldn't find a man like her father—except for our father, and he was taken. Strange, isn't it? I guess people search all their lives for consolation. Father, you, me, Mary—all of us looking for a place that feels like home." Bin stared out of the dining room windows toward the lake, his back to me.

"Home," he said after a while. "Well, a sanctuary, at any rate. Corny as that sounds, we all need one."

I was about to agree with him when he pivoted around abruptly. "And have *you* found a home?" He held out a long arm and pointed at me an overblown gesture. Then he smiled faintly. "Of course you'll say 'of course.'"

"Of course," I said.

"Then why are you running away from it now?"

"Actually . . ." I began. It didn't cross my mind to avoid his question. "I don't know. I guess. I thought I'd found a port in the storm, but things have a way of shifting around. When the kids left, it hit me a lot harder than I thought it would. Once they were gone, reality set in."

"Which is why you're holed up here?"

"Partly," I said.

"And Sam?" Bin said. "Where does he figure in all of this?"

"He's Sam," I said. "You know him. I guess I've always thought of him as a kind of anchor. Without him, who knows? I might be all adrift."

"Then again, you might soar," Bin said. He took a drink of wine. "Face it, Eliza, anchors are dead weight. Sam's just another version of Davidson, more talkative, sure, but not nearly as smart. A nice enough guy, though I've never thought he took very good care of you, or paid much attention, either."

My hackles rose. I didn't want to talk about Sam; I didn't even want to think about him. Bin stood in the doorway to the hall, studying me. I got up and began clearing the table to escape his gaze. "You didn't eat your salad," I said. "Do you want it?"

"Here we go again," Bin said.

I went into the kitchen and began filling the dishwasher, sorry I'd spoken so openly; Bin made things sound far more dire and dramatic than they were. I was okay, basically. My kids were gone; my work had hit a snag; my husband was doing whatever he was doing, which I didn't much care about at the moment. I was taking a breather.

"So," Bin said, coming up behind me. "What do you think of your pal Mary now? 'Of all the songs I'll never sing.' Jesus."

"I still love Mary," I said. "But even if I didn't, I wouldn't blame her for the kind of anger you've cultivated so unremit-tingly." I scrubbed viciously at the roasting pan.

"Fucking home wrecker. I despise that woman."

I slammed the pan down on the drainboard. "Aren't you tired of hating?"

"Not yet, babe," he said and smiled. "Besides, it's better than feeling nothing at all, like some people."

Surprisingly, the next morning we had both calmed down enough to chat civilly as I drove him to the airport. When he mentioned a party he was going to that night in New York, I asked, "How *is* your social life these days?" The last time I'd brought this up, he was dating a woman who worked at the Whitney and another who was a backup singer for a band I'd never heard of. I hadn't seen either woman, but I was sure they looked a lot like Bin. He'd always dated women who looked like him, tall and elegant with dark hair. Angela Aster, the video artist he'd lived with for five years, could have been his twin.

"Boring," he answered. "I'm ready to quit the whole scene."

"Quit?" I said, and he merely shrugged. "By the way, do you ever hear from Angela?" I thought Bin had genuinely been in love with Angela, but apparently he couldn't bring himself to marry her. Which is why they had finally broken up the year before. Bin's view of marriage seemed to involve a disaster scenario, and I was sure Mary's letters had only reinforced that. But Angela and I had hit it off; I liked her, and we still kept in touch.

"She went home, you know," Bin said. "To Tucson. One day, she decided to leave New York, and the next week she was gone. She's teaching at the university."

"I know," I said. "We e-mail each other now and then."

"You do? I didn't realize that." He sighed. "I asked her if she wanted to get married not long ago," he said in a rush. I was so startled I almost slammed into the concrete highway divider.

"That's what therapy will do for you," he added. "Mess up your mind."

"So what did she say?"

"I don't think she thought I was serious."

"Were you?" I turned into the entrance to the airport.

"I guess," he said. "I miss her. Marriage may not be so hot, but the alternative's no picnic either. Being single gets grimmer every year. All the women I know are either twenty-three and totally ignorant, or my age and beyond desperate."

"Listen," I risked saying as I pulled over to the curb. "You should pursue this Angela thing. You really should. She's wonderful."

Bin opened the door and grabbed his bag. "Misery always loves company," he said with a grin. Then he blew me a kiss and was gone.

CHAPTER 14

Mary Talbot was away on the yearly trip to Italy she made with her sister. After my father died, Mary tried to persuade my mother to join them, but as Mary laughingly told me later, my mother had replied, "But Mary, Italy? I've already been there."

Mary and her sister made this pilgrimage for the art (which my mother could take or leave) and for the food (which she had no enthusiasm for under any circumstances). It probably never occurred to my mother to make the trip simply for the company or for a change of scene. With considerable effort, my father had roused himself and my mother several times to travel to Europe, but except for going to New Mexico and occasionally to New York, neither of my parents cared much about leaving Edgecliff. They seemed to enjoy being homebodies.

Mary was ten years younger than my mother. They had met at the Edgecliff Public Library, where they both worked in the mid-1950s. Mary had been the reference librarian then, and later became the head librarian; she was what people used to call a "career gal."

When I was in college, I became intensely curious about Mary's close relationship with her father, probably because, on some level, it called to mind my unrequited devotion to my own. In my know-it-all teenage mind, Mary's unabashed father-worship suggested an analyst's dream: She was Electra, I thought, and proud of it. I used to ask her about her father, and she showed me photographs of him—a large, bald man who was always dressed in three-piece suits. I thought I might discover something about myself in Mary's adoration of him, but I never did. I knew my own father reminded Mary of hers, and I always knew she was crazy about him. I just didn't know how crazy.

In 1953, my mother invited Mary to dinner so that she and my father could meet and Mary could see their new house. I wasn't born yet, but I have heard the story so many times from all three of them—mainly from Mary and my mother—that I feel as if I'd been there.

It was a Sunday, late in May, and the day was unseasonably hot and sultry. The lake in front of my parents' house, into which they'd moved only a few months earlier, lay flat as a pane of glass. The sun was obscured by a dense grayish-green sky that shaded in spots to yellow, like an old bruise.

"It's going to storm any minute," my mother remembers saying when Mary arrived, and she hurried them both out to the backyard so that Mary could see her new garden and the view of Lake Erie from the edge of the cliff before the rain.

I have a framed photograph of the four of us, and although it was taken several years after that day; over the years I have conflated it with the way they must have looked the first afternoon Mary visited our house. In the picture, voluptuous Mary wears a pale-pink linen dress, her waist cinched tightly by a wide belt, her blond hair swept back in wings, so that she looks like a Valkyrie. My mother, so much smaller, has on a light-green strapless sundress that laces up the front, and her dark hair is in braids wound around her head. She is clutching a bundle in one arm—me at three months old in a white sunbonnet. The women look very young. So does my father, in shirtsleeves and natty brown-and-white spectator shoes, who sits between the two standing women on the edge of one of the Adirondack chairs that used to be scattered around our lawn. He is smoking a cigarette and squinting; his hair is dark, and he is smiling broadly. I don't think I can ever remember my father looking so happy in real life. I have no idea who took the picture, but it is dated June 1955, two years after Mary's first visit.

In my imagination, however, that is the way the three of them looked on that Sunday in May, when, according to all accounts, in a matter of minutes the wind whipped up and the temperature dropped thirty degrees—my father swore it, and he was a fanatic about weather details. They rose from their seats on the screened-in porch where they'd been having a drink and walked out toward the lake, which by then had turned pitch-black. There were waterspouts here and there, and a lone motorboat speeding toward shore.

They knew they should head for the basement, but they stood there transfixed. Suddenly, a rushing noise descended on them, like the sound, my mother has always said, of a dozen trains. She shot into the house, calling, "Hurry, you two," and dashed downstairs to the laundry room, but Mary and my father didn't budge. By then, things were blowing around—flowers, branches, uprooted bushes. A small evergreen, newly planted, lifted off from my parents' yard and went spinning upward like a missile.

Later, Mary and my father agreed that staying outside was possibly the most foolish thing they'd ever done, but they were unable to move. Finally, they retreated to the porch, and by then, things were flying around in there, too—newspapers, a lampshade, a patchwork afghan from the back of the wicker couch. They stood in the doorway to the house, yet when my father urged her toward the basement, Mary shouted over the noise, "Not yet!" and he wouldn't abandon her.

Then, with a terrible, wood-crunching crack, a screen was sucked outward, and my father had seen enough. He got Mary inside and managed to slam the door, but he literally had to shove her down the basement stairs. "Good Lord," Mary has always said, "your father was trying to save my life, and there I was resisting! I was hopeless. But I didn't want to miss a thing, not a thing!"

Throughout all of this, Mary had never set down her martini glass, a detail my father particularly liked, and he himself had grabbed the martini pitcher when the wind started up. They found my mother in the basement—the power had failed by then, and it was dark—and my father filled Mary's glass, which she then passed around. My mother, who seldom drank because she had been trying to get pregnant for almost a decade and still held out hope, took several big gulps. Outside, the wind roared and objects pelted the house. They felt what seemed to be a large tree smack the ground with a jolting thud accompanied by the crunch of metal. My mother took another swig of martini and announced that the storm had better be over soon, before she got drunk.

Later, all three of them claimed that they hadn't been frightened. They were having a high adventure, huddled in the doorway between the laundry and the jelly closet, not a bit concerned that the house might collapse on top of them. At some point, my father lit a match in order to survey the contents of the closet, and he sat back down on the floor with a jar of malted-milk balls, which they dug into eagerly. They all had another drink of martini, the wind screaming around the house, things crashing and banging.

The air in the basement was chilly and damp, and my mother managed to hand a clean sheet to Mary and wrap one around herself. She gave another—or at least that was what she thought it was—to my father, but when he unfolded it, it turned out to be a cut-lace tablecloth. It was growing lighter by then, and when he draped it over his shoulders, the two women dissolved into laughter. The last thing my mother remembers is the vision of my father wrapped in her great-aunt Emma's Portuguese lace. Then she passed out.

As abruptly as it had begun, the storm was over, and the sun re-emerged, sending shafts of light through the deep-well windows across the basement floor. The scene was too much for Mary: the three of them wrapped in white, my mother slumped against the wall, the jar of malted-milk balls nearly empty, the martini pitcher on its side. Mary began laughing again and kept laughing even after my father went upstairs to assess the damage. Eventually, she got herself under control, made sure my mother was as comfortable as she could be, and followed my father upstairs.

Everything inside the house was fine, but the front yard was littered with so many branches the lawn was completely obscured. A telephone pole had fallen on top of Mary's car, parked in the driveway. "Oh no!" Mary said, suddenly completely sober. The car was a pearl-gray 1952 Ford, a graduation gift from her father who had died shortly thereafter. "Oh no!"

Evidently, my father said, "Mary, I'm sorry. That damn pole. I'll call someone." The absurdity of his calling anyone when the phones were dead struck them both, and they began to laugh again, Mary so hard that she had to sit down. She claims to have been nearly hysterical, crying and laughing at the same time. "But it felt so good to laugh," she has said. "And your father kept giggling, which made it even worse."

My father giggling is difficult for me to imagine, but I take Mary's word for it. I suppose a crisis and a few martinis could lift anyone out of character. He got hold of himself first and pointed out the wires scattered all over the lawn and driveway. "It looks like you won't be leaving any time soon," he told her.

"I'll be like the man who came to dinner," she remarked.

"Then make yourself at home," he said.

"We ought to get Louise up to her room," Mary finally said. "I don't think she's going to feel too well."

But my father wanted to look at the backyard first, so they walked together through the house. When they opened the door to the screened-in porch, it was no longer screened in; all of the screens had blown away. They stood transfixed by the scene before them. Most of the wicker furniture had vanished, and in its place, perfectly aligned as if it had been deliberately put there, sat a dark green wooden picnic table with attached benches, completely intact. What's more—and Mary found this the strangest thing of all—a half-dozen stalks of pink peonies were arrayed on the table, as if someone had just cut them and run indoors for a vase. Mary claims that my father said, "Odd. No one around here has peonies."

Beyond the porch, the yard was immaculate, only a twig here

and there and a small crater where the evergreen had been. Mother's garden of pansies, which surrounded the old oak, were wind-flattened but not much the worse for wear. It seemed as if everything had blown over the house and landed in the front yard.

The lake was blue, with gentle whitecaps; the sky was clear; the humidity had vanished. The two of them stood and stared. Finally, Mary asked for a vase to put the peonies in, and my father hunted one up. She was filling the vase with water when the sound of sirens began, and it didn't stop until far into the night. My father went to the basement to get my mother. When he couldn't rouse her, he carried her up two flights of stairs and put her into bed, still in her dress, still wrapped in the sheet. "At least he managed to take off my shoes," she always said indignantly, as if he had failed her by not putting on her nightgown and brushing her teeth. She claimed she had a headache for two days afterwards, strictly from the gin.

On the strange picnic table that had showed up out of nowhere, Mary and my father ate the dinner of vichyssoise and chicken salad my mother had prepared earlier. They ate by candlelight, sirens screaming in the distance. The telephone and electric companies eventually arrived and sorted through the downed wires, but Mary's car would be captive for several days beneath the telephone pole.

It was after midnight when my father and Mary left our house. He walked her home through a sea of tree limbs, past uprooted bushes and houses with demolished roofs and garages. They saw weird, out-of-place objects in the beam of my father's flashlight: a bicycle in a tree, a screened door on a lawn, a canoe on a curb. One street, Neptune, was littered with porch swings and gliders, as if there had been a particular call for them. Though it was late, everyone seemed to be awake; candles flickered in the windows, portable radios blared. Mary said it seemed more like a celebration than a disaster.

As they were walking, someone offered them a glass of lemonade, and they stopped and chatted for a while. No one seemed to know why they had not been forewarned about how extensive the damage might be; they were all just grateful to have their homes, whatever shape they were in. The next day the papers reported that over two dozen houses in south Edgecliff had been destroyed, along with the wing of the high school that housed the swimming pool. Miraculously, no one was seriously hurt.

I wasn't born until two years later, but that Sunday in May often seems to me more memorable, more resonant, than many incidents in my own life. Perhaps it's because I've heard the story repeated so many times that, like my mother's hometown, I've made it mine. Or maybe because I sensed in some strange way that it was a day after which nothing would ever be the same.

Whether it was the storm or my mother's "martini caper," as it came to be called, they all became fast friends. They were so different from each other, but in an odd way, the three of them made a perfect couple. They hit it off and the friendship stuck, the glue being not so much my mother's relationship to Mary but rather the bond that Mary and my father had forged on the night of the storm. He reminded her of her father, and she, the least fragile of women, a tall, broad-shouldered, athletic blond to my mother's delicate China doll, was like a pal to him, straight-talking, with an unexpected toughness for all her proper upbringing. She even played golf, something my mother, one of the least athletic people I have ever known, could not have done had she wanted to.

Mary was one of two daughters of a prosperous paper-mill owner in upstate New York. She attended Vassar and then studied library science at Columbia University. After she received her M.A., she came to Cleveland to visit her older sister, who had married a man whose family owned a large tool-and-die company there. Mary decided to stay in Ohio after she was offered a job at the Edgecliff Public Library. She left her sister's and rented a carriage house that belonged to one of the large estates along the lake. She once told me she knew the moment she set foot in Edgecliff that she would spend her life there. She couldn't explain why, but it felt like home.

When I was small, I was awestruck by Mary. With her long red fingernails and bright red lipstick, her movie-star bosom and golden hair, she seemed so glamorous. Plus, she always wore high heels. Mary was vivid and glittery—sexy, too; even I could tell that. Next to Mary, my mother seemed drab and a little old fashioned.

My mother and I look nothing alike, and for as long as I can remember that has led her to pass along—and for all I know, generate—certain stories: the one about the baby nurse who came when I was born and stayed until Bin was six, who joked that perhaps I had been switched in the hospital; the man who approached my mother while she was walking me in a stroller and asked if I were adopted; the people who assumed my mother was the babysitter, or who said, "Such a beautiful blond child! Where in the world did she come from?" My mother clearly enjoyed these stories and told them with relish.

Since childhood, I have tolerated my mother's habit of exaggerating, of turning small moments into momentous ones. (Bin didn't get his talent for theatrics out of thin air.) Though I never seriously doubted that I was my mother's child, for years I permitted myself to fantasize otherwise. I secretly imagined Mary Talbot was my real mother, from whom, I conjectured, I had been separated at birth with the best of intentions on her part.

Mary was perfectly suited to the tasks my own mother wasn't up to, and she was the picture of health. She had many friends, with whom she socialized frequently—at the country club pool, on the golf course, at bridge games. She drove a convertible. She traveled to faraway places, and would always bring back presents for me: a gold bangle from Spain, a set of nesting dolls from Japan, a cuckoo clock from Switzerland, all of which I still have.

The first real trip I ever took, when I was eight or nine, the first time I flew in a plane, was with Mary, who took me to New York City. We saw *The Fantasticks,* and went to Radio City Music Hall, where I was enchanted by the Rockettes. We went to the top of the Empire State Building and the Statue of Liberty, ate at restaurants where the food seemed so exotic it could have been from another planet: oysters on the half-shell, huge shrimp cocktails, steaks that cut like butter (which Mary advised me to always order rare because otherwise waiters would think you were a hick).

Later, in my fantasy in which Mary was my mother, she would go to bat for me in school against the Latin teacher, Miss Caldwell, who didn't approve of the way I comported myself in her class. "Eliza continues, despite legions of warnings, to chew gum in class," Miss Caldwell wrote in a note she sent along with me to the principal's office. The principal's secretary, tired of Miss Caldwell's notes, rolled her eyes and pointed to the word "legions." "What is this supposed to mean?" I told her I was sorry but I didn't know, though of course I did. The secretary just shook her head, as if Miss Caldwell were crazy, and sent me back to class.

At some point Miss Caldwell actually called my mother, who then ordered me to stop chewing gum, which was the right thing to do, as far as it went. But I needed my Mary Talbot–mother, someone who would explain to me why, for a brief time during my adolescence, I repeatedly caused commotions in school. I got straight A's, but I also got in trouble, lapses so benign that no one would even take notice of them these days, but back then such things were considered bad behavior: chewing gum, talking in class, passing notes.

My mother's point of view was relentlessly adult. These things were *my* fault, *my* failure to exercise self-control (one of her favorite phrases). How, she asked, could I be such a wonderful girl at home and then go out into the world and be such a menace?

I wasn't a menace, and we both knew it, but I sensed that within her question could be found its own answer. I had learned early on to take my angry feelings out of the house, to hide them from my mother and father, who seemed too fragile to withstand them.

I used to think that my Mary Talbot–mother would have set me straight, or rather, would have seen that none of this happened in the first place. She would not have been frail or needy or silent. On my birthdays, she would produce lavish parties for me. She would even remember to give me presents, which Mary did, in fact, always remember to do; sometimes my mother didn't recall what day it was, and I would have to remind her. And as I grew older, this same fantasy mother would introduce me to society at the Debutante's Ball, not pooh-pooh it as "gauche," as my mother did. And instead of making jokes about the Junior League, she would have been active in it, as indeed Mary was.

Fairy tales, all of it. And from a distance, comical, too. But as a child, I was not in a position to understand what was going on around me. Mary loved me, coming to our house after work and fixing us all dinner when my mother was flat on her back, treating my ungrateful little brother and me to Indians' games and movies. I hadn't reminded Bin that Mary took us both to see *Brigadoon* at an outdoor theater when he was five, and that he and I were both so thoroughly smitten by it, we begged her to take us back the next night—which, delightfully, she did. Nor did I mention that from that point on, he was hooked on the theater. She taught us both to play cribbage and backgammon, and she often played hearts or Scrabble with my father through the long empty evenings, after everyone else was in bed.

Had I an inkling about her relationship with my father, the faintest hint? No. In the innocent world I inhabited then, even if it had crossed my mind, I would have dismissed it as a preposterous idea, something that could never happen in real life, certainly not in mine.

CHAPTER 15

By the time I dropped Bin off at the airport, I felt as if I'd been run over by a truck. My eyes stung. Even the washed-out sunshine seemed too bright. I decided to drive directly to the hospital, the hell with visiting hours. If I snuck in to see my mother then, I could go home and take a nap and return later.

I pushed open the door to my mother's room; the drapes were drawn and it was dark. At first I thought she was sleeping, but she was just lying with her eyes closed. Slowly she turned her head and smiled wanly at me. She seemed all done in. I pulled up a chair next to her bed and took her hand. Neither of us spoke. After a few minutes, I put my head down on the bed, and she ran her fingers around my ear, just as she had done when I was small. Eventually, we must have both dozed off.

I woke with a start when a white-haired nurse entered the room with my mother's lunch tray. "Rise and shine!" she said and yanked open the drapes.

My mother opened her eyes. "More food?" she said thickly. "Didn't I just have breakfast?"

"Now, honey," the woman said. "It's lunchtime. Just try a little bite of everything. You want to keep your strength up." She winked at me. "You'll help her, won't you," she added. "She's such a sweetheart. We all just love her to pieces around here!"

At some point you had to wonder what hospital workers, nurses especially, were on. Whatever it was—speed? jolly pills?—I needed some.

"When I come back," the woman said to my mother as she left, "I want you to be a member of the Clean Plate Club!"

My mother reached for her water glass. She seemed dazed. "Here," she said, pushing the tray in my direction. I shook my head and pushed it back.

She cleared her throat. "I hope you had a good visit with your brother."

I nodded and managed to say, "It was fine." I wished Bin had burned all the letters and never said a word to me about them. I didn't want to think about Mary.

"I trust you're not just saying that for my sake," she said. Listlessly, she picked up the cover of her main course and then dropped it back. "You must know it's one of the tragedies of my life," she said, looking toward the window, "that Bin and your father got along so poorly."

"He didn't want another child, did he," I said, startling myself. I had no idea where that thought had come from, but once I'd said it, I knew it was true.

She kept her eyes on the window. "He was concerned about my health," she said quietly. "He thought Bin's birth might be the end of me."

"So he punished Bin for having been born?"

"Eliza, what's come over you? He loved Bin. Of course he did. They just . . . he just . . . something in their chemistry. They were a lot alike. Stubborn, both of them. But . . ." After a long pause, she said, "At any rate, it would make me extraordinarily happy if you and Bin could be more than fitful companions."

I wanted to reassure her. "I think we are," I said. "I think we're getting better."

"He cheered me up so much," she said, though she didn't seem at all cheered up that morning. "But it's strange. He put me so in mind of your father, I can't shake it off. I feel like he died yesterday instead of two years ago." She turned and looked directly at me. "I can't believe he's gone. It gets tiresome trying to act like a good sport when half of you is missing. Fifty years is a long time to be married, Sister."

I urged her to eat, which she began to do with painful slowness. Soon enough, she pushed the tray away and shifted uncomfortably.

I had been speaking to Geoff Ewing daily, and he seemed satisfied with her progress. The last time he had said, "You can't expect people your mother's age to heal as quickly as you or I would. She's coming along nicely. But she won't be up and around until that staph infection clears up." And then, as he almost always did when we spoke, he added that he wanted to have me to dinner, though it was clear by then that neither of us had enough enthusiasm for the idea to make it happen. Bin had gone over to Geoff's house for a drink one night when he was in Edgecliff, and after he came back, I asked him about Geoff's wife.

"She's wifely," was all he said. "Kind of dangerously skinny, but nice. Geoff seems happy enough."

Mother leaned back on the pillows and closed her eyes. "I'm not very good company today, I'm afraid."

"Would you rather be alone?"

"If you don't mind, Sister."

"Then I'll come back at dinnertime," I said. The afternoon stretched before me like a wasteland.

"Don't bother, dear. We can talk on the phone. I'll feel better later." I kissed her good-bye, and she turned away.

"Listen," I said. "You're a trouper. I know this is difficult, but it will be over soon. Remember what you used to tell me? That time heals almost everything?"

"Ha," she said. "Time! But I'm *not* a very good trouper today, I'm afraid. I'm just a broken-down old woman who feels sorry for herself. This is beginning to remind me of all those years . . ." She stopped.

"You'll be up very soon," I said. "This isn't a permanent condition. Anyway, there's no harm in feeling sorry for yourself once in a while."

"Yes, there is. I hate feeling gloomy. I hate feeling old. I detest lying here in this bed. It makes me feel like a perfect wretch." She lifted her hand. "Now go," she ordered. "Do something pleasant. And for heaven's sake, don't tell your brother about this sinking spell. I'm really quite fine, just worn out is all."

In the car, I felt a little more awake, and when I got back to the house, I called my children—first Anna in California. It was three hours earlier there, and I thought she might still be in her room. She wasn't. What I got was the ear-splitting noise of electronic music, then her voice with that strange upward inflection so many young people seem to have today. "Hi?" her recording said. "I'm not here? Leave a message and I'll call you back? Or try my cell?" and she recited the number.

I almost hung up but then I said. "Hi, it's me. Nothing important. I'll try you later. Hope everything's good. I love you."

But then I did try her cell and I reached her. She was on her way to class and couldn't really talk. Again, the reception on her end was lousy.

"What about Sean?" I yelled into the phone.

"He's history, Mom. I'm over him big-time. I told you that the other day." She seemed to be talking from the bottom of a hole.

"And you're okay?"

"Excellent," she shouted back. "Actually, I feel lucky. The guy was a jerk."

"Well, great," I said.

"Gotta run, Mom. Talk soon."

Good for her, I said to myself as soon as I'd hung up. Good for her. And I decided not to take that thought any further.

Then I called Jesse, but his phone only rang and rang. His voice mail didn't seem to be working. I wanted to tell him I'd decided it was okay for him to take flying lessons, despite the fact that the whole idea made me cringe. But who was I to inflict my fears on him? Besides, wasn't it statistically safer than driving a car? I'd try him again later. Next I called Will, and hung up when his voice mail came on. Having struck out twice, I decided to take Duke for a walk, but at the end of the driveway, I turned back. I went upstairs and lay down on my bed, where I fell immediately into a deep, blank sleep.

I woke up two hours later, groggy and with a headache. I took some aspirin and washed my face, but that didn't help, so I made a pot of coffee. While it perked, I stripped my brother's bed and took his sheets and towels to the basement. Doing laundry might make me feel better, I thought; it often did, with its good smells and its clear-cut beginning, middle, and end. If my mother had

had a clothesline, I might have hung the sheets out to dry, but she didn't, so I tossed them in the dryer. Then I noticed it had begun to rain.

I didn't know what to do with myself after that. I felt as if I had been stranded on a desert island without even Shakespeare or the Bible or whatever it was you were supposed to take. Henry James, probably, in my case. I thought of trying to walk Duke again, but he was asleep. By that time, it was getting dark and a steady rain beat on the windows.

I paced around restlessly as if I'd lost something and couldn't find it. Finally I phoned my mother. To my astonishment, she sounded bright and chipper, not at all like the person I'd left hours before. Rabi had dropped in to see her, she said, and had brought a bouquet of white freesia, her favorite flowers. "And guess who just called from New York?" she said brightly. "Mary! It was good to hear her voice."

"How did she know you were in the hospital?"

"Oh, you know Mary. She has spies everywhere. But I expect she heard it from her sister's husband, Ed. I called him a few days ago to see when they were getting back."

"When?" I could feel my heart speed up.

"Tonight. I'll be glad to see her. And, of course, you know what that means, Sister."

Frankly, I did not even want to contemplate what that meant.

"It means you can get out of this place. Mary to the rescue! You can go back to New Mexico for a while. Mary's ready and willing to help with things. You know what a take-charge person she is."

"I don't know about going back to New Mexico," I said. "We'll see."

"Don't be silly," she said. "And for heaven's sake, don't even think of coming out on a night like this to visit me. It looks perfectly dismal. I have the books that Bin brought me. You stay put."

"You sound a lot better," I said.

"Better?" she said, a familiar challenge in her voice. "Why, of course, I'm better. I told you I would be. I'm like the phoenix, you know." She laughed.

"You are indeed."

When I hung up the phone, my head was swimming. Mary to the rescue. I didn't know whether to laugh or cry.

I felt so antsy, I would have driven across the city to get out of the house. As I got out the morning paper to scan the movie section, the phone rang. It was Sam. He had gone ballooning in Albuquerque that morning with a client and Pete Campbell, one of his partners who was a serious balloonist and often made cross-country jaunts. The day had been so clear, Sam said, they could see all the way to Colorado. Hot-air balloons frighten me, but Sam loved to go up with Pete. He had even talked about getting a balloon of his own. He was happy floating free, moving silently with the winds that came off the mountains, but I felt utterly out of my element in a balloon, untethered, unsafe.

I couldn't pretend to match Sam's enthusiasm that night. For a moment, I considered telling him about Bin's discovery, but it seemed too complicated, too intimate. In any case, he was in a hurry; he was going out with the client and Pete and his wife for dinner.

Oh sure, I thought. Ms. Gardenia's probably on the menu. I hated being so suspicious.

When I hung up, it occurred to me that I was letting our marriage drift, like a hot-air balloon. I wondered why I wasn't able to summon enough energy to try to salvage our relationship, or even to think about it most days. Either I was too angry, or else I had already abandoned it, and I couldn't bother to figure out which. Instead, I had settled into a fog of indifference.

The weight of a whole evening with nothing to do hung as heavily on my shoulders as if I were eighteen and the only girl in the dorm without a date. Rain battered the lakeside windows, and the wind howled menacingly. The night extended like a wilderness before me, but I decided it was too miserable to go out. I found a bottle of Chardonnay in the refrigerator and was about to open it when the doorbell startled me. The first thing that flashed through my mind was that Mary had come back early, and I wanted to hide. Instead, I went to the door, corkscrew in hand. It was Rabi, and when I saw him, my heart lifted.

"Rabi!" I said. "Come in." His hair was damp, and he wiped off his shoes.

"Hi," he said.

"Was I supposed to be expecting you?"

"No, no," he said, "and I will go in a second. I'm sure you have plans. I just wanted to bring you this." He handed me a package wrapped in brown paper.

"For me?" I felt a little flustered. "I was just opening a bottle of wine. Won't you join me?"

"Of course," he said, "if you have time. But first you must open the package."

We stood in the front hall and he watched while I fumbled with the wrapping. Inside was a small, framed black-and-white photograph of a little boy in short pants, looking shyly at the camera.

Beside him was a dark, handsome man who looked a lot like Rabi.

"Rabi, how sweet. It's you, isn't it? And is that your father?"

"Yes," he said. "It was taken when I was ten, shortly before he was killed." He pointed at the white wall in the background. "That was our house."

"Your house," I repeated. Momentarily, I was at a loss for words. Finally I said, "I'm touched that you want me to have this. Thank you."

He followed me into the kitchen, where I poured two glasses of wine. I put some salted almonds in a dish and set them on the kitchen table, and we both sat down.

"You see," he said hesitantly, "I know all about your life when you were young, from what your mother has told me and from the photos and other things I've seen, and you hardly know anything about mine. I thought I'd try to even things up." He smiled.

Rabi was right; he knew a lot more about my past than I knew of his. "Tell me about your father," I said.

His father had been a neurosurgeon and was on his way home from a conference in Tel Aviv when PLO terrorists attacked two buses. His father stopped to help and was killed by his own people. "A senseless death," Rabi said. "So many senseless deaths."

I shook my head. "The irony of it. His own people."

"Yes, the irony. Because my father was a Palestinian above all else." He looked grave. "Most Americans," he said, "think this whole mess in Israel is about Jews and Muslims, but it's not. It's about Jews and Palestinians, both Christian *and* Muslims. Their destiny is the same."

"I'm afraid I don't really understand it," I said.

"Go back to the British, to the teens and 1920s. They betrayed everyone; they made promises they didn't keep—to the Jews, to the Palestinians, to everyone. And now, it is chaos."

I felt like an idiot, I knew so little about the situation. I had stopped paying attention long ago, and my history was shaky.

"Is it hopeless? Can't someone make a difference?"

"I am afraid only God, if He exists, can make a difference now."

We were both silent for a while, listening to the rain beating on the windows.

"At least you got out," I said at last.

"Oh, sure. The Israelis were happy to get rid of any Palestinians who would leave. Luckily, my mother had a cousin in Hamburg and another in Pittsburgh, so we had a fairly easy time of it. But she was never the same. She lost her spirit when my father was killed. She died five years later of a heart that wouldn't mend."

"I'm so sorry." I paused. "Do you ever think of going back?"

"No, I want to move on. What else can I do? And I am so lucky to be in this country. So lucky." He actually smiled. "But, Eliza? I'm leaving Cleveland. My advisor is moving to Berkeley, and he's asked me to go, too, so that I can finish up my work with him there. I'll leave in April, when the semester is over."

"Berkeley? That's wonderful, Rabi," I said.

"Yes, I'm very excited. My father would have wanted me to go. He went to medical school here, and he liked this country. He often said he should have stayed, but the pull to return home was too strong for him." He ran his hand through his hair. "Be a Palestinian for ten minutes, and you'll know how he felt. But I cannot go back. Maybe I'm a coward, but I'm no fool." He took a sip of wine. "Things are heating up again," he said. "You watch. The terrorists are crazy; they have nothing to lose and plenty of money."

"Yes, well," I said. I was sobered by his story, which rendered so much else trivial.

"I'm glad you wanted me to have this picture," I said again. "Thank you."

He smiled, and told me about his visit to my mother that afternoon. The rain was coming down in sheets, so loudly that we had to raise our voices. I finished my glass of wine, and, to change the subject, told him I had been considering a movie and asked him if he wanted to go.

"Why don't we get to work on the books in your parents' library instead?"

"You want to work?"

"Sure, why not?"

The idea of sorting through books didn't appeal to me at all. "Frankly, I'm a little sick of all this sorting and packing," I said. "I thought I'd take a break."

"Ah," he said. "A lazybones. We can't have that." His good spirits seemed to have returned.

"You're a stern taskmaster, as my mother would say."

He laughed. "Your mother," he said and shook his head. "I have learned more phrases like that from her than I ever could have learned from books. A lot of other things, too. She's wise, and she has so much energy. She's funny, too. Once I told her that grandmothers where I came from wear black and chase chickens around the yard, and you know what she said?"

"What?"

"She said that grandmothers in this country wear bright colors and chase young men." He laughed again. "So," he said, rising, "for her, we do the books."

I poured myself more wine. I felt slightly giddy and realized I hadn't eaten all day. "Have you had dinner?"

"No," he said. "But it doesn't matter."

"Maybe I could order a pizza. How about that?"

"One from Planet Pizza," he said. "Yes! With peppers and mushrooms and anchovies."

"Double cheese," I added.

"Sausage, too."

"Done," I said and phoned in the order. The dispatcher said deliveries were running late because of the weather; it could be at least an hour, maybe longer. I gave them the address.

By the time I got off the phone, Rabi was already in the library. I took my wine and joined him.

"You realize," I said, "that you're forcing me to help you."

"That's a joke," he said and smiled. "As if stubborn you could be forced to do anything."

Rabi and I both liked jazz, though he knew a lot more about it than I did, so I turned on the radio to a local jazz station. A woman whose voice I didn't recognize was singing, "I'll Be Seeing You."

"Ruth Brown," Rabi said, wrinkling his nose. "She's just okay."

We stood in front of the bookshelves. My parents owned hundreds, possibly thousands, of books, some of them valuable ones I knew my mother would want to keep, others I planned to take to the Edgecliff Library for one of their book sales. There were a number of first editions my father had accumulated over the years—the complete works of Mark Twain, Charles Dickens; a set of Jane Austen that, like the collected writings of Henry James he also owned, was probably worth a fortune. It occurred to me that to do this right would require a knowledgeable rare-book dealer. I hung back, unable to imagine where to begin. Sorting through books wasn't what I wanted to be doing that night, although what I did want escaped me.

Rabi began by taking down one book at a time and showing it to me. I, in turn, put it on the floor, one side of the room for books to keep, the other for ones to give away. We would have to box them later, since I'd run out of cartons.

"What's the Arabic word for 'books'?" I asked him at one point.

"*Ketub,*" he said.

"*Ketoob,*" I repeated, rather badly.

"One book is *ktab,*" he volunteered.

"*Kitab.*" I mimicked, and he laughed.

We worked quickly for half an hour or so, not saying much. The rain was so noisy I turned the radio up. Duke Ellington, Chet Baker, Ella Fitzgerald, Miles Davis.

Soon there were piles of books all over the room. I finished my wine and went back into the kitchen for the bottle. When I returned, Bill Evans was playing "Waltz for Debbie" on the radio.

"Look," Rabi said as he handed me a dog-eared copy of *The Odyssey* with my father's name written on the flyleaf, and underneath it, "Oberlin College, 1936."

"This was one of the first real books I ever read in English," he said. "I thought I would go insane. I had to spend so much time looking up words, you wouldn't believe. Maybe that was why it became one of my favorite books. Or maybe it wasn't the time I spent; maybe it was because it seemed like my own story."

"And did you have a Penelope you were trying to get back to?" I asked flippantly.

"No," he said, shaking his head.

"Well," I said, fingering through the pages. "It's old and a little worse for wear, but I'm sure my father would have wanted you to have it. Please, take it."

"Thank you," he said. "I would like that, if you're sure. Especially because it was your father's. He was such a . . . a *deep* person. I didn't know him long, but he was kind to me, though I don't think he much liked my boss, Mr. Barker. I was like a stray your mother brought home, and your father welcomed me. He treated me like a son."

"He did? Bin will be glad to know he treated someone like a son. The two of them didn't get along."

"Really?" Rabi asked, as if that couldn't possibly be true.

"Maybe he saw a second chance in you," I finally said. "But then, you and Bin are as different as night and day."

"He's a star. I'm not."

"It's more than that."

"Sometimes your brother seems a lot like your father. He talks more, sure, but he always reminds me of him."

"Are you kidding?" I didn't want to make a big deal out of it. Perhaps he was referring to a physical resemblance. A stranger like Rabi might have an altogether different take on my family than I did. Still, Bin's caustic attitude coupled with his talkativeness seemed unrelated to my father's silences. But then, Rabi was so cheerful and winning, my father might have simply responded in kind.

"I could be wrong about your brother," Rabi said. "I don't know what went on between them. But *I* thought your father was great. He seemed like a Renaissance man to me. He knew so much."

Rabi's words were so heartfelt, I couldn't dismiss them. Despite my father's flaws, despite the affair with Mary, my father had been a Renaissance man in many ways. I was tired, and I'd drunk too much wine on an empty stomach, and for a moment, I seemed on the verge of falling to pieces.

Rabi must have noticed me falter because he put his arms around me comfortingly. I leaned into him, and everything I had been holding in—worry over my mother, the revelation about Mary and my father, Sam, all my other loose ends—seemed to drain out of me. I clung to him, my face in his chest. I felt limp.

"It's okay," he said quietly. "Everything is okay."

The odd thing was, it suddenly seemed to be. I pulled my face away from his sweet-smelling shirt. John Coltrane's "A Love Supreme" came on.

"Thank you," I said. "I'm a bit of a wreck."

He leaned down and kissed me and, suddenly, it was as if the world had dropped out from under me; nothing mattered except that I hold on to him. He said something I couldn't understand, and we staggered together, half-falling to the floor. I kept thinking, This can't be happening, even as I struggled out of my jeans and sweater, even as he touched my breasts, even as we began to make love so intensely I thought I might fly apart. It was as if I'd never had sex before, never tasted desire. Wave after wave of passion flooded over me until I seemed to be drowning in it. Nothing else mattered: not the thought of Sam, not the lack of protection, not the fact that we were knocking over stacks of books. I wanted to keep him inside me permanently. I licked his hair, his eyelids, his neck. All of him tasted the way sandalwood smells. We came together in a gigantic surge that I thought might kill me, it was so much more powerful than anything I'd ever felt.

Finally, he fell back. I managed to pull a blanket off the couch behind our heads and cover us with it. He reached up and turned off the lamp. The only illumination came from a streetlight outside.

After a while, Rabi broke the silence. "You give me a book, you see what happens?" I smiled into his shoulder, my eyes shut tight.

"I'll give you libraries," I said. "A million *ketoobs*." I hardly recognized my own voice.

He drew me closer just as the doorbell rang.

"The pizza," he said.

"Forget it," I said. "I know it's a terrible thing to do, but please. Don't move."

The bell rang two or three more times, and at last we heard the car pull away. My head was on his shoulder, and I still hadn't opened my eyes, thinking that as long as I kept them shut, this would all be a dream. Gently, he pulled my face toward his.

"Your eyes are closed," he observed.

I nodded.

"Why?"

"I don't know," I said, my eyes still shut. "My father had a word . . . 'struthious.'"

"Struthious? What does that mean?

"It means ostrich-like. That's me. If I keep my eyes closed, I might not notice I'm here. Nobody else would either."

"You have an odd mind, Eliza. What's the word? Quirky?"

"Oh, I'm quirky all right."

"Well, I'm fascinated by your quirks," he said.

"Maybe so, but this is not something I do."

"I know."

"Now what?" I said. It sounded like a large, serious question, and he was smart enough not to attempt an answer. Instead, he turned on his side toward me, and within seconds we were all over each other again. My desire was electric, as if a ferocious source of energy had been unleashed inside me, or a maniac had taken possession of my body. I realized that, without knowing it, I had been looking for something to hold all the turmoil I'd been feeling. And Rabi, so at ease with himself despite his history, offered me what I couldn't find in my childhood home—something rock-solid, uncomplicated, enveloping, safe.

"Now what?" he repeated. "Now we could take a little nap." His voice was low and soothing.

I was cold. "No," I said. "I'm going to take a shower."

He groaned and then laughed. "Absolution," he said.

I wrapped the blanket around me and managed to make it upstairs to the bathroom. My knees were weak, so I sat on the shower floor and let the hot water pound over me. I don't know how long I stayed there; I felt disoriented. My thoughts were jumbled, but I do remember that I didn't think, What have I done? I didn't wonder if I were crazy, nor did I feel disloyal. The desire that had overwhelmed me seemed selfishly something I deserved.

When I went back downstairs, Rabi had rearranged the piles of books. We took one look at each other and fell together. We stood like that for a long time before he said he had to go. I did not ask him to spend the night.

"Oh," I said, suddenly remembering the check I'd written for him the day before and had left on the shelf by the door. I held it out to him. "Here," I said, "please."

He glanced at it, then sat down on the steps and put his face in his hands. I didn't know what he was doing until I realized he was laughing. He laughed so hard, I began to laugh myself, but it was laughter that felt precarious and a little too close to tears.

He stood up and pulled me to him briefly, and then he went out into the night. I tore up the check, turned out the lights, found Duke, and dragged us both upstairs. Then I got into bed and pulled the quilt over my head.

CHAPTER 16

I woke the next morning feeling muddled, as if I had a hangover and could only dimly remember what I'd done the night before. Yet I knew the moment I was fully awake that what I'd done was in an altogether different league than telling your hostess her dinner was lousy or calling your husband's boss a stuffed shirt—neither of which I'd ever done but had longed to.

I didn't want to think about any of it, and I tried hard not to. Yet the ridiculous phrase "unchaste wife" kept churning around in my head. "Bad mother," too, but I chased that one away fast; this had nothing to do with my children. When I permitted myself to remember what had happened, my face would get hot. I was shame personified, but shame mixed with a terrible longing. Rabi's skin, his lips, and the memory of my own explosive need kept barging in.

After a while, I decided that the whole thing had nothing to do with my real life. But then, it occurred to me that maybe the person I'd been last night with Rabi might be the true version of myself, one I'd kept under wraps all these years. That idea startled me. When the phone rang, I debated for a second whether to answer it.

It was Mary. "I'm home!" she said gaily.

"You're home," I repeated. "Great! How was your trip?"

"Fine, just fine. I'll tell you about it later. That is if you'll have dinner with me tonight."

Why wouldn't I want to see Mary, despite what I'd learned? I had to see her. "Of course," I said, and we made a plan.

I floated through the day on a cloud of calm, or perhaps it was exhaustion. My sense of shame dwindled away; by afternoon, I seemed to be on cruise control. At some point, I convinced myself that we all make mistakes, and by the time I went to the hospital, I actually found that flimsy idea consoling.

Mary had already been to the hospital and left, and my mother was all wound-up and bright-eyed from her visit. She rattled off Mary's Italian itinerary, the people she and her sister ran into in Venice whom they'd known as children but hadn't seen for over forty years; she showed me the beautiful handbag Mary had brought her from Florence.

As if she'd been along on the trip, my mother described the quaint little village in Tuscany where Mary and her sister had stayed, a tiny place that had been abandoned during World War II and was now an expensive resort. She reported on Mary's meals in Rome. On and on she rambled, even though she knew I was having dinner with Mary that night.

My mother has always liked the idea of things far more than reality. When she and my father came back from *their* trip to Italy some years ago, her report was heavy on details of dirt, strange food, and endless dull ruins. But Italy became a whole other country in my mother's version of Mary's trip. For my mother, with her immense capacity for vicarious enjoyment, disrupting her life by getting on a plane or changing currency couldn't hold a candle to going secondhand. By the time I left the hospital, she had appropriated Mary's trip so thoroughly it might have been her own.

As I was getting ready for dinner and wondering what I would say to Mary, Rabi called. "Eliza?" he said. "It's me."

"I know." Suddenly I was shaking.

"I don't think I can get there tonight. I'm behind in my work, but I'll try. If not, I'll call you tomorrow."

"Probably you shouldn't," I said.

"I'll call you tomorrow," he repeated. He said something else, which in my zoned-out state sounded like "shut the door" but was, when I replayed it in my head, *"Je t'adore."*

In spite of my better instincts, which seemed to have abandoned me anyway, I found myself melting like a lovesick teenager.

I met Mary at The Gables, one of the few good restaurants in Edgecliff. I was very nervous. She had invited me to her house for a drink beforehand, but I begged off. When I arrived at the restaurant, she was just relinquishing her mink coat to the maitre d'. She threw her arms around me, and I was catapulted by her lovely citrus scent into the same old fondness for her I'd always felt but hadn't expected after Bin's discovery.

"Oh, Eliza, how wonderful you look! Not at all like someone who's been through the mill. Your poor mother!" She hugged me again. "You're quite chic tonight," she added, "but then you always are." Mary herself was, as usual, beautifully dressed and her snow-white hair was bobbed stylishly. My mother called Mary a fashion plate, as if that were a shortcoming. Mary had inherited a lot of money, and she didn't skimp on clothes.

As soon as I was in her presence, I relaxed. All my sharp edges seemed worn down, smoothed over by Rabi. Or maybe not by Rabi, but by something he'd triggered in me that told me for the moment I didn't have to care so desperately about everything.

At sixty-eight, Mary was still taller than I was, five foot nine or more, and wonderfully erect. Her nails were perfectly done, I noted as we sat down, and she looked youthful and refreshed, not haggard, as she had billed herself on the phone.

"Mary," I said, after the waiter had gone to fetch our drinks, "you look terrific. Maybe I should take a trip to Italy."

"Didn't your mother tell you? I had a face-lift last summer. She didn't approve one bit." Mary laughed.

"She didn't mention it. You must have sworn her to secrecy."

"Of course I did," Mary said. "I swore *all* my friends to secrecy." She laughed again. Why wouldn't my father or any man, for that matter, have fallen for this woman? She was so lively, so straightforward and open. Secrets and Mary didn't seem to belong together, although by then I knew that wasn't true. But that had been one of the things I'd always loved about her: She appeared to have no back rooms in her life. By contrast, the world I grew up in was full of them—doors you couldn't open, crannies where things were tucked away, all sorts of forbidden places.

I asked her about her trip, and she skipped the travelogue, talking mostly about the food—white truffles, porcini mushrooms—food so good it practically made her weep, she said. "You know, Eliza," she added, "that's why you have to visit all those churches and museums and ruins. Not because of the art, though God knows, I love the art. But you have to do all those touristy things to work off your dinner and get ready for the next one. Oh, I do so love to eat." Mary was actually trim, much thinner than she'd been when I was a child.

"Me, too," I said.

"But you stay so slender," she said. "And unlike me, I bet you're not perpetually on a starvation diet. Are you still bicycling all over the west?" She laughed.

"Not much anymore. In Santa Fe, I mostly run. Here, I've been walking a lot."

"Please don't rub it in." She extracted a pack of cigarettes from her purse.

Suddenly, I would have killed for a cigarette. I had quit smoking years before, though occasionally I had lapses. I probably would have had more if Sam didn't nag me so.

"May I have one of those?" I said.

"Of course. Then we can both look tacky and out of date. Though one of the things I adore about Italy is that everyone still smokes."

I lit the cigarette she had handed me, and although for a second I thought I was going to keel over, it tasted wonderful. Great, I thought, everything in my life was going down the tubes. But the odd thing was I didn't care. Later I would care, I told myself; another day.

Our drinks came, and I watched Mary take a sip of her picture-perfect martini as I tasted a boring glass of white wine. We talked for a while about my mother, whom Mary called "a good soldier." She told me she felt terrible that she had been away when Bates Barker died and when my mother had her accident. "I'm just grateful you were here," she added.

I honestly hadn't expected to fall for Mary so completely, not after the letters Bin had found, but as we talked, I was perfectly happy to be with her, as if nothing had changed. After we ordered another drink and dinner, Mary wanted to hear about my children.

"So," she said when I'd finished, "your mother tells me you've been doing all her dirty work. And I also heard you've been getting some help from her gorgeous adoptee, Rabi. Talk about swooning! Good God, if I were a few years younger, they'd have to *haul* me off him!"

I felt my face redden and prayed the lights were too dim for her to notice.

"He's cute," I said.

"Cute?" she shot back. "Come now, Eliza, he's better than that. He's movie-star material. And so extraordinarily pleasant. A disposition like an angel and smart as a whip."

"He's been very helpful," I said, sounding prissy.

"I bet," she said in a way that made me wonder if she'd noticed my discomfort or, worse, read my mind.

Luckily, the bread arrived. Mary asked if I wanted a bottle of red wine and made a fuss about consulting me on her choice. We settled on a Tuscan red from Montepulciano. "Who cares if we're having fish?" she said. "I'm absolutely craving red wine."

I bummed another cigarette from Mary, feeling a little drunk though I'd only had a glass and a half of wine. Why was I drinking wine, anyway, I wondered, and not something real like Mary's martini? Since I was running amuck in every other direction, why hadn't I ordered a martini, too? I sat back as she talked animatedly and studied the woman who had had my father's full attention, but I could not find it in myself to feel any differently about her than I ever had.

"You've probably found a treasure digging around in your

parents' house," she said offhandedly. From the expectant way she looked at me, I knew immediately what she was referring to. My first instinct was to play dumb, but I rejected that.

"I'm not sure I'd call it a treasure," I said, a safe answer just in case I'd misread her.

She looked me in the eye. "Well," she said, "it *was* a treasure, a great treasure."

The last thing I'd expected was that this subject would come up, even obliquely. But there it was. "I suppose," I said, furiously searching for words, "we all have secrets."

"Eliza," she said softly, "I thought you'd guessed years ago, but evidently you didn't. He told me he'd saved all those things, and I was counting on getting to them first. I hope this hasn't devastated you. As sophisticated as you are, you've always had a wonderful innocence about you."

Let me tell you how innocent I am, I wanted to say. Let me tell you about your movie-star-handsome Rabi with the sweet disposition. But of course I said no such things. Instead, I said, "Dumb, not innocent. Unobservant, perhaps." And then I added my mantra of the day, "We all make mistakes."

"It wasn't a mistake. You need to know that. My eyes were wide open the whole time. The only mistake was that those letters weren't destroyed years ago. I begged him to at least return them, but he claimed he couldn't find them."

"Maybe he wanted someone to know," I said. Suddenly it occurred to me that perhaps the letters from Mary were the message from my father I'd been searching for all along, the only thing he could leave behind—as always, in someone else's words—that would tell Bin and me what he wanted us to know: I had a heart; there was a side to me I never revealed to you.

Mary took a piece of bread and broke it. "If you're asking me to justify what happened," she said, "I can't. I mean, even I'm not crazy enough to try. All I can tell you is that I adored him. He was my refuge in a way I will never be able to articulate or explain. I miss him with all my . . ." Her voice trailed off, and she sipped her drink. "Well, now," she said after a minute, "this isn't an altogether festive display, is it?" She took a tissue out of her purse and wiped her nose.

Mary's tears almost leveled me. I understood then that she had wept oceans over my father. The waiter brought the wine; Mary tasted it and nodded. Neither of us had touched our salads.

"I hope somehow you can forgive me," she said, holding my eyes with hers.

I didn't even hesitate. "Oh Mary," I said, "of course I can." And if I hadn't already, I did then, just that easily. I recalled how as a child I would follow her around, not wanting to let her out of my sight. How she let me wear her jewelry and her mink stole. She had offered an escape from the suffocation I felt in my home. Sometimes she would invite me to her house to spend the night. We made fudge, and she painted my nails the same bright color as hers; she took me to have my hair cut when everyone else had forgotten about it. She saved all her copies of *Vogue,* and we would leaf through them together for hours. She had seemed perfect in all ways to me as a child, and the truth of it was, she still did. "You positively drooled over Mary when you were small," my mother often said, as if that were a character flaw, or I had revealed shaky judgment early.

"It's him," I said with some difficulty, "that I have trouble forgiving." She started to say something, but I waved her to stop.

"Not because of you. I can understand why he loved you. It's just that I was never sure he loved us. Bin and me, I mean. He was always so distant, so frugal with his words. I don't know what he said to my mother in private, of course, and in many ways she's as cool as my father, just more talkative. But for years, I was a captive of his silence. And you know how Bin felt about him."

"Your father loved you terribly, Eliza," she said, and though I knew she was talking about quantity, not quality, her choice of the word "terribly" seemed ironic. "He needed someone to talk for him, a kind of translator, if you will," she went on. "A lot of men of his generation were reluctant to talk about their feelings. But your father *could* talk about those things, if you pressed him or led the way. He was a sensitive man, maybe too much so, and he needed to keep his soft side hidden."

"He did a good job of that," I said.

"And," Mary said, "your mother is basically a solitary person. She's always been off in her own world. Plus, she was sick for such a long time."

"I know," I said.

"I hope I don't have to tell you that I'm very fond of your mother. It probably sounds odd, but I never felt I was betraying her. I felt as if I was—how can I say this?—filling a gap." She took a bite of her salad. "Oh, the ways we trick ourselves," she said and shook her head.

We ate our salads in silence until Mary put down her fork abruptly. "As for your brother, well, he was a hard, hard case. He grieved your father, you know. Your father really believed that if he remained calm, Bin would snap out of his pouting and histrionics. And maybe he has. I don't know Bin as adult. For years he's avoided me like the plague."

"I don't think my father ever wanted Bin," I said tentatively.

"Eliza, don't say that. Bin was so flighty that your father just couldn't figure out how to handle him."

I imagined if Bin were with us now, Mary and I would have witnessed world-class flightiness, histrionics directed mainly toward me for being such a pushover. "Bin's tough," I said, "but I always thought Father could have found a way to humor him. Or pay more attention to him. Mother did."

"She spoiled him rotten," Mary said. "But he was certainly a bone of contention between your parents, as I'm sure you're aware."

"My mother and Bin have always had this bond."

"Well, they're alike, I've always thought. Quick to criticize. Blunt. But your mother tempers all that with a certain charm I've never seen in your brother, though I suspect it's there now or he wouldn't be as successful as he is. Thank God it was you and not Bin who discovered those letters."

"But it *was* Bin," I blurted out.

Mary looked stricken. "Oh my God!"

I told her Bin had found the letters and destroyed all but the one he showed to me. And how after doing that, he destroyed it as well. "He felt vindicated, I think."

"Vindicated?"

"As if he finally had the goods on our father."

"Oh, Eliza, you don't think . . ."

"No," I said. "If you're concerned he would say something to Mother, I don't believe even Bin would stoop to that."

"Pray not," she said.

"And he seems to be coming around a little. As if all his anger may be draining out of him."

She shook her head. "I hope so. Honestly, though, I don't know what if anything your mother knows. She would never say a word to me. She's a very private person who doesn't deal much in intimacies. I think they make her uncomfortable."

"Maybe so."

"I had this crazy notion," Mary said, "that *I* could find those letters. I'd always thought that if Louise ever moved, I'd be the one to help her." She shook her head. "I had no idea she'd act so quickly. If I'd known, I would have at least postponed my trip. But by the time I learned about everything that had happened, you were here, and I was there, and my sister threatened to kill me if I left her in Siena." She paused. "Those letters. Oh dear. I guess no one ever gets off scot-free."

My stomach lurched. "Unchaste wife" flew through my head.

"I can hardly go back and erase my life, can I?" She raised her eyebrows.

Our dinners came, and again we ate for a while in silence. "Tell me more about your trip," I chirped, wanting to change the subject.

"Oh, forget my trip," Mary said. "Italia: my shrine." She shrugged. "What I'd like to talk about is you," she added. "How are you, really, with . . . all this, everything?"

"Fine, I guess," I said. "It's strange being back in Edgecliff. It reminds me of how I never really understood this place to begin with. I feel a little like a displaced person here."

She eyed me curiously. "Really? Well, one of the things I wanted to tell you is that you can go back to New Mexico now, at least for a while. I'll take over."

I hesitated.

"I thought you'd be wild to get back, but perhaps I'm wrong."

"Sam's away a lot, and the kids won't be home for Thanksgiving," I said. "I might as well stay put. There's still plenty to do."

"Whatever you like. Just know I'm here to spell you if you need a break."

I thanked her. We finished our coffee and she paid the check. Together we braved the windy parking lot, where Mary's sleek, black Jaguar was parked next to my mother's Ford Taurus. She hugged me and said, "I love you. Don't ever forget that."

"I love you, too."

"I can't tell you how much that means to me, especially now." She kissed my cheek, then drew away suddenly. "Eliza look," she said. "That back tire on your mother's car is almost flat."

She was right. "I'll get it fixed in the morning," I said.

"I'm going to follow you home, just in case," Mary said.

"There's no need for that. I'll be fine. I'll drive slowly."

"And I'll be driving slowly right behind you," she said. "I insist."

We promised to talk soon, and I got into the car and drove off with Mary tailing me. The car bumped along, but I wasn't sure I would have noticed anything wrong if Mary hadn't pointed it out to me. I turned into my mother's driveway, and Mary pulled up behind me.

I went to thank her. "It looks like you have a visitor," she said, nodding toward the front porch. I turned to see Rabi sitting on the top step under the light. "Isn't that Rabi?"

"How strange," I said, my heart banging away. "He left some notes here the other day when he was helping me pack books," I tried. "I bet that's why he's here."

I was a terrible liar, but Mary just nodded. Then, it seemed she winked at me, so quickly and without expression I might have imagined it. "Take care of yourself," she said, narrowing her eyes—unless I imagined that, too. I waved as she backed out into the street.

Rabi was on his feet by then. Mary had probably figured everything out. She had always been skilled at reading between the lines, and she knew me so well. She also knew about secrets. I myself was fed up with them, I realized, as I headed for Rabi.

CHAPTER 17

"You weren't supposed to be here," I said to him once we were in the front hall.

"That's a warm welcome, Eliza."

"What are you trying to do? Inflict yourself on me?"

"I'd like to do that, yes," he said, smiling.

For a moment, I felt weary of all his smiles, taken advantage of by his charm.

"So," he said, "do you want me to leave?"

I didn't want him to leave, but I wasn't sure I wanted him to stay, either. "This is a mess," I said.

Rabi's face fell. "You think so?"

"Well, a potential mess," I replied.

"Things happen. Sometimes good things."

"I'm not about to get into a philosophical discussion with you," I said, sounding unusually prickly. "Anyway, a one-night stand is different from . . ."

"A one-night stand?" he said. He sighed. "Okay, I'll go." He reached for the doorknob, but I put my hand out to stop him.

"Wait," I said.

"Wait? For what? For you to go back to New Mexico?"

"But this isn't me," I said.

"*Who's* not you?"

"I mean, I've never thought of myself as someone who would do anything like this. But you, you're footloose, you're young. Why shouldn't you fool around? You have nothing to lose."

"If I believed for a second you had something to lose, I wouldn't be here," he said, looking me straight in the eye.

"Now you're a mind reader?"

"Eliza," he said, "I don't need to be a mind reader to figure out that your marriage isn't making you happy."

Irrationally, I felt insulted by his presumption. My marriage could have been the happiest on earth, for all he knew.

"I overheard you speaking to your husband the other night. You could have been talking to a stranger."

"How would you know how married people talk?" This was ridiculous. Why was I arguing with him? Was this some formality I needed to go through? I was reminded of the martini I hadn't ordered, and all my other safe choices.

"Look, Eliza, I need to tell you that I—"

"Besides," I said interrupting him, "whatever my husband is or is not, nothing entitles me to sleep with every young man I meet." I was beginning to sound like a nut, I realized.

"Just me," he said softly, taking my hands. "Not everyone. But the last thing I would ever do is force myself on you. *Inflict* myself."

"Oh, for God's sake," I said, "inflict away."

Rabi spent the night and every night after that for weeks. I slept in his arms and woke up completely at peace. Either that or pulverized by passion, as they say in sleazy novels. Once, he startled me from sleep when he sat bolt upright in the middle of the night.

"What's wrong?" I asked.

"The dream," he replied. "The awful dream I've had for years."

"Tell me," I said.

He fixed the pillows against the backboard of the bed, and I put my head on his chest, where I could hear his voice reverberating through his body, coming from deep within him.

"In this dream, I am running so fast I am almost flying," he said. "There is tall grass all around me, and I cannot see where I'm going, but I hear the ocean in the distance. I am very frightened." He paused. "Then I am on a beach, and the sand is so white, it hurts my eyes. There is so much light, I am almost blinded. I spot a house in the distance, and I think my mother and father will be waiting for me there." He paused again. "Did I say in this dream I am a child?"

"No, but I knew." In the dark, his speech had a trace of accent that I seldom noticed in the light. He seemed so thoroughly American most of the time I often forgot he hadn't started out that way.

"So I think this will be my house, even if it isn't in the right place. But the closer I get, I see it is not really a house at all, but one of those open-air structures where people sit or find shade— only a roof, no walls."

"A gazebo?" I murmured. "A pavilion?"

I felt him nod. "It has a metal roof that reflects the sun like the sand and the sea, and it is also too bright." He stopped for a second and continued in an altogether different tone. "I don't know why I'm telling you this. Other people's dreams aren't interesting."

"Go on," I said. The way he described his dream reminded me of things my children have told me—their own dreams and

sometimes movie or book plots—which have always aroused infinite patience in me. He resumed his account, his voice finally so
low it seemed little more than an echo through his chest. The
sound mesmerized me. He described filmy white curtains billowing in the breeze, a table set with blue china, light glinting off the
sea in the distance.

"But my parents are not there," he said. "No one is there. I sit
at the table, and there is bread and cheese and fruit. I start to eat,
but suddenly the sun disappears and the world turns dark, and I
am frightened again. Everyone is dead, and this is just one more
empty place." He shifted around. "Such a bad dream, I cannot
tell you."

"But it's a true dream, in a way," I ventured quietly.

"No," he pulled me closer. "No, not anymore. You are everything I've been searching for. The beautiful dream that can make
the other one vanish."

"Oh, please," I couldn't stop myself from saying. Who was this
man, I wondered. And for a split second, I realized I hardly knew
him except physically. Nevertheless, I fell back asleep and oddly,
proceeded to dream his dream. Only in my version I was running
with him, and the sun never disappeared. There was a blue sky and
a soft breeze, and it was Rabi who blinded me, not the light.

Yet if he blinded me, he also opened my eyes. For the first time
in my life I felt sexy, so alive to my body that I seemed to be a different person. Rabi told me he loved me in English and Arabic.
"Bhibbik" he said. Sometimes I almost believed him, maybe because I felt more lovable than I ever had before. All the same, once
when he said that, I turned to him and said, "Don't be crazy. This
is all about sex."

He tilted his head and looked at me. "No," he said.

Another time he told me he wanted me to go to Berkeley with him.

"You know I can't do that."

"Of course you can."

"Have you forgotten I'm married?"

"No," he said, "I haven't forgotten, but . . ."

"You really don't know anything about it," I snapped.

He turned on the lamp by the bed. "You're wrong," he replied. "I know." I believed he did, and why not? He seemed to know everything else, although what his certainty was based on, I had no idea. I began to think he really could read my mind. "The fact is, Eliza—"

"Besides," I blurted, "I'm too old for you. Eight years is a long time."

"Sometimes, you're surreal."

"And you're mad."

"Mad about you," he said, pulling me to him. A long, intense moment followed, during which his eyes met mine, and there seemed to be a universe of emotion between us, so overwhelming and vast, I would have gone to the moon with him at the drop of a hat.

"Listen," he finally said very quietly, "I've seen too much in my life—I've lost too much—not to know what I want. And I want you."

His gaze hypnotized me, and I bowed my head, not to break the spell, but because the weight of it was so immense it frightened me.

"Age is irrelevant, anyway," he said. "You look much younger than you are."

I started to protest, and he put his hand gently over my mouth. "Your husband is also irrelevant," he added.

I couldn't argue with that. "But my children aren't irrelevant."

"Your children are grown," he said softly. "I'm sure they love you, but I'm also sure they are less interested in you than you were in your parents. Something in your life—your mother's sickness, your father's aloofness—made you focus too much attention on them. I bet your children are different."

Was I so transparent that he could see right through me? Because he was right again, though I was startled to hear the business about my parents said aloud.

"If you're so smart," I said, only half joking, "you figure everything out."

"I will," he said. "I am."

What we experienced that November was a crash course in intimacy. Our time was short, and we both knew it. Sex figured hugely. Rabi touched me in ways I had never been touched, in places I had not known existed. I could not keep my hands off him.

We explored each other like cartographers mapping the geography of bodies, like Lewis and Clark tracking every detail of a brand new world. He called me *"Elizatti,"* as he touched me lightly. After that, I almost swooned at the sound of the word, as predictably as one of Pavlov's dogs. His skin was beautiful and golden, so fragrant that the smell of him lingered on me and I hated to shower.

Rabi rendered me breathless; my whole body thrummed with wild cravings. In our little world, which consisted mostly of my old bedroom, but also the kitchen floor, up against the empty bookshelves in the library, and twice on the stairs, we were like bandits hiding out from the law. I wanted to stop the clock. There was a day when we didn't get out of bed until two in the afternoon, and I had to literally tear myself away in order to visit my mother. When I did, she remarked that I was flushed and asked if I had a fever.

I had a fever, all right.

During one of our exhausted time-outs, Rabi asked me about my children and my work, and he wanted to know all about New Mexico. "I'm sure you'll see it sometime," I said.

"Of course I will."

In turn, I asked him questions I'd avoided asking before. When I mentioned that I knew nothing about his work, he gave me a brief explanation of metallurgy.

"It sounds like alchemy," I said, "like some kind of magic."

He laughed. "Alchemy's chemistry, but it's out of favor these days."

He said his thesis was on high-temperature superconducting alloys, but the subject seemed so over my head, I didn't ask him to elaborate. Anyway, as he spoke he was playing with my nipples, and I couldn't concentrate on anything but his touch. I wanted him to devour me; I wanted to devour him, too. I pictured the two of us melting together in a pool of sex.

Another time, when we happened to be out of bed, he told me that his mother was from a prominent Palestinian family but that one of her grandfathers had been German. She was so undone by her husband's death, she never recovered. "She didn't have a chance in Pittsburgh," he said. "It was difficult for her to learn English, and she hated the cold. She had trouble with her cousin and his family who couldn't understand why her grief never ended. She was very depressed."

"That's awful," I said.

"It was. I watched helplessly as she faded away. She died of pneumonia, but I think that was only an excuse. She couldn't go on. After her death, I vowed I would never be that helpless. There is always something you can do."

"But you were so young," I said. "A fifteen-year-old can't save his mother."

"I guess you know that from all you've told me about your parents."

I just looked at him.

"What I meant was that I will never be a helpless child again. My childhood is finished. I can do things now I couldn't do then. And I will."

I found his determination sobering. But even that didn't stop the drunken, steamy passion I felt and the thrilling sense that I'd been born again—seized with lust and greedy for life.

I never spoke about Sam because, really, what was there to say? If I'd loved my husband, I wouldn't have been in bed with another man to begin with.

"What will happen to us?" I asked at some point.

"Don't worry."

Then he told me he loved me again. "*Bhibbik,*" he whispered. "*Bhibbik.*"

I wanted to believe every word Rabi said. Most of the time, that wasn't difficult; it only required that I suspend my disbelief, as you do in a story. So what if we had vastly different histories? So what if he was younger? But while I couldn't read the future, I was sane enough to know idylls like this didn't last.

And was I sane. On some level I was more clearheaded than

I'd ever been. It didn't matter if that was a state Rabi had brought me to or one I'd come to myself; I was in a completely other world than the doggedly dutiful one I'd inhabited for years.

More than once I was caught by a vision of my younger self, the overeager, stubborn girl who had married Sam. I wished I could hold the younger version of me, along with my children, in my grown-up arms, and say, "Now, now, there's no reason to rush, no need to force things. Life will spread out its pleasures soon enough." Strange, because it wasn't like me to have much compassion for myself.

Sam called almost every day, and I found myself speaking to him as if he really were a stranger, one who was interrupting me. On the day he received the perfume I'd almost forgotten sending, he said, "What the hell is this perfume supposed to be about?"

"Just a reminder," I said.

"Of what?" He sounded both defenseless and belligerent, and I wondered why I hadn't anticipated years earlier that the twenty-two-year-old I'd married might stay that way forever, as if frozen in amber. Sam was no wiser than he'd been when we met.

"Of the fact," I said, steeling myself, "that there's someone else. Again. And that she wears that perfume, or something like it."

There was dead silence on the line, and for a minute I thought he'd hung up. Finally, he said, "Come on, Eliza. Get a hold of yourself."

"I have."

"Well, that's good news," he said sarcastically.

"Yes, it is."

"Maybe I should fly to Cleveland for the weekend."

"Don't bother," I said. "There's not much to say."

"There's plenty to say."

Suddenly I was full of resolve in a way I hadn't anticipated was possible. Even if it was Rabi who had emboldened me, I was wide awake. After fuming for years, I could no longer hold in the anger I'd been silently hoarding.

"Plenty to say?" I replied, my voice rising. "I don't want to hear it. It's too late. I'm tired of this pretense." I caught my breath. "I'm sick of having a fourth child. I never wanted a fourth child."

"What are you talking about? A fourth child?" he said, and it occurred to me that he really did not understand. Even in my overwrought state, I realized he was basically dense—dense and naive, annoyingly so. But I was finished with that. I had lived with my youthful bad judgment for too long.

"I want out," I said more calmly. "I'm sorry, but I can't go on."

"*You* can't go on," he said. "Let me tell you, Eliza, if you think it's been any picnic for me to live like I've been living recently, with a virtual deaf-mute, and a depressed one at that, you're crazy. Your idea of reality is straight out of those goddamn Betsy books. Magic seeds, for Christ's sake!"

"Well, then, what more is there to say? And, please, don't go into some routine about being sorry, or tell me you love me." I paused. "I don't even think you know how to love."

"Oh, this is getting good," he said. "But you're right about one thing. I don't love you. You've been like a ghost lately. What's to love?"

"At least you're being honest for once."

"Let me get this straight," he said. "You're leaving me? Is that what I'm hearing?"

I'm not sure why, but I suddenly suspected he might be pulling some legal trick, which maybe he was. I was roiling inside. "Look.

You've refused to grow up. You've screwed around. You don't love me, as you just admitted. Plus, my success somehow diminished you, so that even I could never enjoy it. You're irresponsible, insensitive, and—"

"Whoa," he said, interrupting me, though I could have gone on and on. "Where is all this crap coming from?"

"From my heart, Sam."

"Oh, that's a good one. Would you like to discuss your quote-unquote heart? What heart, Eliza? You complain about your father, but you're just like him. You're two of the coldest human beings on earth."

"My father is no longer on earth," I shouted.

"He is for you!" he yelled back. "He'll never die for you. He's always been in the middle of our marriage like the goddamn elephant in the living room!"

Even as our conversation disintegrated, I realized Sam was right. "That's over now," I said more quietly.

"Then come home, or let me come there so that we can talk sanely."

"No," I said. "It won't get any saner than this."

"I might come anyway."

"Don't you dare," I said, and hung up.

The phone rang twice after that, but I didn't answer it. I couldn't bear to talk to him again. Now that I'd started this, I wanted the whole thing over, fast. Sam could come to Edgecliff or not. Nothing would change my mind.

I felt like I'd flung off my chains. I felt free—free of lost boys, of Sam *and* my father. Free. I had been under a spell for years, or worse, half dead. Not anymore.

I went to the window and looked out at the lake, which was

choppy and gray, illuminated here and there with shafts of sunlight. What I had been waiting for? For Sam to change? For the
kids to grow up? Whatever it was, I couldn't wait any longer.
Time was speeding by, too precious to waste. And I was alive. It
wasn't about Rabi, or it wasn't only about Rabi, though he had
unleashed an astonishing energy in me I hadn't suspected was
there.

And, I thought, if I could be alive to Rabi, why couldn't I be
alive to the whole world? What was holding me back?

Nothing, I realized. Not a thing.

Standing at the window, looking out at Lake Erie, I was daz-
zled by a sense of possibilities, and by something I realized I'd
abandoned long before: hope. My husband had just announced he
didn't love me, and I was the happiest person on the planet.

CHAPTER 18

Sam called the next day to ask if I'd changed my mind. I told him no. "Why would I want to stay married to someone who doesn't love me?"

"Aw, Eliza," was all he said. And then he added, "Well, I guess I tried."

"Tried what?" I snapped. "Tried to be the biggest jerk you could be? Tried to sneak around without my noticing? Tried to shirk most of your responsibilities to your kids? What is it exactly that you tried, Sam?"

He made some noises: I didn't understand him, I'd gotten him all wrong, things like that. And then the kicker: I was impossible to live with.

"Impossible to live with?" I said. "Well, I guess we know how to fix that, don't we?" I slammed down the phone.

If I was tempted to have any second thoughts, I remembered the times over the years when I'd secretly wished for a plane crash or a motorcycle accident, anything to erase Sam from my life. That was a measure of how desperate I'd been. I was ashamed of having been so passive, of believing Sam would disappear without my lifting a finger. I had barricaded myself behind my children and my work and picked at the scab of my childhood while real life was passing me by.

I hadn't wanted to pay attention to the state of my marriage, or dwell on the fact that the best part of it was that Sam gave me breathing room. (Someone else might have called this neglect, but I'd always been grateful for it.) I'd closed my eyes to him years before, and if the extent of my blindness was breathtaking, it was also deliberate, a screen I'd erected to get through the days. We had lived through the children; they were our medium, such as it was. Beyond them, nothing. Now what was I supposed to do? Try to fix the past? I couldn't do that. I wanted to get on with life.

Then I remembered something Emerson had said: that everything has a long foreground. He was right. My decision to end my marriage had been brewing for years. The speed at which things were resolving was not speed at all, but the result of a snail-paced, agonizing, decades-long process.

I didn't say a word to Rabi about my talk with Sam. I didn't say a word to anyone. I figured that when I got back to New Mexico I would do what needed to be done—tell the children, get a lawyer and an accountant, too, since our finances were complicated. All I knew about divorce was that New Mexico was a joint-property state, which, much as I hated the idea, probably meant that Sam would get half of our estate, even though Betsy Blossom and I had earned the bulk of it.

Then I came to my senses, and remembered who I was dealing with. Sam was a lawyer, and he had legal connections all over town. If I were smart I would get my own lawyer, the sooner the better. The following morning, after Rabi left, I called my friend

Barbette, who specializes in divorce, and told her the story. Barbette is an irreverent woman, brainy, funny, and outspoken. Originally from Dallas, she still carried around a load of Texas.

When I had finished explaining what was going on, she said, "Well, listen, sweetie, you know what a small town Santa Fe is. I guess it won't burst your balloon at this point if I tell you that I've seen your guy Sam two or three times in the company of a young woman since you've been gone. Hispanic. Very pretty. I can't remember her name, but I recognized her right away. She's on TV in Albuquerque. Channel Four."

"Not that Mona Whatshername," I said.

"That's it. Mona Ortega."

"My God, Barbette, she can't be twenty-five!"

"Maybe twenty-six. Anyway, who would you expect Sam to fall for? Some old perimenopausal broad like me? I don't think so." She laughed. "A cradle-robber, your Sam. Ugh. But, Eliza, are you okay?"

"I *am* okay," I said. "I really am. Frankly, I'm relieved. This has been coming for years."

"Have you thought about counseling? I have to ask that," she said.

"Honestly? No. We've come to the end of the line here. I've been dragging this large, disorderly child around for too long. You know Sam."

"Yeah. He's a big old huggy cowboy baby; all that testosterone scootin' around. Cute as he is, though, I'm glad he's not mine. But, sweetie, maybe it's your mom's move and all that. This is probably not the best time for you to make a decision. Could be you're under a lot of stress."

"Listen," I said, "the big stress in my life is Sam."

"How *is* your mom, by the way?"

"She's doing fine now, if you don't count the fact that she broke her hip the day after I came here and then got a staph infection on top of it."

"How gruesome. Talk about stress!"

"She should be home by the weekend. Then it's a couple more weeks before she can leave. But she'll be fine."

"Well, that's a relief. But I'm sorry to hear this business about you, because, as you know, I positively *hate* what I do."

"Sure, that's why you're so good at it."

"You know what I mean."

"Barb," I said, "about this Mona person? Next time you see her, smell her."

"What?"

"Give her a sniff. Because dollars to donuts she'll be wearing a heavy gardenia perfume called Tropique."

"What's with the perfume?"

"I smelled it on Sam's clothes for weeks before I left. I smelled it in our house once after I'd been away."

"Come and work for me," she said. "I need a better investigator than the one I've got now."

I laughed.

"Well," she said, "if I see her again, I'll give her a sniff. But you just need to make sure this is what you want. You've been married for a long time."

"Twenty-two years, a large chunk of my life, more than half of it. Too long."

"You sure you don't want to sleep on this?"

"I'm sure."

"And the kids?"

"They don't know anything about it, but I really don't think it will come as a total shock. I'll talk to them at Christmastime. In the meantime, this is between you and me."

"You bet. I'll send you some stuff. Look it over, and we'll talk when you get back."

"Okay." I gave her my mother's address. "And Barb? I don't mean to sound greedy, but I don't want him walking away with *all* of my money."

"Of course you don't, sweetie. And he won't. Not with me going to bat for you."

"Barbette, please. Let's not make this ugly."

"Sweetheart, honey, listen to me: Divorce is *always* ugly."

"Well, I don't want ugly."

"You've already got it, sounds like to me."

That afternoon, when I went to the hospital, my stomach ached and I felt queasy. My mother was all wound-up and on a real tear. When she got like that, which she occasionally did, she could out-do Bin. Here we go, I thought.

She didn't appear to notice I had not been paying very close attention to her all week. Mary had visited every day, of course, and when I'd roused myself to speak to Geoff Ewing earlier in the week, he'd assured me that Mother was on the mend.

"Sister, they're actually going to let me out of this place in just two more days!"

My heart sank. What would Rabi and I do then? Sneak around like teenagers?

"Geoff said when he closed the wound back up, it was clean as a whistle!"

"He told me," I said evenly. Good lord. She herself had told me three or four times. Was she losing her mind?

"I have to leave with that nasty walker, but at least I can leave!" She squeezed my hand delightedly. "And then, he assured me that in two more weeks, we can go. We'll be in Santa Fe in time for Christmas! Oh, how I love Santa Fe at Christmas." She went on to describe Christmas in Santa Fe in detail, as if I had never been there.

She asked me to order a hospital bed for the library because she couldn't climb stairs, and I made a note to do that. She told me that Geoff had already contacted an orthopedist in Santa Fe, and all we had to do was take her records with us when we went. Gaining even more steam, she told me Mary was having her living room and dining room repainted and that we were all invited for Thanksgiving dinner at Mary's, Rabi as well. She mentioned that Bin was flying in for Thanksgiving, something I'd told *her* two or three days before, after I'd spoken to him. She manically rattled on and on, but I barely listened. Get this woman something to calm her down, I thought. Then she started in on an unexpected visitor she'd had, and my ears perked up when she referred to him as "a nice-looking man from the FBI."

"The FBI," I repeated blankly.

"He was doing a background check on Rabi."

"Why?" I managed to ask, but my first thought was, My God, is he a terrorist?

"Why, for his security clearance, Sister," she replied, as if I were daft. "When he goes to Berkeley he'll be working now and then at the National Lab in Los Alamos right near Santa Fe.

Apparently, Berkeley operates it. Which will be nice, because he'll be close by, and we'll get to see him now and then."

I must have looked surprised.

"Maybe he hasn't mentioned that to you," she remarked, as if she and Rabi had many secrets they weren't sharing with me. *Los Alamos?*

"He probably forgot," I said. "We don't talk a lot."

"Well, it will be nice. I was afraid I'd lose touch with him. I thought perhaps I'd leave here and never see him again."

"Wait," I said, "how did the FBI know you were in the hospital?"

"Heavens," she said, slowing down for a second. "I never thought to ask. But they seemed to know a lot. Good gravy, I expect they know everything."

I devoutly hoped not.

"So what did you tell him, the FBI man?"

"Just what I knew. He asked questions, and I answered them."

"What kind of questions?"

"Sister, don't be naive. Questions about a number of things." She said this as if she'd made a top-secret pact with the FBI.

"Like what?" I pressed.

"Well," she said a little reluctantly, "how long I'd known him, for one. Where I'd met him; what kind of work he did for Bates Barker, the poor man. You know, I often think of Bates. He and I had such pleasant times together. Let's see. He asked me about Rabi's integrity, which as far as I know is flawless. And about his family, whom I've never met, though of course he has that cousin in Pittsburgh. About his wife. About his finances, his reliability—"

"His wife," I interrupted. "You mean his cousin's wife?"

"Of course not, Sister. What's wrong with you today? You seem perfectly dense. *Rabi's* wife."

My heart began beating crazily. I couldn't believe my ears. "Rabi's *wife*?"

"I should say so," my mother replied, as if I were demented.

"Really," I managed to say.

"Sister. I don't know what's come over you lately. You're in a fog. I realize it's my fault that you've been here so long, but all week you've been distracted. I don't think you've heard a word I've said for days." She leaned back in her chair. "I know you're trying to be cheerful, dear, but I don't think you feel very well, do you."

"I'm okay. But tell me about the wife."

"A lovely young woman. I met her several years ago. She was studying architecture in Pittsburgh."

For a minute I thought I was going to faint. My head spun and I clutched the arms of my chair.

"Her name escapes me," my mother was saying.

I felt the color drain out of my face. My hands were clammy. My heart raced a mile a minute.

"Oh dear, Sister," my mother said. "You *don't* feel well, do you? You look a little green around the gills. Here, let me ring for a nurse."

"No, I'll be fine. It's just some bug I picked up."

"Well, don't come near me," she said.

"Maybe I'll just slip into your bathroom," I said. I did, and proceeded to vomit violently. When I finally staggered out, my mother *had* called a nurse.

"See how peaked she looks?" my mother said to a bored, over-weight woman who seemed to be dressed in pink pajamas. She'd obviously skipped her dose of jolly pills that day.

The nurse took my hand and led me to my mother's empty bed. "You just lie down for a second. Your mother's right, you look all washed out."

"My stomach," I mumbled.

"I'll go and see if I can't find you something for nausea." She left the room, and I lay with my eyes closed on my mother's bed. I knew she was worried that I was contaminating it.

"Go on," I said to her.

"Go on? Go on with what?"

"You were telling me about Rabi's wife." The word *wife* caught in my throat.

"It seems to have made you ill."

"No, no," I said. "I didn't feel right when I came here."

"I wouldn't think you'd want to drag flu bugs into a hospital."

"Please, go on."

"I'd prefer not to discuss it now. This hardly seems an appro-priate time," she said.

"For Christ's sake, Mother."

"There's no need to talk like a stevedore, Eliza."

An unearthly calm descended on me. I sighed.

"Oh, all right, then," she finally said. "A lovely young woman with the most gorgeous blond hair I've ever seen. The real thing, too; she isn't a bottle-blonde like some people." She cleared her throat meaningfully. "And far be it from me to know what the trouble was, but they divorced. It was sad. Divorce is always sad, I imagine."

"She left him?" I said.

"Or they left each other. I don't really know. I try not to pry. All I know is that they were separated by distance—she was in Pittsburgh and he was here, and of course you can't be married and live like that. Which, by the way, is precisely why I've been urging you to go and see your husband."

"Please," I said, my eyes still closed. "So, was she Palestinian, too?"

"Oh, goodness, no. The Palestinians are Arabs, dear. They don't have blond hair. Rabi's blue eyes are quite the exception. Something in the woodpile there." She laughed gaily.

"An Anglo, then?"

"I should say not. Polish, I believe. Or Czech. Something like that."

"You mean from Poland?"

"For heaven's sake, Sister. From Pittsburgh, I told you. Are you listening to me? Of Polish descent. Or possibly Czech."

Why hadn't he told me, the son of a bitch.

Pink Pajamas swept back into the room. "Here you go," she said. I opened my eyes to find that, incredibly, she was offering me a roll of Tums.

"Tums!" I exploded. "I'm in a great big hospital and you can't find any real drugs?" I'd been up for something that would put me out, for days if possible.

She looked at me levelly. "You are not a patient here," she spoke very, very slowly. "I am an RN, not a doctor. I am unable to prescribe medication. I did the best I could, which was to get these from my purse. If you want one, fine. If not, fine, too."

"I appreciate your efforts," I said in much the same tone she herself had used. "I believe, however, I'll pass."

"Oh, Sister, go ahead. At least chew one. Your bones need all the calcium they can get at your age."

That did it. The FBI. Los Alamos. Rabi's ex-wife. Now my aging bones. I got up in the bed and said, "I'm going back to the house and lie down there." The nurse huffed out of the room.

"I'll call a cab for you, Sister. You can't drive in this condition."

"Of course I can." I was so dizzy, I had to sit on the edge of the bed for a few minutes. "I'll call you later," I said. Amazingly, the minute I was on my feet, I felt almost normal.

"In the meantime, I'll phone Mary and have her bring you some of her nice chicken soup."

"You. Will. Do. Nothing. Of. The. Kind," I said in a far more emphatic and menacing voice than I had ever used with my mother. "Do you hear me?"

"I believe you're so ill, dear, you don't know what you're saying."

"I know what I'm saying, and I'm telling you: Do not call anyone. Please. I'll be fine." And then I added in the softest voice as I could muster at the moment. "I just need to rest. I'm sorry about this."

"And I'm sorry you don't feel better," she said.

There, I thought. We had apologized.

"Erica!" she shouted triumphantly.

"Who's Erica?"

"Why, Rabi's wife. Have you forgotten her already? Her name is Erica."

"What's with the present tense? I thought you said she was his ex-wife."

"Goodness," she said. "You are beginning to sound exactly like your father."

★   ★   ★

When I got back to the house, I went down to the basement and kicked a wall. I kicked it hard, four or five times. I kicked a wall, but it was Rabi I was really kicking.

For some reason, my bizarre actions didn't shock me a bit.

What shocked me was that I never once thought to kick myself.

CHAPTER 19

When Rabi came that night, I wasted no time. "Why didn't you tell me you were married? Why didn't you tell me you would be in Los Alamos? *Why?*"

I felt better than I had earlier, although I was limping.

"But I'm not married." He seemed genuinely puzzled. "You're the one who's married."

"You were, though. You were married."

"I was, but that was over two years ago," he said matter-of-factly. "Unfortunately, things worked out badly." He didn't even look sheepish.

"Well, you should have told me."

"I started to tell you a couple of times, but you interrupted me. I wasn't hiding anything, Eliza. I would have told you at some point. It just didn't seem very important."

I wondered what kind of double standard I was using: I could keep mum about my current husband, but he couldn't do the same about his ex-wife? Still, it irritated me.

"Why are you limping?"

"Because my goddamn bones are old," I shot back.

He pulled me to him and began kissing me, but I tore away.

"Leave me alone."

He tilted his head and gave me a look that suggested I was acting like a crazy person.

"And what's with this Los Alamos business?" I asked. "You're planning to be in my backyard, and you couldn't even tell me?"

"I wanted to surprise you."

"I'm surprised, all right." I stomped awkwardly into the library.

He came up behind me and put his arms around me. "Eliza," he said into my ear, "let's not do this. Please."

I pushed him away again.

"You're just upset," he said.

"You're goddamn right I'm upset. All these secrets of yours upset me. What the hell else don't I know about you? That you're with the PLO? Or better yet, Hamas?"

His shoulders slumped. He stared at a corner of the ceiling for a minute. "That was unnecessary," he said. "I'm going to leave." He started for the front hall.

I was beside myself. I didn't want him to leave, although, yet again, what I wanted wasn't clear to me. I followed closely at his heels.

Abruptly he turned around, so that I bumped into him and fell into his arms. Ah, I thought, this was what I really wanted. Quicker than I knew it, we were making love in the doorway to the library so ferociously we could have been in battle. I wanted to win, but win what? Soon, I was lost in a fog of sex.

Suddenly, the doorbell rang, and Duke began barking. Groggily I raised my head, only to spot Mary's shoulder through the window of the front door.

"Oh, shit," I said. "It's Mary. She knows I'm here."

He groaned.

We untangled ourselves, and I pulled up my jeans. Rabi looked ridiculously disheveled, and I was sure I did, too. There was no way I could sneak him down into the basement without Mary seeing us. "The closet in the library," I ordered, dragging him by the hand.

"You're kidding."

"No. Just go in the closet and wait. Don't make a sound."

I turned on the closet light, thrust a magazine into his hands, and shoved him inside. "This will take only a second," I said. Then I smoothed down my hair and went to the door.

"Mary!" I said as I opened it. She had a basket in her hand with a pot in it—the goddamn chicken soup, of course.

"I hate to bother you, but your mother said you were feeling quite under the weather, so I made you some soup."

"How nice of you." She was still outside, and I reached around the storm door for the basket. As I did, she pulled the door open and walked into the house. "Your mother was right. You look a fright, poor thing."

"Actually, I'm feeling a lot better now. It's been a rough day." We were now in the front hall.

"I'll just put this in the kitchen for you," she said.

"Don't be silly," I said, trying to head her off. "I can do that. I wouldn't want you to catch whatever I have."

As I traipsed after her, Mary stumbled on something. The lid flew off the pot, and soup sloshed all over.

"Oh dear! Look what a terrible mess I've made." There was a puddle of soup on the hall floor, and noodles and bits of carrots slid down the wall. I ran to the kitchen to get something to wipe it up.

When I came back, Mary was holding Rabi's leather jacket in her hand. "Here's the offending party," she said, "the thing

I tripped over." She examined the jacket. "This looks like Rabi's," she added.

I swiped at a piece of chicken and some noodles on the sleeve. "Hmm," she said. "Maybe he left it here."

"Maybe," I replied, sopping up the soup. My life was beginning to feel like a Marx Brothers movie.

"I wouldn't think he'd leave it on the floor, though, or forget it, for that matter. It's freezing outside."

"Beats me," I mumbled.

It was at that point that Duke began barking insistently in the library. I poked my head in the library door to find him clawing at the closet door.

"Duke seems to be having a breakdown," I said, at that point so rattled I could scarcely talk. Mary strode right past me into the library.

"There must be something in the closet he doesn't like." She shooed Duke away and, while I looked on in horror, flung open the closet door.

"Boo!" Rabi said, which I thought was fairly cool under the circumstances. "I've been playing hide and seek with Duke," he added, which seemed to me gilding the lily and not particularly cool. He stood smiling at Mary, holding a copy of *Martha Stewart Living,* the magazine I'd handed him, as if it were perfectly normal to be discovered in a closet, playing hide-and-seek with a dog that could barely navigate.

Mary looked momentarily flabbergasted. Then she said drolly, "I didn't figure you for a Martha Stewart fan, Rab."

"Oh, yes," he said. "I like Martha Stewart. She has many good recipes, a lot of good tips." He smiled charmingly. "Did you know you can make your own Christmas candles? It tells you how right in here," he tapped the magazine. Christmas candles? He was still standing in the closet and I thought, Oh you jerk. The jig is up.

"I think," Mary said with a knowing smile, "I've interrupted you two. I should have called before I came."

"Not at all," Rabi said. "We were just fooling around." You bet.

"Well, anyway," Mary said, "I'm going to dash, but I'm sorry again about the soup. There's still some left in the pot."

"There'd be more of it if some people didn't throw their coats on the floor," I said as Rabi emerged from the closet. "Mary, I appreciate your going to all that trouble. Thank you."

"Your mother seemed unusually concerned about you."

"Boy, was she on her high horse today!"

"She's thrilled to be getting out of the hospital," Mary said as she walked to the door.

"I wish she wouldn't get so revved up when she's excited. She's like a bulldozer!"

Mary turned around. "Eliza, I'm surprised to hear that coming from you. You've always been endlessly tolerant of your mother." The way she said it made me realize that my mother had probably annoyed Mary for years. "By the way, are you limping?"

"I stubbed my toe," I said. "It's nothing."

She stepped out the door. "Good-bye, Mary," Rabi called from the library.

"Bye," she called back, and then she looked me in the eye and in a low voice said, "Eliza, do you want your mother to stay at my house when she gets out of the hospital? I have that first-floor bedroom, and it would be very convenient for her." She paused and cocked her head. "Convenient for you, too, I suspect." She nodded in the direction of the library.

"No, we'll be fine. She'll want to be here."

"Let me know if you change your mind."

"I will," I said.

Oh this was good, I thought. My father's mistress was now a co-conspirator in my own efforts to conduct a steamy extramarital affair.

The following day my mother seemed a little calmer. "But, Sister," she said, "what's wrong with your foot?"

"Nothing. I stubbed my toe."

"Goodness, dear. First that bug and now this."

"I'm fine, actually a lot better." The night before Rabi had told me about his ex-wife and their brief marriage, how long they'd known each other. He had grown up next door to her in Pittsburgh, and he felt more like part of her family, who had sort of adopted him, than his cousin's. She was three years his junior, but eventually they had been at Carnegie Mellon together, where she studied architecture and he chemistry. He said he had confused his affection for her big, happy family with love for her; he'd mistaken romance for friendship. After they'd married, she stayed on to finish her degree, and he came to Cleveland for graduate school. But after a year and a half of living apart, with visits only once a month, if that, they both came to their senses. She was in Paris now, engaged to an Italian architect she'd met there. She and Rabi e-mailed now and then. They were still friends, and he kept in touch with her family.

"That business with Rabi upset you," my mother said.

"No, it just surprised me."

"He and I talk about matters he may prefer not to discuss with you."

"I don't doubt it."

So that my mother would be poised for a morning departure the next day, I busied myself collecting all the things she had accumulated during her stay in the hospital: the purse from Mary, a box of decorative soaps, a useless birdfeeder in the shape of a teapot, an ugly yellow bed jacket with ribbons all over it, a stuffed dog from children in the neighborhood, five boxes of candy. Baskets and vases, books, magazines, get-well cards, notes.

"Do you want any of this stuff?" I asked her.

She surveyed the pile I'd made. "I don't want that bed jacket even though it's from Mary's sister. I never want to see a bed jacket again. But possibly we should save those vases."

"Mother, you had about eight dozen vases at home, most of which I've gotten rid of. I am not lugging these there."

"Then how about the birdfeeder."

"It's grotesque," I said. "Besides, I don't think you'll be needing a wren house in Santa Fe."

"Why not?"

"Listen," I said. "If you need one, I'll buy you one there. But this one is staying in Edgecliff."

"I know!" she said brightly. "I'll give to my neighbor Frannie."

"You can't," I said. "She gave it to you."

"Oh that's right."

"I'm going to see if the nurses want any of this."

"Don't give away all that good candy," she protested.

"Why? Are you planning to eat it?"

"You know I don't like candy, but isn't it nice to have around?"

"No, it isn't," I said and gathered most of the things in my arms. I took it all to the nurses' station, where I ran into Pink Pajamas from the day before.

"And how are we feeling today?" she said in a reprehensibly condescending tone.

"We are feeling terrific," I replied. I dropped the loot on her desk and turned around.

"And just what am I supposed to do with all this?" she called after me.

"If you want it, fine. If not, fine, too," I said. She stared daggers at me, so I gave her a big smile and walked away.

"Well?" my mother said when I went back to her room.

"Oh, the nurses were tickled pink, especially that fatso who offered me the Tums yesterday."

"Sister, you *are* scrappy today."

She was right. I was acting smug and outspoken in a way that seemed foreign to me. Maybe something in the genes had surfaced after years of lying dormant. Or possibly it was because I felt so much better. I fleetingly wondered what would happen, as something surely would, to take me down a peg or two.

I found out soon enough.

When I got back to my mother's house, I tried to rouse Duke who was lying on his side. "Come on, Dukie," I said. "Let's go for a walk." He didn't stir. I repeated myself, louder that time, but still he didn't move. I went over and touched him, but he didn't seem to be breathing. I put my hand on his mouth and felt nothing. Oh my God, I thought, Duke is dead!

"Oh, Duke," I said. "I'm so sorry." I didn't know what to do. He was too heavy for me to get into the car alone, and I couldn't leave him there on the floor. I felt panicky and uncertain.

I walked around the house for a few minutes trying to decide on a course of action. Finally, I called Mary.

"Mary," I said, my voice sounding small, "I think Duke's dead."

"Dead?"

"He isn't breathing, and I don't know what to do."

"I'll be right over."

"Thank you," I said.

I was pacing around the kitchen when Duke stumbled in and began lapping up the water in his bowl. I stared at him as if he were a ghost. Then I went over and touched his head gingerly. "Are you okay, Dukie?" He looked at me with his rheumy eyes, which were so sad I thought my heart would break. Then, abruptly, he fell over in a heap, and appeared to be dead again. I shouted his name: nothing. I put my ear to his mouth: again nothing. Just then, Mary rang the bell, and I filled her in. She, too, kneeled down and put her ear to his mouth. "He's *not* breathing," she said. As we stood in the kitchen trying to figure out what to do, Duke once again resurrected himself and began drinking more water. Then he collapsed.

Eventually, Mary and I managed to roll his body—dead or alive, we didn't know which—into a blanket. With the help of a man who was raking the neighbor's leaves next door, we got him into my mother's car, where Duke suddenly rose on his haunches, as if we were going on a big excursion, except that he was panting too hard. We drove to the vet where we had to get more help to move him, since he had collapsed again.

Mary and I sat in the waiting room, while a parade of pets

trooped in and out. She tried to make conversation, but I couldn't talk. Instead, I thrust my nose into a copy of *Your Pet* magazine. My eyes kept tearing, and I couldn't read. After what seemed like hours, the vet came out to talk to us. She was a tall, raw-boned woman, and she didn't mince words.

"Duke seems to be going in and out of a diabetic coma," she said. "His pancreas is shot. I warned your mother about this the last time she was in."

"I didn't know he had diabetes," I said. "Did you, Mary?" Mary shook her head.

"Diabetes and heart trouble and hip displasia," the vet said. "He's practically blind and seems deaf, too." She stood and looked at me. Her eyes were kind. "But right now, his worst problem is that his pancreas is failing."

"And?" I said.

"Look," she said, "I don't want to influence you, but if he were mine, I would put him down. He's suffering. It won't get any better than this, not now. Do you think your mother could have forgotten to give him his insulin shots?"

"Insulin?" I said. "She's been in the hospital with a broken hip for over two weeks, and she never said a word to me about insulin."

The vet led Mary and me to a back room, where Duke was lying on a table. When he saw me there was a flicker of recognition in his melancholy eyes. I ran my hands over his flank and patted his head, murmuring his name.

"Eliza, dear," Mary said as she took my hand. "Your father adored this dog. If he were here, he wouldn't let Duke suffer."

"I know," I said. Suddenly everything I'd been trying so hard to gloss over in my own life—the end of my marriage, my

uncertainty about how my children would react, my mother's accident and her setback—seemed to be lying on the table with
Duke. I began sobbing as I had never sobbed before, so hard the
vet finally shoved a chair under me and pushed me into it gently.
I knew what had to be done, but I was unable to speak. I kept
rubbing Duke's side and crying. For the first time in my life, I was
making a spectacle of myself, and I didn't care.

Finally I nodded through my tears and got up and stroked
Duke's head. "Excuse me," I said, surprised I could talk.

I might as well have said, Excuse me, World, for all of my
omissions, for my cavalier attitude, for enjoying sex with Rabi,
for having been happier than I could remember. I was pouring
all my emotions into Duke, as if this big, dying dog were a vessel
that could contain them. I lay my head on his side, and his tail
flopped up and down wearily. I kissed him on his ears. I rubbed
his head.

Then I asked the vet to put him to sleep.

Later I called my brother, and when I told him what I'd done,
I began crying again.

"Sweetheart," Bin said softly. "You did the right thing." He
told me we would do something with Duke's ashes on Thanksgiving.

"I'm a wreck," I managed to say.

"I know," Bin said comfortingly. "Things like this are really
hard. You give your heart to a dog like that; you're unprotected. I
understand. You couldn't have known about the insulin."

"But I wondered about this bag of hypodermic needles I
found at the back of a drawer. I meant to ask mother what they
were for, but I forgot."

Then he said something that even in my ruined state caught my attention because, like his calling me "Sweetheart," it was so uncharacteristic of him. "Thank you for taking such good care of Duke, Liz. Mom was lousy with him. I knew that. I should have brought him back to New York after Davidson died. You were the best thing to happen to that dog since then."

We talked for a while longer, and then I forced myself to go and see my mother again. I didn't want to tell her about Duke on the phone. When I got there, she said, "What a long face, Sister."

"The vet put Duke to sleep," I said.

"I know," she replied. "Mary was here and told me. I guess in all the confusion, I neglected to tell you about the insulin. But it sounds as if you became quite overwrought."

"Of course I did."

"Well, pep up, dear. You can't let things like this get you down."

I stared at her, unbelieving. "But—"

"Sister," she interrupted, "he was only a dog."

I recognized this as the attitude that had largely determined my life: Minimize everything, pretend it's nothing.

"By the way, did you order that bed?"

I turned on my heels and left.

CHAPTER 20

Late the next morning, I took my mother home from the hospital. I hovered over her as she awkwardly maneuvered her walker on the stone path to the side door where there were no steps. She was determined to go it alone, and it turned out that she didn't need my help. When she entered the house, she seemed astonished by how bare it was—the rugs rolled up, much of the downstairs furniture jammed helter-skelter into the living room, the bookshelves nearly empty, pictures gone from the walls.

"My goodness, Sister, you *have* been busy," she said, her voice echoing in the empty hall.

I half expected Duke to mosey out and greet us, but my mother didn't remark on his absence. Still in her coat, she clumped around the first floor with her walker, examining things. If I had been my mother I would have been heavyhearted surveying my life in heaps: the dining room table and the small chest of drawers her great-great-grandparents had brought by wagon from Connecticut to Ohio in the 1830s, the brass table from India that had been my paternal grandfather's, my father's desk, and so much more.

My mother treated the whole thing as if it were a curious exhibit, a stranger's, perhaps. Nostalgia wasn't for her, not since she'd stopped talking incessantly about the town where she grew up. What got her through was a kind of stoic forbearance, nothing to sniff at in times like this, but I myself no longer felt wedded to that kind of detachment.

The bed I had ordered for her had been delivered early that morning, and I'd made it up with pink-flowered sheets that I thought would make the library seem cozier.

"Where on earth did you get those sheets, Sister?"

"They were in the back of the linen cupboard," I said. I didn't want to hear a lecture on sheets, although I was sure one was coming.

"Why, they're lovely," she said. "I'd forgotten all about them. I ordered them from Neiman Marcus years ago."

I helped her off with her coat, and she hitched herself around the library, stopping to look at the empty bookshelves, then out one of the windows toward the lake. "I missed seeing the lake while I was in the hospital," she said. "I'm afraid I'll miss it in Santa Fe, too. The way it changes all the time."

"You'll have the mountains," I said. "They change, too."

She nodded with a kind of resignation that surprised me. When she let her guard down and stopped being spunky or infuriatingly feisty, she seemed fragile and vulnerable. My heart softened.

"Well, now," she said straightening up.

"Let me get you a cup of tea."

"In a few minutes, dear."

She toured the downstairs again, with me following, and at last we wound up in the kitchen where Duke's water bowl was still on the floor. I'd meant to throw it away but hadn't, and I didn't think she'd noticed it until she said, "That dog," and shook her head. I helped her into a chair. "Davidson so enjoyed Duke. I suspect he'd shoot me if he knew I'd forgotten about the insulin."

"Duke was old."

"I'm old, too," she replied, "but I'm not ready to die."

"Of course you're not."

"I don't suppose anyone ever is," she said. "Your father wasn't. He died in the thick of things. Strangely, that gives me some peace."

A dreamy silence descended on the room, and for a while we sat without speaking. She took my hand. Through the big kitchen window, we watched the wind flinging the barren treetops around and the seagulls wheeling above the choppy waves.

In my mind's eye, I caught a glimpse of the two of us years before, on a gray, wintry day like this one. I must have been five or six, and in a rare burst of energy on my mother's part, we had walked to downtown Edgecliff. On the way home, we explored a tiny old graveyard she had read about. It was tucked away on a hill near the main street, Saturn, and most of the gravestones were tilted or had fallen over. Dry stalks of weeds were everywhere, and it appeared that no one had tended the place for years.

She and I had poked through the brittle underbrush and read the inscriptions on the stones, some of which had been worn away by the years. I remembered tracing the mossy letters with my mittened fingers. I remembered the painful expression on my mother's face when we discovered the grave of a baby. Odd things about that day, like the dark green coat my mother had been wearing, seemed indelibly etched in my memory, probably because it was so unusual to see her out of bed. I remembered a sharp wind rattling through trees, and scattered beer bottles glinting in the gray light amidst the gravestones; an old shoe, a piece of rope, an empty potato chip bag. After a time, we walked home, holding hands as we were doing now, bucking the cold wind that came off the lake.

Despite its neglect, the graveyard seemed to me then not scary but strangely comforting: all the dead dwelling peacefully with the angels in heaven. And though sitting in the kitchen with my mother years later I no longer believed in angels or heaven, I could suddenly imagine my father and Duke happily ambling through billowing white clouds and golden shafts of sunlight, like those in the picture I used to stare at in my Sunday-school classroom. The idea of the two of them together consoled me.

My child's vision would do, I thought. It was innocent and peaceful, a fairy tale, but it would do.

My mother cleared her throat and asked if we could have lunch, and we did, the two of us eating our cottage cheese and sliced tomatoes, sipping tea, talking about nothing more important than the weather. Time arced over us, all those years, and seemed to enfold us in its arms.

"I don't want you to get the wrong impression," she said while I was putting our plates in the dishwasher. "I'm eager to get to Santa Fe. You might even say I'm excited."

"Good. You'll have a brand-new life."

"Ha! I could use one about now." She laughed and hoisted herself up with her walker.

I helped her get settled in the library, and propped her up in bed with pillows. She asked me to hand her the book she'd been reading.

"Mother, do you remember that little graveyard you and I discovered years and years ago?"

"It was a sight, wasn't it? I can't believe I dragged you there. Bin was just a baby, and I was going through a morbid phase, although physically I'd felt better than I had in some time."

"Whatever happened to it, I wonder."

"Why, they moved the whole thing to Edgecliff Park when you were in high school. Don't you remember? Maybe not; you were so busy then. It's behind the historical society. You've passed it hundreds of times."

"I guess I forgot."

" 'Forgetting those things which are behind, and reaching forth unto those things which are before, I press toward the mark.' "

"What's that from?"

"The Bible." She paused. "I wish I could forget more," she said. "Sometimes my head seems chock-full of things I'd like to get rid of." She leaned back and closed her eyes. "But I'm sorry I forgot about Duke's insulin," she added. "That was a dreadful omission on my part. Dreadful." She sighed and closed her eyes.

After a minute, I pulled a light blanket over her. I thought perhaps she had fallen asleep.

"Well," she said, opening her eyes, "that's over and done with now. I can't dwell on it, can I?"

"No, and you shouldn't," I said. "But why were you feeling so morbid back then? I would have thought you'd been happy about Bin."

"I *was* happy about Bin, but there were other things . . ." Her voice trailed off, and she shut her eyes again.

I waited for her to continue; when she didn't, I asked, "What kind of things?"

"Your father wasn't the easiest man to be married to," she said.

"Probably not," I said. "But, then, who is?"

"Well, I myself was no picnic, sick all the time. I know how difficult that was for him. But still."

"But still?"

Her eyes opened. "I shouldn't be talking like this."

I stood silently, afraid she would stop what she'd haltingly begun. "Go on."

"I have no intentions of going on," she said. "All I'll say, since I started this, is that sometimes it's better to ignore things, or rise above them. Not dwell on them, at any rate. Besides, I was sick, what else could I have done? I didn't have the strength to do much of anything." She paused. "In the end, we had a very compatible marriage in many respects."

"*What* did you ignore," I pressed.

She raised her eyebrows and looked at me as if I was far too inquisitive. Then she relented. "I've ignored a lot of things. Call it hubris, call it the easy way out, call me lily-livered. Whatever you call it, it's gotten me this far."

"You never ignored me," I said, trying to offer her a little comfort. At this point, I was certain she was talking about my father and Mary.

"Oh, you," she said. "You have been the joy of my life. I don't know what I would have done without you. But, don't kid yourself, I *have* ignored things about you."

"Like what?"

"Well, I shouldn't say this, but your marriage, for one thing. To someone I deemed quite ill-suited to you."

"You were right about that," I said. "But why didn't you ever say anything?"

"Do you have any idea how headstrong you were? You wouldn't have listened. You were so determined, no one could have stopped you."

"I must have been a pain."

"I thought if I so much as opened my mouth, Sam would have seemed even more attractive to you."

"I expect you're right," I said.

"But your lovely children. Really, Sister, look what wonderful people you've brought into the world!"

"My children are lovely," I said. "My husband isn't."

"You've had to learn to ignore things, too, I'd guess." She sighed. "It's not the best way, but often it's all we can do."

I wanted to tell her about Sam then, but this seemed to be her story, not mine. Mine could come later.

"He's an unusual young man," she said brightening. "Quite exceptional."

I thought perhaps she was talking about one of the twins. "Who?"

"Why, Rabi, dear, who else?"

"Rabi?" I was so shocked, the hair on the back of my neck stood up.

"Eliza, everyone thinks I'm oblivious, but I don't miss much. You can't pull the wool over my eyes."

"I guess not."

"But we can talk about that another time. Right now I'm going to take a little nap."

I lay on the floor next to her bed, full of love for her, and wonder. Then I dozed off, too.

★ ★ ★

Later I called Ellen to check on Snickers.

"You sound so cheery," she said. "What's wrong?"

I laughed and told her my mother was finally home. "Great," she said. "I just FedExed some papers for her to sign."

"Good. We should be there for the closing." I asked about Snickers, and was amazed to learn he was now sleeping happily with her and Shep.

"In your bed? Seriously?"

"Right behind my head on an extra pillow," she said. "It's cozy."

"Sam would have fits if I even let Snickers *near* the bed!"

"Oh, Sam," she said dismissively.

"He's never called you, has he?"

"Of course not."

I told her about putting Duke to sleep, and she said, "I'm so sorry, Eliza. I didn't even know Duke, but that makes me so sad."

"Me, too."

"But you sound really good," she added.

"Yeah," I said. "Everything considered, I feel good, too." At which point, I willed myself to shut my mouth.

Rabi came that night, and the three of us chatted for several hours while he and I packed silver and china. My mother regaled us with the latest news; she was always avid about it, and a day without the *New York Times* and Jim Lehrer on PBS was lost as far as she was concerned. At that point, Clinton's indiscretion with Monica Lewinsky was one of her favorite topics. She was incensed about it, adultery understandably being a sore point with her. I tried to steer the conversation in another direction. The subject seemed too close for comfort for all three of us, but she wouldn't budge.

"I could just lambaste the man," she huffed. "Take him behind the woodshed! Such a fool to believe he wouldn't get caught. And then to lie about it. Goodness. To think that I voted for him, not once but twice! So did you, Sister, and you, too, Rabi. Can I be the only one who feels betrayed?" She looked at us expectantly.

"Of course not," I said.

Rabi shook his head no. "Possibly your expectations are too high?"

"My expectations of human nature are *low,*" she said. "I'm no fool. But I refuse to countenance lying. Adultery is one thing; I know about adultery," she added, without giving that statement any particular weight. "But lying to the American people is beyond the pale!"

"Mrs. White," Rabi said, "he was ashamed."

"Please, Rabi, dear, how many times have I asked you to call me Louise? You make me feel ancient when you call me Mrs. White."

"Okay. Louise." He said her name a little uneasily. "I'm not saying what he did was right, but he lied—"

"Don't make excuses for the man," she interrupted heatedly. "He lied because he's a liar, and a coward to boot."

"Maybe we need to forgive him," Rabi suggested, "so we can all move on."

"Oh, forgiveness," she shot back angrily. "That's a lot of guff, some religious concept that's lost on me. Frankly, I have never understood the meaning of the word. When you get down to brass tacks, we can *forget* things, we can *ignore* them, but do we really *absolve* people? I don't believe that's humanly possible. 'To err is human, to forgive divine.' Well, I am not divine, and I don't know anyone else who is, either." She paused to catch her breath. "After all, Rabi, can you forgive the Israelis for taking over your homeland?"

He looked up from the silver he was wrapping. "I've tried to understand their point of view," he said solemnly. He was wearing a white button-down shirt under a black sweater, and the white made his coloring even more vivid, his eyes bluer.

"That's not forgiveness," my mother said. "That's just an intellectual exercise."

"Perhaps forgiveness is also," Rabi replied.

She turned abruptly and looked at him for a moment, then barreled right on, "And then, on top of everything else, we have that sex-crazed Kenneth Starr with his prurient mind. He may be the worst of the bunch!"

"Mother," I cautioned, "don't get so wound-up. It's almost bedtime."

"Don't tell me when to get wound-up," she shot back.

I busied myself assembling another carton, aware that her energy for this harangue probably had less to do with Bill Clinton than it did with my father and Mary. I couldn't imagine what it had cost her, keeping all that resentment inside for years. It was a wonder she hadn't exploded. I wanted to say something to calm her down, but what? That getting her anger out was therapeutic? She'd have a fit if she heard that one.

Somehow, however she'd done it, she had learned to live with the fact of Mary and my father. I sensed she believed she had chosen the high road, the road I could not conceive of taking with my own husband. She had compromised out of need and love, and she had loved my father deeply, with an element of self-sacrifice unknown to later generations of women. At least unknown to me.

In an effort to change the subject, I held up a small Blue Willow serving plate and a saucer that matched nothing else. "Where are these from?"

She peered at it for a second. "Oh those," she said. "That's all that's left of the servants' china from home." By "home" she meant the house where she'd grown up, a curious figure of speech sixty years after the fact. I wondered whether she'd ever really left "home" at all; I suspected that she had simply decided not to talk about it, just as she'd chosen not to talk about my father and Mary.

"We could use some servants about now," I said, swiping at a strand of my hair that had come loose.

"Good luck," she said, getting up slowly and shuffling toward the library with her walker. "I'll say good-night now. You two are working too hard. It's time to quit."

"We will," Rabi assured her. "I have to go."

My mother disappeared into the library, and Rabi called good-night to her. He and I went to the front door and I said good-bye loudly; then I opened the door and slammed it shut, motioning for him to go upstairs, which he did very quietly.

I helped my mother get ready for bed and tucked her in. She wanted to read for a while, so I moved the lamp where she could reach it; then I pulled the blinds and turned on a small bathroom light. "I guess that about does it," I said, leaning over and kissing her.

"It's been a long day," she said. "I can't tell you how thrilled I am to be out of that hospital. It was so noisy at night, it was hard to sleep."

"Well, it's quiet here."

"Good-night, Sister dear. You get some sleep now."

I pulled the door closed, but she wanted it left open.

"No high jinks," she said pointedly as she picked up her book.

"Of course not."

After a few minutes, I turned out all the lights and called out, "Goodnight. Sleep well." Rabi was waiting in my bedroom, and we fell on each other. Soon we were making love so quietly, it was like a whole other way of having sex; each movement hushed and extraordinarily delicate, like touching without actually touching— a torment of arousal. I was spellbound; we hardly moved. Everything was as gentle and tender as if we were imagining it—so muffled and slow, I wanted to scream. But even not screaming became electric; seeing how much I could hold in sent me down alarming avenues of ecstasy. This slow, deliberately muted sex seemed more erotic than anything we had experienced before. I was destroyed, out of my head, gone. It was as if I were only *body*. When it was over, we were both panting and covered with sweat.

"Now, there is something new," he whispered after a while.

"Yes," I said. I could barely talk. "Yes. Yes, indeed."

CHAPTER 21

B in arrived around noon on Thanksgiving. He hadn't shaved, and he seemed out of sorts. Almost immediately he began grousing about having to go to Mary's for dinner.

"Was it you who cooked up the idea that we should all be together, the sinned-against and the sinner?"

"Give it up, Bin," I said without batting an eye.

"Wait just a second here. You know how I feel about her."

"Mother and Mary arranged the whole thing. I had nothing to do with it."

"Well, it sucks."

"My, that was pithy," I replied. "Why don't you try acting like a grown-up just for today."

He looked at me closely. "What's eating *you*?"

"I'm tired of your whining."

"I don't get it. You, I mean. What are you doing?"

"What I am doing," I said, "is peeling potatoes so that I can mash them. Then it's on to the green beans." I bustled around the kitchen. "If you'd like to help, you're welcome to."

He appeared stumped. Of all the things I was no longer

interested in, putting up with my brother's crankiness and litany of complaints was near the top of the list. I refused to humor him.

"Well," he said, "don't forget to put garlic in the potatoes."

"I will *not* put garlic in the mashed potatoes today. This is Thanksgiving, for Christ's sake, not some Mediterranean saint's day."

He stared at me.

"Why don't you go outside and find some place in the garden to dig a hole for Duke's ashes," I suggested. "And while you're at it, think of a few words to say." Get him on stage, I was thinking; that might calm him down.

He paced around the kitchen, then went into the library to see our mother. After a while, he got her bundled up and took her outside, Mother clumping with her walker over the uneven grass. The day was cold and windy but, by some fluke, the sun was shining and the lake was a brilliant blue. Fluffy white clouds scudded across the sky, and bright red cardinals darted around the birdfeeder.

I watched my mother and Bin through the window. He loomed over her, but it was clear who was leading whom. Bin was carrying a shovel, and he pointed to the side rose garden, but my mother shook her head. He strode over to the edge of the cliff and poked around, and she shook her head again. In the end, my mother selected a spot under the big oak tree in the center of the lawn, where she had always planted pansies. Bin gestured with his hands in protest, but she stood firm. He attacked the hard earth with the shovel, and though the ground wasn't frozen, it took him some time to dig a small hole. After he was done, he disappeared, and my mother stood alone in the backyard, braced on her walker, her red coat flaming in the sunshine. She looked up into the bare tree and out at the lake, and I wondered if she were thinking she would miss this place.

Just then Bin burst into the kitchen. "Hurry," he said. "Get the ashes. We're ready, and Mom's getting cold."

I put on my coat and retrieved the metal canister the vet had given me, black covered with pink and red flowers and tied with a raffia bow. I joined Bin and my mother at the edge of the garden. The cold wind whipped around us, but it really was an unusually beautiful day for Edgecliff in November.

"Gracious," my mother said. "It's freezing out here."

"Would you like to go inside and watch from there?"

She looked at me and rolled her eyes slightly. "No, but let's get this over with fast."

We both looked at Bin. I had no idea what he was about to say, but like my mother, I hoped he would make it snappy. He pulled the raffia off the metal box and cleared his throat twice. Then his voice boomed out, "We are about to consign the ashes of our friend Duke to the earth." He sounded ridiculously earnest. "Duke was completely unselfish as friends go; he was loyal and true and his heart was huge. He was a great companion, one of the best, and we will never forget him."

My mother nudged me gently with her elbow. I glanced down at her to see what she wanted and realized she was on the verge of laughing.

"That was very nice, Bin," my mother said, assuming he was done.

"Wait, I'm not finished." Bin sounded offended.

My mother bit her lip, and I had to bite mine as well, because by then I was on the verge of laughing, too. I straightened up and made myself look serious.

"He was a great companion, one of the best. And we will never forget . . ."

A gust of wind came along and whipped my mother's black beret off. I bolted after it as it skipped across the lawn. When I returned with it, my mother plopped it on her head and pulled it down over her ears in such a way that she looked, well, odd. "Pardon me," she said to Bin.

"Oh, it's quite all right," Bin said in a tone of voice that let us know it was not a bit all right.

"Please, dear, go on," my mother urged him.

"You're sure you two are ready?"

My mother and I both nodded. I was no longer standing next to her because by then I was afraid that we would both burst out laughing if I did. Bin's fervor was comical, far too heavy for easygoing old Duke.

"We will never forget our fine companion Duke, who brought so much happiness into our lives and graced the house with his presence."

"Graced the house with his presence" appeared to bring my mother closer to the edge. I chewed the inside of my mouth and glanced away. As I did, I spotted a bright red balloon, its string trailing, sweeping this way and that, being pulled up over the lake by the wind.

My mother followed my gaze. "Why look!" she said, and Bin craned his neck.

"It's somebody's balloon, Mom," he said disgustedly.

"It's Duke's spirit rising," she countered.

That seemed more appropriate than all the words anyone could say. "She's right," I piped up.

"Okay," he said very slowly, as if his patience were entirely de-
pleted. "It's Duke's spirit."

"Good-bye, Duke," my mother called as the balloon spiraled
upward and grew smaller and smaller. "Good-bye." She waved.
"Good-bye!" In another voice entirely she said, "That was such a
fitting image."

"And he," Bin shouted, quoting something, I had no idea what,
"shall see the sky sparkling with diamonds!"

I almost lost it at that point.

"Amen," my mother said. "Beautiful, Bin. Just lovely." She ap-
plauded. So did I.

Bin looked at us as if we were the most unruly audience he had
ever encountered. "I give up," he said and opened the little box. He
dropped a handful of ashes into the hole, but unfortunately the
wind blew most of them in his face. My mother made a little snort-
ing noise, and I actually began to laugh. Bin wiped his mouth and
handed the box to my mother, who suddenly appeared confused.

"What am I supposed to do?" she asked as if she'd forgotten
what we were there for.

"Just put some of Duke's ashes into the hole," Bin directed her.

"Goodness no. I don't want to get my gloves dirty."

By that time I was feeling a little sorry for Bin, so I took the box
and dropped a handful of grit into the hole. Bin grabbed the box
out of my hands and upended the whole thing. Most of the ashes
missed the hole and blew into the garden and across the lawn.

"Every dog has his day," my mother called gaily as she hitched
off across the lawn toward the side door.

"That wasn't funny," Bin grumped, his teeth clenched, "you
two horsing around like that."

"It was a sweet little ceremony," I lied.

"I don't know what you were up to, but I resent the way you completely broke the spell. She could have done without her hat for thirty seconds."

"The balloon was a nice touch," I said. "Besides, the wind's unpredictable." If looks could kill, I would have been dead. "Like life," I added after a second and smiled at him.

"Like you, you mean," he said. "One minute you're in tears over the dog, the next you're laughing." He made a show of being disgusted. Then he thrust the empty box into my hands and began vigorously shoveling dirt back into the hole.

And that was our good-bye to Duke, which, thanks to the red balloon and despite Bin's snit, seemed a fitting tribute to a dear old dog.

At 4:30, we were all dressed up and ready to go. Lazy snowflakes had begun drifting down from a sky that was by then ashbin gray. Bin had showered and shaved and he looked better, though he was still complaining to me about having to go to Mary's. He helped my mother into the front seat of the car, and I put the pot of potatoes and the parboiled green beans in the trunk. Then I climbed in the backseat with the walker and off we went.

I knew that Mary had invited Rabi, but I didn't know until we arrived her house that she had also invited an older man with whom she had worked years before, who subsequently became the rare books librarian at a nearby college before he'd retired. I'd heard her mention him but had never met him. Jim Withers was his name, and he was quite handsome, gray-haired and trim; he and my mother had met before. Mary's sister and her husband were absent because they'd gone to Philadelphia to see one of their children. Rabi arrived shortly after we did, and, weirdly, he and I shook hands as if I hadn't seen him for weeks, when in fact, he'd snuck out of my mother's house early that morning.

"Great to see you," I said. "How are you?"

"Quite fine," he said, "and you?"

"Just dandy," I replied. By that time the others were talking, and Mary had sent Bin to fix drinks.

I pretended to be making pleasantries with Rabi, but actually what I said was: "Don't come near me, okay?"

"Really," he said, smiling affably.

"Concentrate your energies on Bin. He's in a foul mood."

"Of course," Rabi said, and laughed. Then he made a beeline for the kitchen to help Bin.

After drinks were served, I talked to Jim Withers for a while. He told me in detail about the collection he'd overseen, mostly manuscripts of plays I'd never heard of and letters of obscure playwrights. He was very proud of the whole thing. "They were like my children," he said. "Say," he added, "don't you have *real* children?"

I nodded. "Three." I went through my children and told him I had spoken to them that morning, and they were fine, each of them off with friends for the holiday.

"And your hubby?" he said.

"Back in New Mexico. He couldn't get away. He's busy." I neglected to say he was probably busy licking gardenia perfume off someone young enough to be his daughter.

"My partner Richard couldn't come at the last minute," Jim said. "He has a nasty cold."

"Too bad," I said, watching Mary and Bin out of the corner of my eye. Bin in particular seemed unusually stiff. I wanted to shout at him to loosen up. Jim and I wandered over to talk to my mother who was only eyeing her glass of sherry. Five minutes later, the two of them were deep in conversation, so I left and went into the kitchen.

The smell of roasting turkey filled the room, and I began mashing the potatoes and sautéing the almonds for the green beans. Mary had insisted I put on a big white apron, which had HOT! written across the front.

"God, I just hate Thanksgiving dinner," Mary said. "Everything has to be done at the same time. It's so annoying. This is the one meal of the year when it would have paid to go to culinary school."

"You and Bin okay?" I asked.

"Hard to say," she said, lifting an enormous turkey out of the oven. "He pulls these actor's stunts. Who knows what's really on his mind?"

"Probably nothing you need to hear."

"I just wish I could figure out a way to make some kind of peace with him." She hoisted the turkey onto a serving platter.

"Don't worry about it."

"I wish I didn't." She started in on the gravy. "Your mother always fixes this. I have no idea what I'm doing."

"Should I get her?"

"Sure. Bring her in. She can supervise at least."

I nipped into the living room, where my mother was talking to Rabi, and Bin and Jim Withers were deep in conversation—about the theater, naturally—and I asked my mother to come into the kitchen to oversee the gravy. As I was helping her up, the back of my leg brushed Rabi's knee, and I was nearly leveled.

"You come along with us," my mother said to Rabi. "I'm sure there's something you can do."

"I don't think so," I said to him, under my breath.

He smiled and leaped up.

So, then there were four of us in Mary's small kitchen, not to mention the walker, which took up a lot of room. My mother stirred the gravy, Mary carved the turkey, I beat the potatoes, and, at Mary's direction, Rabi opened three bottles of wine. "Goodness gracious," my mother said, as he was lifting the cork out of the third bottle. "You'll all have to go to AA after you drink that!" When everything was on the table, Mary called Bin and Jim Withers into the dining room.

"Smells delicious," Jim said as he came into the room. I noticed there was an extra place setting for Jim's partner that Mary hadn't removed.

Mary began serving the turkey. "Bin?" she said. "Light or dark?"

"Whatever," he replied sounding surly.

I was sitting next to him and kicked him under the table.

He looked at me. "Why are you kicking me?" he said in a loud voice, though everyone pretended not to hear. I wanted to brain him.

"Oh," Mary said. "We forgot grace! We really need to say a blessing. Why don't you do that, Bin."

"Me?"

"No, no," I said quickly. "I'll do it." I couldn't stand to hear another of Bin's perorations that day, and I was also afraid of what he might come up with.

I rose and with no idea what I was going to say, launched right in. "This Thanksgiving, we are thankful for old friends and new,"

I said, "for our family, those who are here and those who can't be with us tonight." I glanced at the empty place setting. I was not doing well. "We are thankful for our wonderful hostess and this bountiful feast," I trudged on. Bin was playing with his fork. Across the table, Rabi gazed at me encouragingly. I wanted desperately to sit down. ". . . For our good fortune and health. We are thankful for the privilege of living in a great country. And finally, we are thankful for all the love we share and are able to give away. Amen."

"Here, here," Mary said. "I'll drink to that!" She lifted her wineglass and everyone but Bin joined in.

"Jesus," Bin said under his breath as I had sat down. "That was horrible. 'The privilege of living in a great country.' Good God."

Silver clinked and everyone began to eat except Bin and me. I'd had it. "You are such an asshole," I shot back in a voice that was not as low as I'd intended and, what's worse, came during a lull in the conversation. I was horrified. My mother's head jerked up from her plate as if she'd been shot. Jim dropped his knife. Rabi looked at us curiously.

Mary didn't bat an eye. "My, Eliza," she said, "these are delicious mashed potatoes! What did you do to them?"

My mother rose swiftly to the occasion. "How do you like these lumps she leaves in them, Mary? Apparently, it's the latest thing. In our day, you just about killed yourself getting them smooth and creamy. But I like this texture. It's more interesting."

What followed was a very deliberate discussion between the two women about mashed potatoes, almost choreographed, stagy but heartfelt in its effort to right things: Russets versus reds, peeled versus skins, electric beaters versus ricers, hot milk versus cream; how much butter, the strange things some people put into them—cream cheese, blue cheese, chiles, green onions, bacon, garlic. My mother scoffed at all those. "I guess I'm a purist," she said. "Or an old fogy." She laughed.

Seated between the two women, Rabi swiveled his head back and forth as if he were watching a tennis match. Jim pitched in and made a case for garlic, which my brother joined. Tensions eased. Rabi brought up mashed sweet potatoes, and everyone booed. Jim voted for chives. If you'd been there, you would not have believed the subject could have been so deeply plumbed or that the discussion could have lasted for almost ten minutes. Thanks to my mother and Mary and their energetic small talk, the mashed potatoes salvaged the dinner. I began eating and so did Bin.

I had never seen my mother and Mary working together like a tag-team, literally towing a group I had almost capsized into the calm waters of civility. But they'd done it, and don't tell me these little gestures don't count. The two of them were even better together than they were separately: charming, resourceful, comfortable with one another as only old friends who have spent years together can be. In light of her ease with Mary, I wondered at my mother's recent outburst about not believing in forgiveness. I also wondered at Mary's recent suggestion that my mother annoyed her. But there was no reason to doubt the regard they felt for each other; it was clear as a bell—they had come to terms long ago. Even Bin couldn't ignore it, though I was sure he would later insist, again, that my mother had been an unwitting victim of our father and Mary.

I watched Rabi watching the two women. I watched Jim eyeing Bin and Rabi, but except for eating, I kept my mouth shut; it seemed only prudent after my outburst. The conversation eventually shifted from mashed potatoes to Israel, then segued into a discussion of Bin's latest career move, a series of ads for a cell-phone company. Briefly we spoke about Duke, and settled finally on my mother's upcoming move, about which, I was pleased to note, she sounded enthusiastic.

"Richard and I adore Santa Fe," Jim said. "It always feels like our spiritual home."

"I can imagine," my mother replied drolly.

"I'll see Santa Fe soon," Rabi said. "I've never been there, but now I'll go." He told Mary and Jim about leaving for Berkeley and how Berkeley and Los Alamos were connected. At that point, Mary kicked me.

Increasingly, I became aware of the empty place at the table and decided it was not Jim's partner who was absent, but my father. And then, I knew he *was* there, moderating between my mother and Mary, cheering them on, encouraging their easy banter. So what if he hadn't paid much attention to Bin and me, I thought. At least he'd kept those two lively women reasonably happy and friendly with each other—friendly enough that together they could save a dinner from my newly unruly mouth.

Bin and I cleared the plates. Alone in the kitchen, I said to him, "Look. I'm sorry about what happened."

"Don't be," he said. "It was my fault." And then he did the most unexpected thing. He gave me a peck on the forehead and squeezed my shoulder. "You did fine," he said. "I was just pissed it wasn't me saying grace. What a jerk. By the way, what's with you and the Arab?"

"Rabi?"

"Yeah," he said, scraping the plates.

"Why?"

"Because the two of you are generating enough electricity across the table to light up the whole town."

I stared at him.

"Eliza, you can't bullshit a bullshitter like me."

I debated for only a split second before saying, "Apparently not."

"Later?" he said, as Mary came through the door.

I nodded.

Later. Later would have been after my mother and Bin and I went back to Mars, and Rabi took off for Moon, the first night we hadn't spent together in weeks. Later was after my mother's lecture, mild compared to what I'd expected, on my inappropriate outburst, and after she asked Bin why he persisted in provoking me, for which he apologized. Later was after my mother went to bed with a book, and Bin and I opened another bottle of wine, and went to the basement so as not to disturb her.

"So," he said once we were settled. "Tell."

"Why would I want to tell you anything? I never know when you're going to turn on me."

"Eliza," he said quite soberly, looking me in the eye, "I swear I will never, ever do that to you again. I'm very sorry."

"Why should I believe you? You yourself already acknowledged you're a bullshitter."

"Come on, Lizzie. I really meant what I said."

Suddenly it no longer seemed important to hide anything from my brother. "I'm leaving Sam," I said. "We're getting a divorce."

"You're kidding!"

"Don't I wish. I mean, I *hate* to do this to the kids."

"I expect they'll survive. But good for you. To tell you the truth, that's a big load off my mind. Ever since we talked a couple of weeks ago, I've been worried about you. Before that, too."

"Really?"

"I've always thought you were way too good a sport when it came to Sam. All his adolescent rocketing around." His eyebrows shot up. "Probably screwing around, too."

"How did you guess?"

"It wasn't hard. He was always flirting with someone wherever we went. Women would come on to me, and *he'd* be the one paying attention. I'm no prude, but I found it distasteful. It wasn't like I was a stranger."

I sighed.

Bin called Sam a lout and a number of other things, all of which fit. During his little outburst, I never once wanted to defend the man I had been married to for more than twenty years. When Bin calmed down, he asked if there was anything he could do to help, which startled me, although this seemed a night for the unexpected. Eventually, he circled round to the subject he'd raised in Mary's kitchen. "So, what about Rabi?"

I hedged. "He's been a big help."

"I bet he has."

"Let's just leave it there," I said.

"I'll leave it anywhere you want. But are you in love with him?"

I made a face.

"*Are* you?"

I honestly didn't know how to answer him. "It's too soon to know. I can't tell. Don't ask me that now."

"Well, for what it's worth, I like the guy, although I don't know how much he has to talk about beyond metallurgy, or whatever his field is. But he seems solid. And he's kind, too, which might seem totally revolutionary to you after Sam."

I nodded.

"Is Rabi the reason you're leaving Sam?"

"God, no. I've wanted to leave Sam for years."

"Well, something's changed. You seem a lot more decisive and outspoken, more confident. Face it, you never would have talked like this to me in the past."

"Come on, Bin. You haven't been the most sympathetic ear. Always criticizing me, always trying to get my goat. And on my end, I've taken you far too seriously."

"Let's call a truce."

"No," I said. "I don't want a truce. I want it *over*. I'm sick of our bickering."

"Okay, it's over. I'm ready. But, look, Eliza, it's been hard to deal with someone who's always so distant, always 'fine,' always holding herself in check."

"I expect so," I said. "But I need a friend, I don't need an enemy."

"Lizzie," he said softly. "I'm not your enemy and never have been. I admit that sometimes I've taken stuff out on you that was meant for old Davidson. I'm sorry about that, I truly am, but when I was little, you seemed exactly like him, off in never-never land, leaving me to fend for myself. I used to get so lonesome."

"I'm sorry," I said. "Probably I *was* off in never-never land. Most of the time, our family seemed too much for me."

"Yeah," he said. "A heavy group, with Mom sick and Davidson so resentful of me he could hardly be civil. You know, if I had to guess, I'd say he never wanted another child—me, I mean. Look at it this way: One child, and he might have been able to leave Mom. Two, no way." He took a drink of wine.

"Don't you think that's a little theatrical?"

He shrugged. "Possibly. But it makes sense, doesn't it?" I put my hand on his. "And speaking of Davidson," he went on, relieving me of having to answer him, "I still can't get over how mother buys into Mary's quote-unquote friendship."

"She knows all about it, Bin. She's known for years. About father and Mary, I mean."

"She has?" He looked incredulous.

I nodded. "And if *she's* come to terms with Mary, I think it's about time you did, too."

"How do you know all this?"

"I know," I said. "She and I talked. Obliquely, but we talked. She's astonishing in her way. Amazing."

"Well, that's a shocker."

"What? That I find our mother amazing?"

"No, that she knows."

"I'd just drop the whole thing if I were you. It's over now, anyway. You saw them tonight, carrying us through."

"You mean their mashed potatoes routine?"

I nodded.

"That was something," he said. "Quite a performance."

"They're genuinely fond of each other."

"Yeah, but Mom's borne the brunt of all this."

"Look, let's just drop it."

He thought for a moment and then said, "Okay, but I still don't get it."

"You don't have to get it. Trust me on that."

"I guess I will," he said. "But what's come over you? You seem like a different person."

"Things change. I came to my senses."

"Well, however you did it, I'm impressed."

I asked him about Angela, his old girlfriend in Tucson, and he told me they were in touch again. He added that she'd invited him to visit her after Christmas.

"Great," I said. "Maybe you'll work things out."

"I don't know about that. But it'll be good to see her, even if the thought of it gives me the jitters."

"Jitters? *You?*"

"Jitters might as well be my middle name."

"And I thought you were cool as a cucumber, at least when you weren't around me."

"Ha! Don't I wish." He finished his glass. "Then again," he added, "I thought *you* were incapable of dumping Sam."

I asked him if he wanted more wine, and when he shook his head, I corked the bottle. He put his arm over my shoulder as we climbed the stairs.

The light was still on in the library, and my mother called, "What's going on out there?"

She put down her book as we entered her room, Bin's arm still slung over my shoulder.

"Goodness gracious," she said, "will you look at this. My two little ones. I never thought I'd live to see the day when you'd look so much like pals."

"We *are* pals," Bin said and grinned.

"My, that took a long time," she said.

We talked for a few minutes, then both of us kissed her good-night and went upstairs. In bed, I recalled what I'd said about love in my corny Thanksgiving grace. I had come to Mars depressed, confused, and nearly out of steam; certainly I hadn't been thinking about love. Yet look at all the love I'd discovered. The secret love between my father and Mary, which revealed he was far more human than I'd thought. A saner, less needy love for my children, which I'd arrived at once I stopped pouring all my frustrations over Sam into their absence. Peace with Bin, whom I'd always loved but had never completely trusted. And this: a renewed flowering of love for my mother—a rare gift I hadn't expected—after years of taking her for granted.

As for Rabi, did I love him? I wasn't naive. Sex was one thing, love another. Yet on some level he seemed to understand me in precisely the ways I had always wanted to be understood. He'd come out of nowhere like a whirlwind and swept me off my feet, stirring up storms of new feelings. He'd startled me awake when I hadn't realized I'd been sleepwalking. Was it possible to confuse gratitude with love?

Of course, I thought. Of course.

But the whole question of Rabi could wait. It no longer seemed important for me to know right this second what I was doing or where things were headed. I remembered something Mary used to say to me when I was small and became impatient: "Hold your horses, Eliza. The last dish of ice cream in the Western world isn't melting. Slow down!"

I was a lot more patient now, and there was no need to hurry.

CHAPTER 22

Over the next two weeks, my mother and I managed to accomplish dozens of last-minute things. We went through the piles I'd set aside for her to look over, and she decided to throw away almost everything. I arranged for a rare-book dealer to come to the house. He offered my mother an enormous sum for all of my father's first editions, but she refused to sell them. So I trudged back to Packer Man, where I was by then on intimate terms with Mr. Packer, as I called him, and bought more cartons for those first editions, though I had no idea where they would go in her new house.

We studied photographs Ellen had taken of that house, searching for walls that might accommodate bookcases. "Oh, Sister, I can't wait to see the place," she said. "It seems more cunning every time I look at these pictures." I had scheduled a painter, and the plan was that mother would stay at my house while hers was being painted. Other than that, I'd thought the place needed very little.

"You know," my mother announced one morning, "I've decided I want to move in as soon as I get there and not camp at your house. Let them paint around me; it might be faster that way, and I could keep an eye on them."

Suddenly, there seemed to be a million things neither one of us had thought of: I needed to find someone to clean the house and wash the windows, someone else to measure the windows for shades. I needed to round up a chimney sweep, an exterminator, and now a carpenter to build bookshelves. I was on the phone to Santa Fe several mornings, making all the arrangements.

Mary had insisted she would drive my mother's car across the country until I convinced her that wasn't a good idea, especially in December. So I found someone else to do it, a colleague of Rabi's at the university. Rabi himself had offered, but the last thing I wanted was to go back to Santa Fe and have to worry about him on top of Sam and the children, who would be coming home for Christmas vacation at about the same time my mother and I arrived. I told him that, and he understood.

Rabi still stayed at night, most of the time. By then, we had practiced slow, muffled sex so often, we were astonishingly good at it. The mere thought of it sent me into a swoon. Frequently, however, I found him receding into the background of the dozens of details I had to attend to. My life was confusing, and I was frazzled; there wasn't enough of me to go around. During the night, I would lie awake for hours, anticipating all I had to do beyond the physical act of getting my mother moved—deal with Sam, which I wasn't eager to do, and talk to my children, which I dreaded. I longed for a couple of Betsy's magic seeds to make Sam disappear into thin air and my children happy, all of it over and done with. Unfortunately, real life wasn't like that.

I had no space in my brain to worry about Rabi, even though

he still rendered me witless with longing. I fretted and fussed through the days, making lists, and then lists of lists. Characteristically, my mother seemed rather blasé about things, assuming either that I would do them or that they would somehow get done by themselves.

A physical therapist came to the house every afternoon and coached her. By then, she was flying around with her walker, so agile she would be able to graduate to a cane as soon as Geoff Ewing gave her the go-ahead.

One evening over dinner, my mother said to me out of the blue, "Sister, do you remember me when you were small?"

"Of course I do." I was surprised by her question.

"What do you remember?"

I told her I mostly remembered that she was sick much of the time, and that I had worried about her excessively. (I did not mention that everyone in our house seemed melancholy and lonely.)

She was shocked. "Goodness, no. I wasn't sick *all* the time! For weeks at a stretch I often felt fine. Around the time Bin was born and for several years afterwards, I felt almost decent, physically."

It was my turn to be shocked. "Are you serious?"

"As I told you, I had things on my mind then, so it wasn't all smooth sailing. But don't you remember the picnics at the beach, or the antiwar rallies I dragged you to? The gun-control petitions you and I went door to door with after all those terrible assassinations? Don't you remember playing croquet together? Or our trips to Florida? The wonderful boat rides we took there with your father's friend, Mack?" She stared at me expectantly.

"Now that you mention it, of course I do." I was mystified. How had all that faded from my mind?

"Memory is so strange," my mother said, "especially a child's memory. By any chance, do you recall the stories about my home-town I used to tell you?"

I nodded. "Of course I do."

"Embroidered, I expect. I was so homesick when you were small, I was grasping at straws. I fell back on my childhood to avoid my adulthood," she said matter-of-factly. "I don't know whether that was the cause or the effect of your father's . . ."

"Well, that's not an issue now," I said feebly.

"I got over it somehow. Maybe I made myself sick, or sicker, I should say. Then I had my surgery, and I got well. And that was the end of it. For me. I was simply glad to be alive."

We sat in silence for a minute or two.

Finally, I said, though I knew I shouldn't, "Tell me more."

"I've told you too much already." She took a drink of water and cleared her throat. "Now then, I believe we were speaking about how unreliable children's memories are."

It was clear that she was not going to say anything else about it.

"I didn't think mine were that off," I said.

"Sister, your memory is as selective as anyone's."

"I suppose so, but why did you ask me about this in the first place?"

"Curiosity, nothing more."

"You were always a good mother," I said, wanting somehow to right this peculiar conversation.

"I was probably merely adequate, but I certainly did love you."

"I always knew that."

"And so did your father. He was crazy about you, just wild."

"He was?"

"Of course. You couldn't have escaped knowing that."

"I think I might have."

She looked at me askance. "Sister," she said. "My, oh my."

We proceeded to talk about other things, but her words haunted me. She claimed she wasn't sick nearly all of the time, only "now and then." Had I gotten everything all wrong? Or were her memories the ones that were skewed?

Who would ever know now?

Later I mulled over our odd exchange and began to wonder about my own children. What would they remember?

That night, nestled next to Rabi, I woke up around two A.M. Actually, I'm not sure I was awake, but I didn't seem to be asleep either. In what might have been a dream but seemed more like a trance, I saw my children as adults. They were talking about me in, of all places, an airport bar.

"Remember," I imagined my daughter saying, "her striding around in those yellow running shoes?"

"Remember," Will piped up, "how, day after day, she would drag us to tennis courts, with our crayons and toy cars and shovels?"

"Remember," Jesse said, "her bicycle trips? She practically went across the whole country and never did learn how to change a tire very well."

"Remember," they variously chimed in, "the marathon swims? The weights? That red Snoopy hat she wore when she ran in the winter? The silly pictures she drew of us, how we always looked so mad in them?" And they dissolved into laughter.

I knew that what I remembered about my own mother—her

illness, her sadness, her dislocation—might have been true, but perhaps not the whole story. Yet, my own memory mostly held me in thrall to moments of her in beds, in hospital rooms, in doctors' offices. But what if she had been like that only occasionally? What if she had been as energetic and lively as she claimed she'd been, as she was now?

The scene shifted, and I saw my children in a strange kitchen. A dishwasher hummed softly in the background, and the three of them sat at a table drinking beer out of cans. No one else was around; everyone else in the household, whoever it belonged to, seemed to be far away or asleep.

"Remember," Jesse said, shaking his head and smiling faintly, "how she would scream and carry on in the mornings, trying to get us off to school? And go red in the face stamping her foot?"

"Like Rumpelstiltskin," Will said and laughed.

"Remember the way she whacked me that day when we were fighting in the car?" That would be Anna, who was always somehow climbing out of her car seat.

"My God, the car," one of the boys said. "Remember how she would drive us around for hours and sometimes cry, though she pretended not to? I used to be afraid we'd crash."

"Remember," Will piped up, "how she would go into her office and work all day long? Or read?"

"Or sleep? Remember how she would sleep?"

"Poor thing, she seemed unhappy."

"Maybe we did that to her, do you think?"

"Maybe it was Dad, but who knows, who knows?" A puzzling silence hung in the air until one of them changed the subject.

In the strange dream-state I was in, it occurred to me that the memories you live with are the kind that you, the rememberer,

deserve. Maybe I deserved only memories of a sick mother, always on the verge of dying, of stopping, of leaving me behind.
Maybe so, but my children deserved something better, some kind
of reassuring perfection. They deserved my Italian red bicycle for
instance—sleek, shockingly expensive, well-oiled—my only ex-
travagance during those years when Sam was so touchy about the
money I'd earned from Betsy Blossom. My red bicycle. Yes.
Astride it would be only some hazy figure my children knew to
be me, waving—not good-bye, never good-bye—but waving,
whether at the remove of distance or wild exertion, waving I love
you, I love you, I love you.

The next morning my mother said, "By the way, Sister, I've
been meaning to ask you to sketch a picture of this house. And
maybe also, if it wouldn't be too much trouble, the view from the
backyard toward the lake."

I should have thought of that myself. Late in the morning, I
found the sketchbook I'd brought but hadn't picked up for
weeks, and went outside. The day was cold and gray, and a faint
smell of snow was in the air. I sat on a rock at the edge of the
driveway and drew the front of the house with its shutters and
deep porch. But suddenly as I sketched, the trees around it became
leafy, not barren as they actually were; ivy surrounded their trunks
the way it did in the summer. I drew my mother's climbing roses
blooming in wild profusion on the side of the house, and although by then I was conflating summer and spring, I sketched
the lilacs by the front porch and the dogwoods in flower along the
drive. Summer, spring: What did it matter? I wasn't a camera.
This was the way the house begged to be remembered.

Then, on a whim, I added a bicycle leaning against the garage door where Bin used to leave his, much to my father's irritation. My mother wouldn't know it, but it was not Bin's boyhood Schwinn, but my own adult Italian bicycle, stylish and severely sleek. As perfect as in my dream.

Without thinking, for by then I was in a suspended state of absorption that wiped away time and thoughts and everything else, I added Duke, lying on the lawn. Next to him, I drew our old yellow Lab, Blossom, both of the big dogs eyeing Snickers, who was on his hind legs clawing at the elm, as if he wanted to climb right up it.

And then, out of the blue, it hit me: My book about Lily running away from home, which I hadn't thought about for weeks and which had always stumped me, wasn't about people! It was about dogs. A whole town full of them: restless dogs, homeless dogs, settled ones, bossy ones, kind ones, too; big and little and all sizes in between. At the end, there would be a parade with a dog marching band, and a huge party, with goofy hats, noisemakers, cake, and ice cream. Fireworks, too. Perhaps the mayor, a German shepherd or a Rottweiler, would speak and tell the homeless dogs that he was planning to build a comfy place in the park where they all could live. Or, maybe not. In any case, at least while the party lasted, all of the dogs would feel safe and at home.

And for the first time since I'd been fooling around with the story of Lily, I actually felt interested in it.

When I went inside to warm up, my mother was on the phone. I drank a cup of lukewarm coffee, sharpened my pencils, and found a scarf, then I set out for the lakeside. I hadn't thought I missed drawing but I must have; I was so eager now, I could hardly contain myself. Outside, I only glanced at the choppy gray

lake. What I drew was the lake as it was on one of those rare
windswept days in summer, blue with whitecaps and gulls soaring
above it. On the water were sailboats with their spinnakers rigged
for a Saturday-morning regatta. The sky was cloudless, the sun
shone brightly, and the July air—I could feel it even in the December cold and damp—wasn't heavy and humid as it so often
was in summer, but soft and benevolent as in my childhood dream
of all summer mornings, mornings when the white curtains in
my bedroom billowed gently in the breeze, and Mr. Eckles's old-
fashioned lawn mower clanked comfortingly next door. I would
listen to the sound of it for a few minutes, growing increasingly
more excited, and finally I would leap out of bed and jump into
my overalls. Then, without putting on my sandals or brushing my
teeth, I would race outside across the wide back lawn to the edge
of the cliff, where I would stand hypnotized by the sight of
dozens and dozens of sailboats gliding by in the golden morning,
the air so clear I could sometimes hear the sound of the water as
their bows cut through it. Eventually, my father would appear
around the corner of the house, always, it seemed, with a pair of
pliers or a hammer. I waited for him to scold me for standing too
close to the cliff. Instead, he joined me and took my hand.
"Mighty nice little breeze they've got this morning," he said. We
stood there, the two of us, watching the boats go by, holding
hands, everything quiet except for the birds and the sound of water. My father and I.

I went back into the house and showed my mother the sketches.
She studied them for a minute and then looked at me quizzically.

"Sister, I see you've tampered with reality a little."

I laughed. "I didn't think you'd mind."

"I don't mind at all, dear; they're beautiful and I'll treasure them. They'll be reminders of this house and, even better, of the lovely inclination you've had ever since you were a child to turn the dullest day into one that's sunny and hopeful."

"Me?"

"Oh, pshaw," she said and laughed. "Who are you trying to kid? You're basically a cockeyed optimist, just like your old mother."

I didn't think of myself that way at all, and the expression on my face said so.

"Take it from me," she said. "I've watched you your whole life."

"I don't think Sam would buy that version of things."

"Sam," she said dismissively, waving her hand. "That man's enough to take the wind out of anyone's sails. But you've borne up. You've done what you had to."

"Dutiful. That's me," I said. I still hadn't told her about Sam.

She reached for my hand. "You're a good girl, Sister," she said, and then added in a quieter voice, "Now get out while you can."

I was stunned. Except when she was on one of her manic tears, my mother hardly ever offered advice.

"Yes, well," I said and then told her the whole story.

When I'd finished, she simply looked at me and nodded. "I see," said the woman who had made the best of a troubled marriage. Even though she'd murmured, "Get out while you can," I wasn't sure she approved, and I realized I wanted her approval.

"So," I said, "what do you think?"

"What do I think? Only that I trust our friend Rabi hasn't clouded the picture."

"No," I said. "He hasn't."

"In that case, I think you'll do the right thing, Sister." As if to signal that she was through with the subject, she picked up the sketches of the house. "I do so like these," she said. "I'll have them framed in Santa Fe."

"I can do them over again, if you want. I can draw what I *see*."

"My no, Sister. These are perfect." She took my hand. "Anyone can remember a gray old day. There's no trick to that. None at all."

CHAPTER 23

A few days before we were to leave Edgecliff, my mother had an x-ray, and the following afternoon I took her to Geoff Ewing's office. It was all decked out with poinsettias and draped with fake garlands and silver bells. Christmas cards were taped on the edge of the reception desk, and in the background, carols were softly playing. I kept being startled by signs of the impending holidays, since I felt so un-Christmasy myself, but the season was spinning along without my help. I shuddered to think of everything I would have to do when I got back to New Mexico: buy presents, a tree, wreaths; make sand-and-paper-bag farolitos to set around the yard with the kids—assuming they were still speaking to me by then. I didn't know what to do about the Christmas party we gave every year. Would a celebration like that be considered in bad taste? Would Sam be there? For the moment, it all seemed too much to worry about.

We sat in Geoff's waiting room for almost half an hour, my mother deep in another detective story Bin had given her. I was reading George Eliot's *Daniel Deronda,* lost in all that wonderful nineteenth-century dithering about the charmingly haughty Gwendolen's prospects for romance.

When we were finally admitted to Geoff's office, he apologized for keeping us waiting, and announced that my mother was healing beautifully. He told her she could throw away her walker and use a cane until she felt steady enough to throw *it* away. But he cautioned her to take things slowly and to follow the directions of the orthopedist he'd referred her to in Santa Fe.

While the two of them were talking, I scanned Geoff's office. On the wall behind him was a framed photograph of his very thin, pale wife and his children, posed in front of one of those marbled backgrounds you see in photos from Sears or Wal-Mart. There was another of his parents in golf clothes. There were diplomas, of course, and two rather bad landscape paintings, one of a river and autumn trees, and another of a sunset and mountains. The furniture was Early American, the walls were papered in green with a pattern of chevrons. The couch behind me was covered in orange and green plaid. I don't know why people's bad taste always astonished me, but it did.

I suddenly realized Geoff was talking to me. "You've had a long visit, Lizzie," he was saying. "I trust it's been a good one. Sorry we never got around to that dinner, but another time, I hope."

"Definitely," I replied.

"I enjoyed seeing Bin," he said. "He seems terrific."

"Oh, he is," my mother said. "Bin's finally growing up."

Geoff laughed. "He needs to get married. That would solve his problems."

"Why?" I blurted out. "Whose problems has marriage ever solved?" Both Geoff and my mother stared at me.

"You mustn't mind Sister," my mother said, raising her eyebrows in my direction as if to say be quiet.

Ever the peacemaker, Geoff said, "You may have a point. I just meant that Bin might be ready to settle down."

"Maybe so," I responded.

The three of us chatted for a few more minutes; then Geoff gathered my mother's records and x-rays and stuck them in a large envelope, which he handed to me. He also gave her a little card saying that she had a metal plate and screw in her hip, in case she needed it to get through airport security. As he ushered us out of his office, he gave my mother a peck on the cheek and shook both our hands.

"Keep in touch," he said warmly.

When we were in the car, my mother said, "That little outburst about marriage wasn't called for, was it? I'm surprised at you."

"It was stupid, you're right," I said, "but his supercilious tone got my goat."

"I'm sure it was well-intentioned. He's a good-hearted young man."

"You know," I said as I drove, "I find it curious that he kept saying he was going to invite me for dinner and never did. Don't you think that's a little odd?"

"Not if what one of the nurses told me is true," she said.

"What was that?"

"I hate to repeat what could be a rumor," she replied.

"Oh, go on."

"Well, she told me that Geoff's wife, Marcia something— Marcia Sue—that's it—has some kind of eating disorder and recently was packed off to a hospital in Maryland for several months."

"That's terrible," I said, wishing I could take back my remark about marriage.

"We never know what others are going through."

"I guess not. Maybe it's hard being married to a doctor, even a nice one like Geoff."

"Eliza," she said sternly, "it's hard being married to *anyone*. You should know that." She unsnapped her seatbelt as we turned into her drive. "It's full-time work under the best of circumstances."

I didn't know about the best of circumstances, I thought, as I ran around the car to help her out. Slowly she made her way up out of the seat. "Damn this thing," she muttered, as I handed her the cane. She looked up at me. "It's a little like this, a limping arrangement. I got used to it, perhaps because I was cowardly, but I—"

"*What's* a limping arrangement?"

"Marriage, Sister," she said. "Wasn't that the subject?"

I stood with my hand on the car door and watched her limp down the walk, her red coat brilliant in the sodden light. A few flakes of snow wandered down from the sky. We had one day left in Edgecliff, and then I would have to face my own limping arrangement—by then crippled or, more accurately, paralyzed—a fact which simultaneously made me uneasy and buoyed me up.

I helped her with the stairs, and we went through the house, room by room, she reluctantly. I'd made her promise we would do that, though I knew she was simply going through the motions to humor me. The movers had come the day before and taken everything but two beds, the old kitchen table and chairs, garbage bags full of clothes and boxes of pots and pans, all of which Mary would give to the Salvation Army after we left.

In each room, dozens of memories came to mind, and I selected one and thought about it for a few minutes. As my mother hobbled around, inspecting empty closets, I went through my little ritual: I recalled the time I had measles, when I was five or six, and lay in my bed half delirious with fever. The time Bin finger-painted the walls of his bedroom in red and yellow, sending my father into a fit of anger and my mother, to my astonishment, into gales of laughter. My mother lying in bed early in the morning, while my father was in the shower, on the dresser his watch and pocket change, which I could see as clearly as if they were there now. The summer afternoons when, as a teenager, I read book after book on the enclosed sun porch. My parents' large bathroom where I'd gashed my head on a sharp corner of the wall when I was four or five, and our next-door neighbor, Frannie Eckles, had rushed me to the emergency room because my mother was too sick to get out of bed. "Be a good soldier," my mother told me before we left, my head wrapped in a towel. "Keep a stiff upper lip."

After we had completed our circuit of the upstairs rooms, I asked my mother if she wanted to go to the third floor, but she said no. Alone, I climbed to the attic, where instead of all the rainy days I'd spent there playing house or school, with the sweet, musty smells of wood and old papers and the rain beating on the roof, I chose to remember the night a month earlier when Rabi had inadvertently touched my hand and sent me into a tailspin. After that night nothing was the same. The world had lurched, pitching me not upside down, but right side up. How odd and unexpected.

I knelt down at one of the little dormer windows and looked out onto the roof below, then beyond through the skeleton trees, to the street where I'd grown up. I struggled to raise the window.

The snow was falling in earnest by then, making a comforting sound of stillness. Like a child, I stuck my head out into the cold and opened my mouth to catch the snow on my tongue.

This was the place where I'd grown up, I thought, and there would be no next time to get it right, no next time to turn it into the fairy-tale place I'd longed for when I was young, no next time to make my family the happiest on earth. This had been my home for almost eighteen years, and it was what I had—it was my past, my childhood. Suspended above the treetops, with the snow fluttering all around, something eased in me and, almost as if a spell had lifted, I realized I'd made peace with my life on Mars.

"Sister?" my mother called from downstairs. "Sister?"

I pulled my head inside. "Yes?"

"Where are you?"

"In the attic."

"Come down here, please."

I closed the window and descended the stairs. Good-bye, attic.

My mother was standing in her bedroom. "Look at this," she said, holding out a photograph. It was a picture of her and my father, both of them young and good-looking, his arm around her.

"Odd, isn't it?" she said. "I found this tucked in the corner of your father's closet, by the shelf. I guess you . . . we . . . missed it. Turn it over."

I did, and on it was written, "May 1943," with a fountain pen. Beneath that, in ballpoint, my father's writing tiny and spidery, as it became when he grew older, he'd added:

Though trees turn bare and girls turn wives
We shall afford our costly seasons . . .

I recognized those lines immediately. They were from a
W. D. Snodgrass poem my father had admired.

There is a gentleness survives
That will outspeak and has its reasons.
There is a loveliness exists,
Preserves us, not for specialists.

My mother was staring up at me. "I was twenty-three when
this picture was taken," she said. "He had just finished law school.
We were visiting his aunt in Columbus, and I remember the day
as if it were yesterday." She paused. "What do you make of it?"

"That he was crazy about you," I said. "And not only when he
wrote the date, but later, whenever he wrote this in ballpoint pen.
You recognize the lines, don't you?"

"I think so. They're from a poem your father enjoyed, though
I can't remember what came next."

I told her, and she looked slightly mystified.

"Mother," I said, "he loved you. He always loved you."

"Perhaps he did."

"Of course he did."

"And the other?" she asked, obviously referring to Mary.

"I don't know about her. The point is he loved you."

" 'Costly seasons,' indeed," she said, turning to a window that
overlooked the lake. "How strange."

I wasn't sure what to say.

"Though what's so strange, after all, Sister? You get to be my
age and nothing is strange. Or everything is."

"He did love you," I said again.

She turned away from the window and smiled at me wistfully,

then nodded abruptly as if to right herself. There was no self-pity in her gaze, nothing but pluck and determination. "Let's leave it at that, then," she said, tucking the photo into her sweater pocket.

"Yes."

"Why, your hair's wet, dear. What on earth have you been doing?"

"The snow," I said. "I had my head out the window."

"Your father was always so fond of the snow," she said dreamily. She turned toward the door and as she did, she dropped her cane; it made a loud, rattling sound as it hit the floor of the empty room. I retrieved it and put it in her hand, and for a moment she and I were both holding the cane, my fingers on hers.

"Mother?" I said. "I think you know more about forgiveness than you let on."

She raised her eyebrows. "You do, do you?"

I nodded.

She looked away. "I recognized my own culpability," she said. "I was ill."

"But that wasn't your fault."

"As I said, I was ill, off and on, for years." She shrugged. "Why wouldn't he have wanted a normal relationship? It wasn't difficult to see how attractive she was."

We were still standing, holding the cane together.

"When I realized what was going on," she said, not meeting my gaze, "it was painful, terribly so. I was brokenhearted. But suffering didn't suit me, and I couldn't leave your father, for all sorts of reasons." She paused. "After a time, I made some accommodation. Don't ask me how I did it, but I did."

"Isn't that a kind of forgiveness?"

"I don't believe so, dear. I don't know. But after I had my surgery, I was so happy to be alive, I refused to dwell on . . . that. I can't put a rosy face on it, even now, and, remember, I had you and your brother to think of."

I squeezed her hand.

"Time has a way of smoothing things over," she went on. "It surprises me. But I couldn't bear the burden of bitterness, so somehow I managed to cast it off. I have no anger now. Pride can be a terrible thing, but in this case it's served me. I never said a word to your father, and I never will to Mary."

Slowly she began making her way toward the door. "Come now, Sister," she said. "It's time to leave. Enough of this."

The snow, which had not been forecast, came down so heavily that by midafternoon, everything was blanketed in white. Places of business shut down, the freeways closed; so did the airport. With only an old radio left in the house, we listened as cancellations and school closings were announced. I phoned Rabi at his office but got no answer. Mary was to have brought dinner, but she called around five to say she couldn't get out of her driveway.

"You stay put," my mother cautioned Mary. "We'll be fine."

The two of them talked for a few minutes, but I heard only my mother's end of their conversation. "No, dear, of course not," she said. "And if we don't, we don't. One of these days Sister and I will get to Santa Fe." She laughed. She listened for a moment and then said, "Now, Mary, we can talk about that when you come to see me in February."

"Mary's like you, Sister," she said when she got off the phone. "She wanted to have a last dinner here, for old times' sake. Where is all this sentiment coming from?"

"Some things are worth memorializing," I said.

"She first came to this house in a storm; I think she wanted to go out in one, too. You remember the story."

I nodded.

"And I don't want to ever hear about her guilty conscience," she said. "Ever."

Slowly, we made our way downstairs.

"Water over the dam, at any rate. Done," my mother said. "I've kept house with the past too long."

"Maybe we all have," I replied.

I tried to call Rabi three or four more times, but there was still no answer, which made me a little nervous. Around seven, I fixed a can of soup, and my mother and I ate it with stale crackers and tea. As we were finishing, the doorbell rang, and I ran to answer it. To my relief, there was Rabi, covered with snow.

"My God," I said, flinging open the door. "I've been so worried about you! How did you get here?" I hugged him. His cheeks were like ice.

He stamped his feet vigorously, stepped into the front hall, and shook out his jacket. "I drove most of the way," he said and smiled. "But I had to abandon my car down the street when the person in front of me ran into a snowdrift and blocked the way. He said he'd be right back with an SUV to pull his car out, but on a night like this, who knows?"

"You came," I said. "I didn't think you'd make it."

"I'd cross Antarctica to get to you." He laughed.

My mother walked in from the kitchen. "Rabi," she said. "Gracious! Come in. Sister will fix you some nice hot soup.

Other than that, we haven't much to offer. I'm afraid the cupboard is as bare as old Mother Hubbard's."

Old Mother Hubbard seemed to baffle Rabi, so while I was heating another can of soup, my mother gave him a lesson in English nursery rhymes.

"There was an old woman who lived in a shoe," my mother recited, and, laughingly, he repeated it until he seemed to have at least that one nursery rhyme down pat. There had been a time when my mother would have driven me crazy with this kind of routine, but that night in the cozy kitchen, with the wind howling outside, it seemed sweet and somehow appropriate.

"I love the snow," Rabi said as I gave him his soup. "It's amazing for someone like me who grew up in the desert."

"Ha!" my mother said. "As for the beautiful snow, it makes me sick," she added, quoting something out of my childhood.

"No, no," Rabi said. "It's a miracle!"

"One that, quite frankly, I could do without," she replied.

Rabi cupped his hands around his eyes to peer out of the window. "I think it's letting up a little," he said and went back to his soup.

I had been wondering how he and I could find some time alone, so I suggested we take a walk in the snow. "When you're done with your soup, let's go see about your car."

"Sister," my mother said, "don't be ridiculous. This poor man just came *in* from the snow."

"You'll go with me?" he said to me.

"Of course I will."

I scrounged around in a garbage bag of old clothes until I'd found a pair of boots and an old down jacket, mittens, and several moth-eaten scarves. We both bundled up, Rabi wearing a black woolen cap, me in an orange one that said P on the front. When we were ready to go, my mother stood by the door, shaking her head.

"You two should have your heads examined."

"We won't be long," I said. "We're just going up the street."

Rabi and I went out into the night. The temperature had been dropping all day long, and by then it was freezing. We clumped through enormous drifts, and at the end of the driveway he took my hand, pulled me to him, and kissed me hard.

"I'll miss you," I said, a little breathless.

Holding hands, we trudged through the snow. It was beautiful, perhaps the most gorgeous snow I'd ever seen, everything still except for the sound of the wind whirling the flakes around, dimming even the streetlights. The world looked unfamiliar, as if we'd been transported to another planet. Snow flew in our faces, and after only a block or two, we were covered in white. Our breaths were steamy, and I felt tongue-tied. We walked down the center of the street, but the oversized boots I was wearing—my father's? Bin's?—were difficult to walk in and at one point, I slipped. Rabi rescued me as I was on my way down.

"I love you, Eliza," he said when he'd righted me.

Suddenly something occurred to me. "Have you ever seen an angel?"

For a second, he looked confused. "An angel?" he said. "Only you."

"No, no," I said, "I mean a snow angel." I threw myself down on the nearest lawn and scissored my feet and arms. Then I got up very carefully so as not to ruin what I'd made.

"There's a snow angel for you," I said.

He seemed delighted. "I want to make one, too!"

"Be my guest."

He fell to the lawn and, next to mine, made his own bigger angel; then he too got up carefully. "Oh, that's good," he said. "I like this. We could do it all the way down the street."

"We probably don't have that kind of time," I said.

"We have very little time," he said. "At least for now."

"I know. And I don't see how you can spend the night."

"It doesn't matter," he said.

"It does to me."

"We have a whole store of nights, a treasure of them. And we'll have more. Think of it that way."

"But I'm greedy for you," I said, kissing his cheek. The two of us clung together as a gust of wind threatened to blow us over.

We moved on, and after a while, I said, "This is like a fairy tale, this night."

"Every night with you is like a fairy tale."

"But how does this one end?" I caught myself asking.

"It doesn't," he said. "We just take a little break, and then we'll be together."

For some reason, in the freezing cold, with the wind whipping the snow around, I pictured us at a fabulous hotel in San Francisco, the kind I would never have splurged on for myself, where I'd once stayed while on a book tour. High above the bay, with windows all around, the room had views that seemed to go on forever. There would be no sneaking around like thieves in the night, just Rabi and me alone together.

"I have a lot to get through before we're together again," I said.

"Yes," he said, "but you'll get through it. And I'll help you however I can."

"I don't know," I said hesitantly.

He stopped walking and pulled me to him. "Listen," he said. "This is real. This is not some trivial thing. This is important, Eliza. And it will all work out."

"You believe that?"

"Yes," he said solemnly. "Because you're a strong person. Because I love you. Because I believe you love me."

The wind blew fiercely. I had seldom heard Rabi speak with such conviction. I realized that part of my hesitation about him was that he was so agreeable I wasn't certain he had it in him to be forceful. But this time he was, and I knew I had to stop avoiding things, as I'd done for years with Sam. It wasn't as if Rabi had asked me to marry him, for heaven's sake. Then the strangest thing happened: In my answer, I seemed to discover the truth in myself.

"Yes," I told him. "I do."

He laughed. "Where have you been?"

"On Mars," I said, and we both laughed as we slipped and slid down the dark, deserted street, snow billowing all around us. His hand in mine was solid, and I leaned into him.

When we found his car, the one that had blocked him in was gone. Rabi's engine started right up, and by rocking the car back and forth, he maneuvered it out of the snowdrift; we ploughed slowly back down the street. Miraculously, he made it into my mother's driveway.

"You're a pretty good snow driver for a desert guy," I said. By then, the heater was blasting away, and melting snow was dripping all over the front seat.

"I'm a pretty good guy, period," he joked. "I thought you'd never notice."

A powerful blast of wind off the lake rocked the car, and he held me. "At this rate," I said into his jacket, "the airport will be closed for weeks. My mother and I will never get on that plane tomorrow."

"Don't worry," he said, stroking my neck reassuringly. "This will all be okay in the morning. It will. In the meantime, I'll miss you and long for you. *Rah ishta'lik*."

"Yes," I said. "Yes. I'll miss you, too."

CHAPTER 24

By the following morning, the main streets had been plowed, and the airport was up and running. Our plane didn't leave until early afternoon, and there was no more snow in the forecast. Outside, the sun shone blindingly, making everything sparkle; each branch of every tree was outlined in white, and a wonderful silence lay over the world. Edgecliff seemed enchanted.

After I'd shoveled the front walk, I helped my mother pack her remaining things, and I packed mine. I called Will, who was already home from school, and we arranged where we'd meet when he picked us up in Albuquerque that night.

"Say good-bye to the house for me," he said. "I always loved going there. I always felt so safe with Boppa. I have such good memories of him."

"I'm glad."

"And, hey, Mom, guess what? I got an A on that paper I was agonizing about."

"Terrific! What did I tell you?"

I was so excited to see him. I hadn't missed missing my children in recent weeks, but now I couldn't wait to have them close. I was counting on their understanding.

I phoned Rabi, too, at his office, but he must have been teaching. I left a voice mail saying, not good-bye, but simply, "I'll see you soon." Mary, who had wanted to take us to the airport, still couldn't get out of her driveway, so I called a cab, which came right on time.

After the cab driver and I had loaded the suitcases into his trunk, I helped my mother outside. She was wearing sunglasses against the glare, and she looked quite jaunty. As we pulled out of the driveway, she asked the driver to stop, and he braked. She turned and looked back at the house on Mars; instead of doing the same, I watched her. For a second, she appeared a little bewildered. Then she rearranged her face and smiled. "You remember what happened to Lot's wife, Sister." And then, to the cab driver, she said, "I trust you know about Lot's wife."

I felt myself shrink, an automatic response. But it turned out that the driver, a heavyset older man, *did* know about Lot's wife—and plenty more. In fact, all the way to the airport he regaled us with an extraordinarily detailed account of how he'd accepted Christ into his life and read the Bible daily. By the time we arrived at the airport, my mother had managed to get his life story, and the conversation—or more precisely the monologue he'd delivered at her urging—seemed to delight them both. Another example, if I needed one, of my mother's winning ways. As I paid him, he vigorously refused the tip. Wouldn't hear of it. He blessed us both, carried our luggage to curbside check-in, rounded up a wheelchair for my mother, blessed us again, bowed ever so slightly, and went on his way.

I tucked my mother into the wheelchair and piled our purses and carry-ons in her lap. "Looks like you did it again," I said. I was wowed by her friendliness.

"Sister," she said, shaking her head as if I were hopeless, "what did it cost me? Nothing."

When the time came for our plane to board, I pushed my mother down the ramp, and at the door of the aircraft, she struck up a conversation with the flight attendant. Then, before I knew what was happening, we were somehow upgraded to first class. "You'll be a little more comfortable there," the flight attendant told her.

"Why, goodness," my mother said, "what did we do to deserve this?"

"Don't ask," I muttered, concerned there was a mix-up.

"Why, you're a VIP," the attendant said and smiled, her white teeth blinding.

"Oh, I am, am I?"

"You sure are."

I helped my mother get settled; she wanted the aisle seat. Then I climbed over her to the window seat.

"Nice going—again," I said to her.

"It's just because I'm so aged, Sister," my mother said.

"No," I replied, "it's because you're so friendly."

"It never hurts. Try to remember that."

"I will."

Before the plane took off, my mother had talked not only to the captain but also to the man across the aisle, who looked up from his laptop, so startled that someone was actually speaking to him that he spoke back. By the time we were airborne, she'd gotten most of his particulars, I noted, though I already had my book out and was huddled by the window. I wasn't actually reading; I was thinking again how amazing my mother was, and how I had spent so much of my life being embarrassed by her charm when, in fact, all along I should have been proud of her, even emulated her. Was I like my father, who, if not an outright curmudgeon, was put off by strangers? Not rude, exactly, but always cool? If so, I didn't want to be like him any longer.

My mother took out her own book and began to read, but as we flew south, she nodded off. I had so much to worry about that I didn't know where to begin, so I didn't. For a while, I thought about Rabi, recalled the feel of his golden skin, surveyed the length of his lovely body, recollected the scent of him. For the first time in my life, I felt cherished by a man, and that overwhelmed me. But thinking about him seemed a torment I didn't need, and, besides, who knew what would happen? So I dove into my book and read almost all the way to Houston.

Half an hour before we landed, my mother roused herself, asked for a cup of tea, and drank it slowly. "I must be tired," she said.

"Yes."

"It's been a long haul, hasn't it? I've kept you from your work, from your home, your life." She sighed.

"No," I said. "I'm so glad I came. You have no idea."

"Are you're nervous about seeing Sam?"

"Nervous? I don't know. I'd like to get this over with."

"He's a wonderful man," she said.

"Sam?"

"Good grief, not Sam. Rabi. I told you I've never liked Sam. No, that's not true. I have found him . . . wanting . . . as far as you're concerned. A person whose moral fiber I've always questioned."

"Moral fiber" sounded like something my father might say, but she was right. I shook my head.

My mother took my hand. " 'Costly seasons,' " she said. "We all have them. You'll get through this. I have great confidence in you."

"Thank you. That means a lot to me. But it's my kids I'm most worried about. I hate to disrupt their world."

As if she hadn't heard me, my mother said. "Perhaps you can be more peaceful now. Even as a child, cheerful as you were, you sometimes seemed anxious. Distant, too, as if someone had instructed you early on to keep your own counsel. Did I convey that message? If so, I didn't mean to. But I've always known it would take a far cleverer man than Sam to get through to you. I think you may have met your match now." She raised her eyebrows.

"We'll see," I said. "But I *am* worried about the kids."

"Don't be silly," she replied. "They're young, they're sturdy, and," she paused, "they understand a lot more than you think they do. They're not idiots, Sister. I expect they've known something was fishy for years."

"You do?"

She nodded. "They want you to be happy. You can depend on that."

"You haven't said something to them, have you?" She had spoken to each of them many times since I'd been in Edgecliff.

"Of course not. I may be a lot of things, but I'm not a meddler. I told them to take good care of you, but don't I always? I know your children, and they *are* your children; they're as kind and loving as you are. And you're a far better mother than I've ever been."

The plane bumped along the runway.

"No," I practically had to shout over the noise of the engines. "Not a better mother than you."

"Ha!"

After we'd landed, I gathered our things, and, with her cane, mother limped out to the wheelchair that was waiting for her at the foot of the jetway. Then we dashed off through the Houston airport, which, even if I'd been blindfolded, I would have recognized, because it always smelled like popcorn.

It was twilight when we boarded the plane for Albuquerque. This time, we were not upgraded to first class, but since the plane wasn't full, we had a row to ourselves. I curled up by the window and my mother was on the aisle, so there was an empty seat between us.

We both read for a while, but stopped when drinks were served and then, shortly after, some kind of sandwich made of processed meat. I watched as my mother stripped the contents of her sandwich and ate half the bread and the apple. She gave me her chips, and I devoured them along with mine.

"I don't know why they even bother," my mother said about the meal.

"Me neither."

She shifted in her seat and leaned over toward me. "Sister," she said, "I am getting *so* excited!" We were flying in the dusk, but ahead of us was the sunset, the horizon brilliant with oranges and reds and violets. "I feel like a pioneer," she added. "I expect that sounds silly to you, but I do." As she spoke, she took my hand.

"Can you see out this window?" I said, tugging at her. She ducked her head and looked outside.

"Why, it's breathtaking! And look! Stars!"

I peered out at the night sky, and sure enough, there was a handful of stars.

" 'The forget-me-nots of the angels,' " she said.

I gave her a questioning look. "What's that?"

"Oh, I don't know," she said. "Someone, maybe Longfellow. " 'Silently,' " she recited, " ' One by one, in the infinite meadows of heaven / Blossomed the lovely stars, the forget-me-nots of the angels.' " After a moment, she added, "The sky's the limit, Sister. Who knows what the future holds?"

I certainly didn't, but I leaned across the seat and kissed her cheek, which, as always, smelled of freesia. Then I looked out the window again and stared at the stars sprinkled across the clear night sky. Most of them were little more than remnants of light from ages before, but they were all the light those intrepid explorers had to guide them when they set out to find new worlds. Ancient light, but enough to go by.

Ahead of us, the colors of the sunset deepened, spreading a gorgeous array across the western sky. I motioned for her to look again.

"Oh, Sister," my mother said, gazing out of the window. Then she squeezed her eyes tight and raised her shoulders in a gesture of delight. "This is such an adventure!" She sounded so thrilled, my heart spilled over.

Suddenly, we were both pioneers, holding hands, fearlessly chasing the brilliant light. My mother and I together, blazing a trail into the unknown.

Acknowledgments

Enormous thanks to my editor, Trena Keating, and to my agent, Esmond Harmsworth. Also to Roxanne Shaw Apple, Susan Emerling, Edward Feil, Alex Gancarz, Glenn McMillan, Mayo Miller, Ghassan Sarkis; and with special thanks to Maudwynne Metcalf, Arden Reed, and Rebecca Friedman.

ABOUT THE AUTHOR

Alicia Metcalf Miller lives in Santa Fe, New Mexico, with her husband. They have three children.